WRESTLING WITH WEREWOLVES
HAVEN EVER AFTER - BOOK FIVE

HAZEL MACK

COPYRIGHT

© Hazel Mack Author 2024

EBook ISBN: 978-1-957873-54-1

Paperback ISBN: 978-1-957873-57-2

All rights reserved. No part of this publication may be reproduced, stored or transmitted in any form or by any means, electronic, mechanical, photocopying, recording, scanning, or otherwise without written permission from the publisher. It is illegal to copy this book, post it to a website, or distribute it by any other means without permission.

This novel is entirely a work of fiction. The names, characters and incidents portrayed in it are the work of the author's imagination. Any resemblance to actual persons, living or dead, events or localities is entirely coincidental. However, if I get the chance to become Ever's newest resident, I'll take it!

I don't support the use of AI in book, book cover or book graphic creation. If you love human generated books, please feel free to learn more at my website at www.annafury.com/ai. I do not approve the creation of derivative works based on this book or series without consent.

Editing - Krista Venero at Mountains Wanted

Proofreading - Marcelle - BooksChecked

Cover - Anna Fury Author

Cover Art - Linda Noeran (@linda.noeran)

❦ Created with Vellum

AUTHORS ARE NOW FACING AN UNPRECEDENTED CHALLENGE - ARTIFICIAL INTELLIGENCE (AI).

AI-based "books", which are computer written, rather than human, are flooding the market and reducing our ability to earn a living wage writing books for you, our amazing readers.

The problem with AI as it stands today? It's not capable of thinking on its own. It ingests data and mimics someone else's style, often plagiarizing art and books without the original creator or author's consent.

There's a very real chance human authors will be forced out of the market as AI-written works take over. Yet your favorite authors bring magical worlds, experiences and emotions to life in a way that a computer can't. If you want to save that, then we need your help.

LEARN MORE ABOUT THE HARMFUL EFFECTS OF AI-WRITTEN BOOKS AND AI-GENERATED ART ON MY WEBSITE AT WWW.ANNAFURY.COM/AI

SYNOPSIS

Lola

Music is my life. At least, it would be if my father's politics didn't dictate every minute of my day. When I sneak out to live my dream for the night, consequences follow. Papá's Second, Eliel, challenges him for the throne, putting me at risk of being forcibly claimed by the devious, disgusting male.

To keep me safe, my father sends me to the one person he trusts—his best friend, Richard. Yet, Richard isn't the wolf I remember from my childhood. The moment I see him again, a tether forms between us, twisting our souls into a bond so rare, it hasn't been seen in thousands of years. Barely there touches, smoldering looks, and soft growls become something more, something intense and powerful that draws us together like moths desperate to burn.

But as with everything in my life, our connection is complicated. We have to keep it hidden, because when my father finds out, he won't understand. Worse yet, he won't give us the chance to explain. I've got to succeed in my quest for harmony to drown out the discord. Like my best friend Leo says, when words fail, music speaks.

GET THE FREEBIES

WANT SPICY EPILOGUES?

Sign up for my newsletter to access the FREE bonus epilogues to every Hazel Mack book I write.

CONTENT NOTICE

While this book is very sweet and lighthearted, there are a couple heavy themes to mention. In particular, there's reference to past parental death (off page), some light violence, threat of a forced relationship and unwanted sexual commentary.

If you have any particular questions, feel free to reach out to me at author@annafury.com!

Lola is one of my most favorite female characters I've ever written. She's brave, smart, strong, and loyal. A literal and figurative rockstar. I hope my Mexican readers see a bit of themselves and their beautiful culture in Lola and Santa Alaya.

CHAPTER ONE
LOLA

The cramped dressing room vibrates with the drums and bass playing onstage. Nerves flutter in my belly, my skin peppered with goose bumps. My guard will be here soon—I hope that this time they're slow enough that I get at least a song or two with my friend Leo's band before Nuñez forces me home to Santa Alaya.

Standing in front of the ramshackle room's only mirror, I remove the tiny gold crown from my curly black hair, tucking it into a hidden pocket in my midnight leather corset. Reaching into my bag, I pull out my favorite extra—a gauzy, translucent bustier-style skirt. The front is a simple belt, then fabric drapes in increasingly big swathes to the floor. From the front, the audience will see my black leather leggings and the belt's gauzy green snaps. But from the side, it'll trail long like I'm some human princess from a storybook.

It's beautiful.

A brisk knock at the door announces the stage manager's arrival. When I open the door, he dips his head respectfully, looking at me from beneath dark brows. "¿Lista, Princesa?"

I rub his shoulder thankfully. "Ready as I'll ever be. I can't thank you enough for arranging this."

Luís, whom I've known my entire life, grins at me. "I'm fully expecting a call from your father, so I'm going on vacation for a month right after your set."

I laugh loudly at that. "Good idea." I don't know what my papá will do to me for breaking his rules so thoroughly—again—but I imagine I'll be locked in the castle until I'm old and gray. It can't get much worse, though. I already feel like I'm locked in a gilded prison whenever I'm home.

The steady drumbeat changes, and a solo guitar begins a refrain I've always found hauntingly beautiful—it's from a human band called Transcendency.

"That's your cue," Luís says, lifting his head. "Knock 'em dead, Princesa."

Grinning, I spin into the room and grab my turquoise electric guitar. I slip the black strap carefully over my huge hair and wink at myself in the mirror.

"You got this, girl," I mutter as nerves flutter impatiently in my belly. They'll disappear the moment I step onto that stage, though. Being in front of people, immersed in the music, it's heaven on earth.

I scan my face in the mirror, grinning. Dark makeup lines my nearly black eyes. Between the see-through belt-skirt and all the leather, I do look like a princess. A badass rocker princess.

I fucking love it. This is me, in my element, shoving aside shifter court politics and all the other bullshit that comes with being the sitting king's only daughter.

Turning, I follow Luís out of the dressing room and down a cramped, smelly hallway toward the stage. The scents of stage smoke and hundreds of gathered monsters send a thrill through me, my wolf rising up from my consciousness. Of the two of us, she's more stoic, but even she loves it when I play.

Luís leaves me just behind the stage curtain. On the main

stage, my best friend Leo's band, The Lovestruck Lobos, plays the stunning first minute of "Crash and Burn." There's a fantastic, complicated riff about fifty seconds in where I'll come onstage with a big bang. Then we duet. Leo's bass voice is amazing in harmony with my higher tones. I'm biased, of course; I've been lucky enough to sneak out and make appearances with the Lobos for the last few years.

Whenever I can escape Papá and Nuñez, that is.

Somehow, I think the way I randomly show up to play actually intoxicates the crowd. Leo says the times I join are always their best concerts.

My fingers dance along my guitar strings in anticipation. Onstage, Leo's lost to the music, black eyes closed as he sways from side to side. The tattoos snaking up his neck tell the story of his love affair with music, starting from when we were pups. All the women love them. I was with him when he got every single one of them. I never got any, though, because Papá didn't want me to.

I glance at the audience. From my vantage point, monsters of a dozen or more species are clear. It's harder to see those standing toward the back, but when the strobes illuminate the crowd, I catch a glimpse of a few vampires, centaurs, and—holy moons! The tiny monster haven of Ever's elusive Keeper sits at the bar with a stunning red-headed woman in his arms.

Hot damn.

A giant boom sounds from the stage, echoing off the walls and ceiling and forcing goose bumps to the surface of my dark bronze skin. That's my signal. A joyous smile comes to my face as I stroll onto the stage, grinning at the crowd.

The roar that goes up when they see me overloads me with joy. It sparks and sputters deep inside, my wolf preening at the attention and focus and obvious excitement. My fingers pick at the strings—I've practiced this song a thousand times. Leo's inky eyes flick open and meet mine, wrinkling happily in the corners.

At his back, the other three members of the Lobos are way into the music, eyes closed as they rock out.

We've been planning this for a while. There will be repercussions; we know that too because there always are. But for now, there's only the music.

And it is *everything* to me.

I join them, fingers moving faster on the strings as Leo belts out the bridge. Our notes dance together, rising and falling as the music consumes me. Leo growls into the microphone, the crowd going wild as the song twists and morphs into the chorus.

When I join in, the screams rise louder, my instinct on a knife's edge. I become the song, pure harmony and balance as we duet. This is it; esto es lo que quiero hacer con mi vida. I want to play, tour, and choose where to go without anyone telling me I shouldn't or can't.

"We serve the people, mija." My father's voice rings in my head. "Sobre todo, familia." Above all, family.

Tonight, I only have to serve the music.

Leo and I lean into his microphone as my wolf spins in my chest, her soft growl pulling my attention from the song.

No. I refuse to look at where she's focusing. I know what I'll see.

The song crescendos into my solo. I match my notes to the chorus as we close the final refrain. Leo's background growls amp up the sound of my higher tones as the crowd screams along with us. I'm in my blessed element, and I swear to the goddess, nobody can take this from me.

But eventually, my solo ends. The crowd roars, but I feel Nuñez coming before I even see him.

Leo bumps me with a hip, his version of "good job," before his dark eyes flick over my shoulder, his expression growing sorrowful.

My bodyguard's fury precedes his presence onstage, raising my hackles. He swoops onto the stage, cutting a massive figure in his navy three-piece suit as he grabs me by the elbow. "What the fuck, Lola?" Nuñez snaps quietly in my ear.

Surprise snakes through me. Nuñez has never uttered a curse word in my presence.

I give the crowd a final wave as Leo starts up a new beat. He and the Lobos will crush the rest of this set. We practiced it together, and I had high hopes I'd get to join in a few more songs before Nuñez found me.

Sighing, I allow my head bodyguard to guide me off the stage. My wolf slinks to the corner of our shared consciousness, eyeing him with confusion and hurt. He says nothing, his much bigger frame laced with tension. Behind the curtain, three more guards from my personal retinue stand tensely. Not a single one looks at me as Nuñez pushes me gently toward an open door. The side of a black SUV is visible through it.

Something is different about tonight, though. They're all focused and tight-looking, as if they expect someone to swoop out of the sky and scoop me up.

I look up at my bodyguard. "I've got a bag and my guitar case in the dressing room. May I go get it?"

"No," he barks, putting a finger to his earpiece. "Grab the princess's things from dressing." With that, he stops at the door and glances around, as if snipers are waiting on every rooftop to off me.

This is really a new level of paranoia I wouldn't have expected from him.

Goddess, help me keep my cool and find some way to exist where I can be the real me, Lola, and not just Lola, First Princess of Pack Santa Alaya.

I resist the urge to bark at Nuñez that I'm not in danger, but he's doing the job my father hired him to do, and I made it harder tonight by disappearing. It's a game we've been playing for the better part of ten years—I disappear to find the music, and

Nuñez tracks me down, gives me a speech, and then we do it again.

I don't know what's different about tonight, though, so I hop into the SUV without a word. I can read a room as well as the next omega, I've been practicing my entire life. My only hope is that tonight's repercussions don't break my heart.

CHAPTER TWO
RICHARD

I stand at the giant circular window in my bedroom, staring at the dense forest behind my treehouse. Pressing a button in the window frame, I select the option for rain. The magical window overlay can produce all varieties of weather, but pouring, pounding rain is my favorite. I love the tiny monster town of Ever, but the perfect sunny weather sometimes gets to me. I miss the wilder weather of my home haven, Acadia. I sometimes even miss the tropical heat of my adoptive haven, Santa Alaya.

The moment the rain hologram begins to play over the surface of my window, a sense of peace steals over me. I love staring at the rainy forest—it quiets my mind, most notably my wolf's voice, which has become loud and demanding on the best of days. But even he falls silent when it rains.

Sometimes, I stare into the downpour and wonder what it would be like to share everything I've accomplished with someone, a partner. But it doesn't seem like the goddess Alaya has someone in the works for me. As if she can sense my melancholy, the treehouse creaks and groans, her version of a comforting hug.

A chirping sound from the living room makes me twitch my ear. It's my communication disk—someone's calling from another haven.

Muttering, I leave the rain behind and jog out of my bedroom and into the giant rustic living area. After grabbing the flat metal comm disk off the wall, I set it on the floor. A single name hovers over its smooth surface.

Marco.

Running a hand through my salt-and-pepper waves, I direct the comm disk to answer. The moment I do, a life-size hologram of my oldest friend rises from the disk.

"Mi rey," I say with a teasing lilt, dipping my head to one side as I grin playfully.

"Cut that shit out," Marco barks. "I'm not in the mood."

I lean against my fridge and cross both arms, flipping to alpha mode. It's been a long time since I was the king's Second, but it's easy to fall back into that role. "What's wrong?"

He runs both copper hands through his hair, the mirror of mine. "Lola fucking took off again tonight. Nuñez found her putting on a godsdamned concert in another haven. Huge crowd gathered. They knew she was coming, which means she planned it. Yet again."

I grimace. Marco's daughter Lola has always had a wild streak. I've reminded Marco plenty of times that she gets it from him. It's not the first time she's snuck out to play music and I suspect it won't be the last, either. She's something of a rock star, despite her father's wishes otherwise.

Pitch-black eyes find mine. "I'm going to be challenged soon, probably by my Second, Eliel. I'm hearing things."

I nod. It's the way of our people, but being challenged as the sitting king is a whole different ball game, to use one of the human sayings Thea, a new resident, recently taught me. "You've been challenged before. What makes this different?"

Marco's eyes flash with irritation. "This pendejo has always had an eye on Lola. I'd fight to the death to not cede the crown to him, but, moons forbid, he wins, he'd force her into a bonded arrangement."

I snarl. "I take it she doesn't want that?"

Marco scoffs. "The only thing that girl wants is to play music. My Second is a raging asshole, but he's good at his job, so I keep him close. I cannot have her end up as a political bargaining chip." His fierce look softens. "Can I send her to you?"

My mouth drops open, but I zip it quickly.

"You're the only one I trust, Richard," he croons in that same convincing tone he used to get me in trouble when we were pups. He was the brains and I was the brawn, and we got into our fair share of bullshit.

I glance around my treehouse, considering all the angles of allowing the shifter princess to come to Ever. Finally, I look back at Marco. "Ever isn't without danger, old friend. We've had increased thrall attacks, and a warlock recently orchestrated multiple battles here."

Marco grins wickedly. "Word on the streets is that the Keeper's new mate killed him with black magic. Is that true?"

I think back to the events of last week. What I saw Morgan do to Wesley will haunt me for the rest of my life.

"Yeah," I admit. "She obliterated him. She was able to—"

"So that's no longer an issue," my king interrupts. "I'll stop worrying about Lola if she's with you. No place is completely safe. I just need her out of here until I can deal with this threat. Then she can come home and resume her duties." He gives me a soft look. "Hey, it'll be a good chance for you two to reconnect. You haven't seen her since she was a pup."

I smile at that. "Remember that time you fell in a fucking hole on a pack run, and I had to carry her home for you?"

He scoffs. "She's not that little anymore. She's a grown-ass woman, as she likes to remind me on a daily basis."

I smile bigger. I was around a lot when Lola was young, but

then I gave up my position at court and left Santa Alaya. So, I haven't seen her in many, many years. "When do you want to send her?"

Marco's eyes wrinkle at the corners with what I assume must be relief. "Tomorrow, if that isn't too soon?"

I hold back a sigh as I consider all the things I'll need to do to prep Shifter Hollow for a royal visit.

"Works for me," I say.

We make small talk for a few more minutes before I leave to call my Second, Connall, and begin the preparations.

I had hoped, after recent events, I could take the next few months slowly. Spend time with my pack, rebuild after the recent loss of our packmate, Leighton. The unofficial shifter motto is "Above All, Family". I wanted to keep my insular community slash family, well, insulated.

As much as I'd like to reconnect with Lola, my duty and drive is to my pack first.

Fucking great, my wolf snarls into our bond, butting into my thoughts. **Babysitting is my favorite.**

Indeed.

CHAPTER THREE
LOLA

I slept like the dead after Nuñez dragged me back home. A soft, repeating chime helps wake me as I flutter my eyes open. Above me, the arched wooden ceiling is painted the faintest of pinks.

"Good morning, amor," I purr to the castle.

The pink ceiling beams ripple and shimmy, her version of a hello. Across my expansive room, a wall of double doors shakes, the doors opening and shutting on an imaginary breeze.

"What time is it?" I groan. The sun is barely peeking above the turquoise waters of the Bahía de Santa Alaya.

Five creaky chimes ring out from somewhere in the room's depths. I sigh and roll out of bed, pulling to a stand and stretching from side to side. My room is still the same pink and turquoise it was when I was a teen—we've lived in the castle since I was little. I keep thinking that since I'm well past coming of age, I should redo it to be more adultish. But somehow, I can never bring myself to do so.

Striding across the pink-painted wood floor, I step out onto a long, thin balcony that runs the entire length of my suite. A breeze drifts in from the ocean, just visible across the city from the castle. Below me, tall, thin townhomes in every shade of pink, blue, purple, red, and yellow make up the village of Santa Alaya.

Soft music echoes up from somewhere below. That's probably the wolves who own the panadería, baking conchas and all sorts of other delicious treats. I can almost smell the sugar from up here.

A noise behind me draws my attention. The doors on my turquoise armoire swing open. The castle tosses an outfit out—a long cotton ruffled skirt and fitted tank top. I smile and cross the room to pick up the clothes.

Fingering the ruffles, I let my memory pull me back to last night and the amazing green gauze bustle one of the omega seamstresses in town secretly made for me. Smiling, I change and pick my fingers carefully through my boisterous curls. Taking a quick peek in the mirror, I make sure I don't look one-hundred-percent a hot mess before grabbing my bag and guitar and heading for the door. It's time for the rounds I do every morning as part of my duties. Truth be told, it's the one part of being a princess I love—connecting with our packmates in the city. Santa Alaya is so big, it's hard to know them all well. Sometimes I wonder if living in a smaller haven feels different...

I open the door and step into a hall overlooking our center courtyard. Papá's room is directly across the open space from mine. Palms soar up into the sky from the first story, plants spilling out of every crevice and climbing up the round white columns. Oversized agaves placed artfully around the room lend the feeling of the castle being part of the landscape itself. When Papá won the throne, he brought in a designer to bring Santa Alaya *into* the castle. It never fails to make me nostalgic when I look around.

Heading to my right, I wind through a myriad of sun drenched hallways toward the exit.

Colorful birds swoop in and out of the columns, cawing their delight at flying into another day. I smile as I watch them, only a little jealous that they can spread their wings and disappear into the sky. If I could do that, there would be so many places I could visit.

The guard at the exit door smiles at me from behind a newspaper. "Buenos días, Princesa."

I wave at him as he lifts his comm watch to his lips, speaking quietly. "La princesa ya sale."

I've got all of five minutes before two or three of Nuñez's team trail me into the city. It's a regular rotation for them, but I've always hated it. Maybe it's just that nothing quite says family like armed guards going everywhere with you. I huff at the thought. I've never felt unsafe in Santa Alaya. Papá smothers me.

Hurrying, I leave the open front gates and jog down the cobblestone street into the residential area, heading toward the bay. On either side of the main road, Calle Santa Alaya, colorful homes rise three and four stories high. Very few monsters are out this early, which is why I like to make my rounds as the sun comes up. Less opportunity for my packmates to stare as guards trail me through my home haven.

Rounding the first corner, I smile at the open doors of La Iglesia Santa Alaya, so named for the patron wolf goddess of all wolf shifters.

"Good morning," I croon, ascending the steps to tickle the carved wooden doors playfully.

The building responds with a series of happy groans, the double front doors shimmying on their hinges. Inside, candles flicker faintly in front of a dais piled high with offerings for our goddess.

I step into the building, my sandals slapping softly against a terra cotta tile floor. Moving past rows of intricately carved wooden benches, I pace to the dais and admire the many offerings others have left. Pan dulce, flowers, even a few plates of dried meat. There are paper notes too, folded in the traditional way to represent a star. They litter the floor, full of monsters' hopes and wishes and prayers.

Taking a few steps to the right, I grab a candle from the offering box and drop a handful of coins in its place. I return to the dais and seat myself in front of the offerings. A small box of matches sits in a tiny hole in the floor, there for those who wish to leave a candle offering for Santa Alaya.

Grabbing a match, I strike it on the floor and light the candle, poured into a tall glass container with an image of Alaya on the front. It never fails to hit me how beautiful she is. Her wolf is black like mine, her ears tapered to long points. Her ears are bedecked with beautifully crafted silver jewelry. A silver medallion with a green gem hangs around her neck.

Setting the lit candle down among many others, I close my eyes and pray for peace and harmony for my people. I pray for good weather for the farmers and happiness for those in troubled times. And when I'm done, I sit quietly for a few minutes, basking in the tangible presence of our beneficent goddess.

Eventually, voices drift in from outside. Santa Alaya is waking up. It's time for me to get going.

Leaving the church, I admire my haven's tropical beauty as I stroll casually through a network of cobblestone roads, all the way to Calle Mercado, the boardwalk facing the bay. In a few hours, a lively market will pop up right on the bay's edge. Vendors sell everything from sleeping potions to blocks of white cotija cheese to Santa Alaya's hallmark silver jewelry. My favorite leather sandals vendor is at the far corner of this market. It's a good thing, too. Santa Alaya's weather is always sunny and eighty-five degrees. I've never worn a closed-toe shoe.

Shops and restaurants line the street, waves washing quietly up on a pink sand shore. Breathing deeply, I search for my wolf, longing for connection. I always feel her so strongly when I walk my city's streets. Perhaps it's the innate sense of serving my people that comes with being the king's daughter. Maybe it's just that she also seems to enjoy our morning rounds.

Either way, when we walk the streets early in the morning, I almost imagine I can hear her voice. Although, that's incredibly rare for our kind. Not even my father can hear his wolf's precise thoughts, and he's the most powerful shifter I've ever met.

I head for my favorite café and order two coffees. This shop sells coffee made from the traditional Santa Alayan beans, grown in the dry hills behind the castle. The depth of flavor is my absolute fave.

The minotaur barista smiles at me as he mixes up the troll whip-infused concoction on my first stop this morning.

His sausage-thick fingers brush mine as he passes me both cups. "Lola. Take me up on that dinner offer, please. I'm learning to cook, if you can believe it."

I beam up into his hopeful, curious gaze. "Good for you, Rafa. But you know I'm married to the music."

His smile grows softer, like he expected the answer. Probably because every time he asks me out, my answer is exactly the same.

It's not like I wouldn't date, if the monster interested me. But my wolf takes no notice of the males in Santa Alaya. If she doesn't care to pay them any attention, then, neither will I. Her instinct has always been spot on.

"Another time, perhaps," he says carefully.

"Perhaps," I agree, winking as I turn from him and exit the cafe's back door. Outside and to the left, a rickety iron staircase leads to a set of luxurious residences Papá built for the older solitary monsters in our community. Most aging shifters live with their families; that's the way of our people, having all generations under one roof together.

But not everyone is lucky enough to have a big family in Santa Alaya. For those who don't, the community home offers what they cannot get otherwise. It's always my first stop.

I ascend and push through a set of carved wooden doors, smiling at the beautiful shifter omega seated at the front desk.

"Princesa, good morning!" she chirps, dipping her head politely.

I smile, even as footsteps behind me announce my guards' arrival. I force my smile even bigger. "How is Lupe today?"

The girl's smile falls a little. "Morose. She's been sitting at the window, looking out at the bay since the sun began to rise."

I lift my chin and nod. It's what I expected. Of all the shifters at the community home, Lupe is my favorite, but her story is sad. Her sons mated and moved away from Santa Alaya, leaving her behind. It's hard to fathom one's children behaving so poorly. I'd slap them if I had ever met them. But that happened a long, long time ago.

I pace through the halls until I reach the open common room. It's empty save for a single, hunched figure seated in front of the window.

"Lupe," I call softly, knowing her excellent hearing will pick up my tones even from this far.

"Don't shout, girl!" she grouses back. "I'm old and falling apart, not deaf!"

"What about caffeinated?" I cross the room and hand her her favorite drink.

She takes it with an appreciative look. "I'm never caffeinated enough, corazón. Thank you." Her dark eyes flick over my shoulder. "I see the nitwits are following as usual."

I tuck a stray lock of white hair behind her tapered ear. "Tsk, Lupe. They're just doing their jobs."

Her smile goes wicked, eyes wrinkling in the corners. "And how was the concert?"

I sigh and flop down into the seat across from her, staring out the window at the turquoise waters of the bay. "I managed to get a full song in, but that's it before Nuñez showed up."

"Well…fuck," Lupe says.

"Mhm."

She sighs loudly, lifting a middle finger toward the open room behind us. I can only assume my guards stand in the doorway like always. She loves to taunt them. To their credit, they ignore her obvious insults.

"Lupe," I chide again. "Calma, por favor, and tell me what you've been doing since I last visited."

She snorts and takes another sip of her latte. "Oh, you mean since yesterday? You do too much, Lola." Leaning down, she swats playfully at my thigh. It's so grandmotherly, I almost laugh. She's not *my* grandmother, but she might as well be with that move.

Instead, I feign growly irritation as she lifts her coffee. "Serving my people feels right and good."

"You are your father's daughter," Lupe says softly. "But don't forget that you need to serve yourself as well, Lola."

"I tried," I muse. "I managed five whole minutes of song before Nuñez dragged me home. That's something, I suppose. Time to start planning my next escape."

Lupe falls silent, and for once, I'm happy to sit quietly with her, sipping our drinks and staring out at the horizon as the sun emerges from the sea. Eventually, I play her some songs while she falls asleep in her chair, her cup dipping to one side as her grip loosens.

I take it from her wrinkled fingers and set it on the windowsill before dropping a kiss on her forehead. "Rest well, my friend," I murmur before turning to leave the room.

In the doorway, my guards stand with even expressions. I can't imagine they enjoy trailing me around any more than I enjoy being followed, but they're good-natured about it.

For the next three hours I make the rounds of the community home. My guards are always patient until lunchtime. Then they start grumbling until I take them to a little spot on the corner that sells shaved meat street tacos.

That's our routine, so it doesn't surprise me when one of the guards bumps me with his hip as we cross from the community home and head toward our next stop. "I'm starving, Princesa. Can we take a break?"

I open my mouth to respond when a voice surprises me, ringing clearly from the other side of Calle Mercado. "Why don't you all head back to the castle? I can keep an eye on the princess."

As a group, we turn to see Papá's Second, Eliel, standing on the sidewalk, leaning against a lamppost.

Like always, a chill skirts down my spine at the way he looks at me. Eliel is classically handsome—russet skin, dark hair, dark eyes, dimples on either side of a broad, plush mouth. His angular nose tilts slightly up at the end—nearly all the omegas have the hots for him.

But it's the lascivious way those black eyes trail down my body and back up that sets my teeth on edge.

Thankfully, one of the guards comes to my rescue with a quick retort. "It's our job. We're happy to do it, and we have lunch plans, Second." He spits Eliel's title like a cuss word.

Eliel shrugs, waving the guard's comment away. "No matter. I'll join you."

Ugh.

Technically, as Papá's Second, he ranks higher than my guard. They can't tell him no.

But I can.

"No thanks, Second," I say cheerfully, using his title to remind him that he doesn't run this pack.

Eliel steps off the sidewalk and slips both hands into white linen slacks that accentuate the bulge between his thighs. His cock is hard, the swollen edges of the fleshy knot at the base of his penis clearly visible through the thin fabric. He probably thinks I find that hot, that if he shows me what he's packing, I might throw caution to the wind and beg him to knot me.

Gross.

I don't think there's ever been an alpha who appealed to me less than this one.

My guards hover behind me. They work for the crown, not Eliel, but the lines of seniority blur this high up the shifter food chain. Technically speaking, Eliel isn't a threat. I just find him skeezy.

He stops in front of me, so close we're almost touching. Dark eyes travel a path down to my chest and back up, his full lips curling into what he likely thinks is a seductive smirk. "You should really give me a chance, Princesa. I could be so good to you."

Yuck.

I beam brightly and wink at him. "I'm married to the music, Eliel. There's no place in my heart to test out your theory."

His smirk grows into a full, fang-toothed smile. "For now, Lola. But not forever. At some point, you'll be expected to take a mate. You're not getting any younger, you know."

Boiling fury joins the chill traveling down the back of my neck, all the way down my spine as my body violently rejects his suggestion. Still, I know when no reaction is the best reaction. When I say nothing, Eliel chuckles and curls his upper lip backward, showing me his fangs.

"Step away from the princess," one of my guards orders.

Eliel mock salutes and turns away, but he'll be back, I know it. Because that sinister look in his eye? I've seen it before.

~

Hours later, a knock at my bedroom door draws my attention. "Come in!" I call as I turn. I'm struggling to get the vision of Eliel's commentary out of my head. Fuck, that's the least of my troubles based on the grim look on Nuñez's face as he enters my room. I suspect I'm about to get an ear chewing from Papá about last night. Seems like today is the day of rough conversations. Not even a morning of rounds absolves me of what I did.

My head bodyguard cuts me a harsh look. Dark circles underscore both of his eyes. "Your father wants to see you immediately."

I cross the room to gaze up into his weathered face. "I'm sorry if I made your job difficult, old friend." My apology comes out as a whisper.

Nuñez runs one hand through his sun-kissed dark hair. "Yeah, well, it doesn't matter now because I'm no longer your head bodyguard."

Shockwaves ripple through me, my mouth dropping open. "What do you mean? You've been with me since I was a child!"

His expression flattens, his nostrils flaring. "Yeah, that was before you planned an entire concert and escaped the castle right under my nose for the millionth time. The king no longer trusts me to guard you, and I don't blame him. Last night was the last straw, Lola."

Oh moons. I bring a hand to my mouth. "Why? What's different this time? Nuñez, I'm so sorry."

My guard waves the question and apology away. "Get dressed, Lola; let's not keep him waiting."

He steps out as I grab my crown. It's still in the pocket of my skirt from the concert. Shock and shame war within me. I thought through the consequences of what I did, but I never expected Papá to go this far. He never has before, and I've probably snuck out two dozen times in the last decade. He loves to remind me that my future is the people of Santa Alaya, not a musical career, but he's never come down that hard on me for pursuing music.

Two minutes later, I follow my bodyguard through breezy, sunkissed hallways from my suite to my father's office on the far side of the castle. Every archway we pass through shimmies and shakes, almost like a reassuring pat on my back. But by the time

Nuñez and I get to the door to Papá's office, even the castle is quiet.

My heart pounds in my ears as Nuñez grabs the door handle and swings the whitewashed door open, gesturing for me to enter. I walk quickly down a short hall filled with bookshelves on either side. It opens into the office, a giant open space, the back wall of windows looking out onto the city and the bay.

Papá sits at his desk, a thunderous look on his face. He rises as I enter the vaulted room. A figure kneels to the left of his desk.

Oh fuuuuuck.

My bandmate Leo lifts his head. One eye is swollen and completely shut. A gash through one of his dark brows bleeds heavily, a trail of red dripping into his mouth.

I dash across the room and slide onto my knees in front of him, cradling his face between my hands.

"Lola," he croaks. "I'm fine; it's not that bad."

My father rounds the desk as I spin toward him and glare. His black eyes, the same obsidian shade as mine, move to Leo. "Get the fuck out of my office."

Leo puts his hands over mine, squeezing me gently, then rises and jogs out of the room. I watch in shocked silence before I'm able to face my father.

He leans against the edge of his desk, warning flashing through his expression. "I have begged and pleaded with you to be careful. I have shared with you the political challenges of holding this throne. But you seem bound and fucking determined to flout the rules I put in place to keep you safe."

Fury fills me. Fury for Leo and fury for Nuñez. I plant both hands on my hips. "I've done this before and you've never come down this hard on anyone. Why is it different now? And what use is holding the throne if it makes you a raging asshole?"

I've never spoken to my father like this, but in my entire life, he's never hurt anyone outside of an official challenge. An alpha's job is to protect his family, not whatever happened in the office before I entered. It's so wrong I resist the urge to scratch at creepy-crawlies skittering over my skin.

He snarls and shoves off the desk, bumping me with his chest, demanding I submit to his wolf's will. His wolf's purple sheen flashes through his irises, a reminder that they're on the same page about this.

How? Why?

My wolf rises inside me, upset and angry and in complete disagreement with our pack alpha's behavior. "What you did isn't okay," I press. "Sobre todo, familia. Leo is our *family*, Papá."

"No, it's not okay," he says on a hiss. "But I'd do worse to keep you safe."

"I'm not in danger here," I snap.

"Wrong," Father barks, his alpha command a near-physical slap to the face. "Eliel is going to challenge me any day. If he wins, he'll bind you no matter how you feel about the situation."

I reel backward in shock. Eliel?

Eyes wide, I stare at my father. "He wouldn't. Forced bondings are illegal."

"What's legal won't matter because I'd probably be dead," he says roughly. "I've shielded you from some of this, Lola, because I didn't want you to worry. But Eliel won't play fair. I sense it."

I look out the wall of windows. "I didn't realize," I murmur, voice trailing off. "If I had known…"

"I'm not sure you'd have done anything differently," he says, his tone wry. "You've always been strong-willed."

"Not to the detriment of those around me, I hope." I turn to face him again. "What do you need from me? How can I help thwart whatever Eliel is planning?"

Suddenly, my father looks exhausted. His shoulders slump, his eyes hooded. "I need you out of trouble so I can focus fully on Eliel and uncovering what his plan really is. I'm sending you to Richard in Ever. I trust him to keep you safe."

Keep me in line, he means.

I nod slowly. I haven't seen Richard since I was a pup, but he was a staple of my childhood. I understand why Papá wants to send me there, even if it rankles a little.

"I love you," he whispers. "So damn much, mija. I could not stand it if Eliel forced you into something you didn't want. If I fall, I need to know that Richard will be the second line of defense between you and the new king."

I gulp. The idea of my father falling to Eliel is unfathomable. What would happen to Santa Alaya, if Papá fell? Eliel hides a snake's deadliness beneath his simpering smiles. He's not fit to be our king.

"I'll go." I wrap my arms around myself, but Papá pulls me into an embrace, purring the way he has since I was a tiny pup.

"It'll be fine, mija. This is just a precaution, okay? I trust Richard with my life and yours. You'll be as safe as you *can* be there. And when you get back, we'll talk a little more about the music, hmm?"

He strokes my curls away from my face, tilting my chin up so that I'm looking directly in his eyes. "Please, please do not leave Ever under any circumstances, okay? Promise me, Lola."

"Se lo prometo," I swear.

I promise.

CHAPTER FOUR
RICHARD

Connall's big strides eat up the distance between us as he crosses the street toward my bar, Bad Axe. I've been standing out front, waiting for him to arrive.

He runs a hand through his auburn waves, green eyes flashing. "Lola's guest house is ready, and I've notified the rest of the pack about the timeline."

I open my mouth to respond just as hoofbeats announce the arrival of Ever's current Keeper, Arkan. He halts next to Connall, who takes one look at his shirt and snorts.

I almost don't look…almost. Because every damn day the innuendo on Arkan's tees seems to get worse and worse.

The dark coated, inky skinned centaur shifts from one front leg to the other, his horse tail swishing around his black-coated sides. He winks pale eyes at me and points to his shirt.

And I look. Despite my best efforts.

Spread cheeks. Not hate.

I groan and slap a hand over my face. "Arkan, the *princess* is arriving. Princess, as in shifter royalty."

He stomps a foot and crosses his muscular arms over the tee.

"I've met Lola a half dozen times through my work with Hearth HQ. She's cool as fuck. She's not gonna care about my shirt."

I give him a stern look. "You know, your predecessor was a little more…" I cast around for the right words to describe our former Keeper, Ever's version of a mayor.

"Stick in the mud," Arkan offers helpfully. "Tortured by his demons? Desperately in love?" He shrugs. "You know I adore Abemet, but just because he did it one way doesn't mean I need to."

And there's the rub. I worked with our former Keeper since right after the Cerinvalla Act created the monster haven system. We've partnered for hundreds of haven-years.

Arkan and I are still finding our footing.

He rips the shirt over his head, revealing an upper body tight with muscle. Flipping the tee inside out, he beams at me. When he throws it back on, I growl.

Jackass, my wolf snaps in our shared mindspace. **Break one of his legs.**

"Stop it," I growl to myself.

Arkan and Connall cock their heads to the side. Arkan smiles. "And how's Big Daddy today?"

Connall chokes and looks off into the distance.

I groan. "Don't call him that; you'll egg him on."

Arkan beams and stares deeply into my eyes, scanning my face as I resist the urge to follow my wolf's instruction and kick him in the foreleg.

The big centaur sighs. "I'm headed to the portal station. Hana's already there, making sure everything is ready for the princess."

I nod, lost in thought about Lola's impending arrival. Connall and I watch Arkan take off up the road at a canter, his black tail streaming like a flag behind him.

"I like him," Connall states, grinning at me. "Even though he antagonizes Big Daddy."

"Stop it," I hiss.

Connall beams. "Listen, I've never known an alpha whose wolf talked to him. It says a lot about your strength, Richard. If your wolf wants us all to call him Big Daddy, I'm down."

In my mind, my wolf preens and prances like an asshole. **That's right, Second,** he quips in my brain.

Connall stares deeply into my eyes. "He's saying something about me, isn't he?"

You keep staring that hard, I'm gonna think you wanna suck my dick, my wolf growls.

"Nope," I say aloud. "He's bitching about the weather."

Liar.

"Liar," Connall says with a snort.

The reality is that my wolf has only been talking to me since Leighton died. I don't know why he chose that moment to make himself more present. I can only assume it's because a pack alpha's first and primary objective is protecting his pack, and Leighton's death revealed the threat of dark magic.

It should have been a blessing to receive that level of power with my wolf. But in the short time he's been vocal, Big Daddy has overwhelmed me with commentary that almost never matches my own thoughts. We're still finding our footing too, and it's really fucking frustrating.

Thankfully, he falls silent as Connall and I head up Shifter Hollow's main drag toward the portal station where Lola and Marco will be arriving. By the time we get there, a small crowd is gathered despite the fact that I specifically told everyone not to come. I need to cover some details with Marco, and I don't want to do that in front of my entire pack.

When I growl at the gathered shifters, Connall takes the hint and shoos the onlookers away from the portal station's door. Two stories of windows line the front of the giant one-room building. Inside, it's just an open room, the round green portal on the far side. Its surface glimmers and ripples peacefully. At each side stand members of my pack. It's our job to guard the portal door that connects us to one other haven.

Hana, Arkan's lovely centaur wife, smiles when Connall and I enter the station. "Hello, Alpha and Second."

What a smoke show, Big Daddy growls. **We've never mounted a centaur. We should see how Arkan feels about sharing.**

Oh my goddess, he's insufferable.

"Hey, Hana," Connall says.

I give her a friendly smile, keeping my lips zipped, lest some of Big Daddy's stupid internal monologue leaves my mouth.

Hana tucks a strand of dark hair behind her pointed ears. "Hey, Big Daddy."

He howls inside my mind, so damn loud, I wince and clap a hand over one ear.

Hana chuckles. "Seems like he's really loud in there, huh?" Her expression goes serious. "Vikand might have suggestions for you. I'm sure he'd love to find a way to be useful, if you wished for some insight into Big Daddy's…strength." Her dark eyes wrinkle mirthfully at the corners.

"Noted," I say agreeably. I'll find her father-in-law, Vikand, later, because the extra voice in my mind is making me crazy. I always felt at peace with my wolf until I could hear his specific thoughts—they seem to center primarily around sex, something I haven't had with another person in a very long time. For now, I'd like to evict him and get some peace and quiet.

The portal creaks and shifts, the surface rippling outward in waves. Hana, Arkan, Connall, and I take a few steps backward. A green tunnel shoots into the room and then retracts, the portal's surface becoming almost mirror-like. A trio of shifter males walk through carrying luggage. A woman follows, stepping gracefully through the doorway.

Sound muffles as I blink slowly. The omega's black curls are stacked high, framing her face like a halo. Night-black eyes scan the room. Her lips are dark too, a tiny, familiar freckle on one side of her plump mouth.

Hubba hubba, Big Daddy purrs. **Let me out.**

No, I bark, reality slapping me.

That stunning woman who just stepped out of the portal, the woman whose eyes meet mine as she smiles? That's Lola.

Lola, who I carried in my jaws when she couldn't keep up with the pack.

Lola, who I haven't seen in decades.

Lola, my best friend's daughter.

My mouth goes as dry as a desert.

Connall kicks my foot. "That her, Alpha?"

Lola's longtime bodyguard, Nuñez, trails her out of the portal. He's the highest-ranking male in this group, apart from Marco, whom I realize with a start isn't here.

But I can't pull my eyes from the female who stalks gracefully across the portal station floor, a soft-sided guitar case slung over her back.

She beams at me and, when she gets close enough, hops up and throws both long arms around my neck, pecking my cheek with lips as soft as silk. She floods my nose with the scents of oranges and sweet cream.

"Richard!" she exclaims, her tone excited. "It's been too long!"

Something deep aches and breaks free inside me. Shock, I think. Even Big Daddy is silent.

I wrap my arms carefully around Lola and squeeze. "Good to see you too, kiddo."

The word hangs awkwardly between us as she eyes me with a curious, careful expression.

Kiddo. Ugh. This woman isn't a child. She hasn't been a child for a long time, almost two decades by shifter standards. And it's been longer than that since I've seen her.

She slips out of my arms with a wry look, placing both elegant, black-nailed hands on her muscular hips. "You haven't aged a day." Her smile falls. "Thank you for agreeing to host me. Papá is swamped with things; I'm sure he told you."

Alaya blessed this omega, Big Daddy croons. **Look at those tits.**

I swallow hard, shaking my head to clear my thoughts—and his—forcing my eyes firmly above her neck. "So he said. Where is Marco, Lola?"

Her smile falls, dark lips turning downward. She shoves both hands into the pockets of her jeans. "He didn't come. He said he has all the confidence in you being able to protect me." Her lips twitch like she'll say something more, but she doesn't.

I look at the three males who arrived with her. Lola's bodyguard, Nuñez, frowns. "His Majesty is preparing for a challenge. He wanted Lola safe quickly."

I give Nuñez a harsh look. "So the king isn't coming?"

He purses his lips and shakes his head no.

I'm shocked Marco isn't here, but I don't want to make it awkward for Lola, so I gesture to her things as I look back at her. "Let's get you settled, alright?"

Nuñez clears his throat, pulling my attention back to him. "As you might imagine, we've got to return to aid his majesty with the preparations. We're leaving now."

Lola purses her lips and shifts from one foot to the other.

I look between her and the guard. "I'm missing something. You're not staying? You're dropping her off and leaving?"

Out of the corner of my eye, I notice Hana and Arkan back away to give us privacy.

Lola gives me a look that's somewhere between imploring and desperate.

"We're leaving immediately," Nuñez says on a growl. "Marco needs us. She'll be fine here with you as long as she doesn't *leave*."

Lola winces and shoots him a look. "I promised I wouldn't."

I bet Marco kicked Nuñez's ass for allowing her to slip out to put on a concert, given what's going on with Eliel.

He gives her a shitty look that pulls a growl from my throat. Now that she's here under my protection, she's my packmate, and I don't like the way he's fucking looking at her.

Connall reaches for one of Lola's bags with a big smile. "We've got it handled, man, thanks. Hey, Lola, I'm Connall, Richard's Second." He reaches for her hand with a big, friendly smile.

Good boy, Big Daddy purrs in my brain. **Second protects. Second welcomes. He's pretty good.**

Thankfully, Big Daddy seems to approve of Connall despite the regular chest beating to remind him we're the Alpha.

Nuñez gives Lola another rough look, then makes the "round 'em up" gesture over his head. "Let's go, team."

I resist the urge to snap about them leaving Lola like they are. She stands beside Connall and me, watching her lifetime protector leave her behind, seemingly without a care. I could never dump a packmate like he's doing, even if I thought I was leaving her somewhere safe.

This is one of the million reasons I left Santa Alaya. Innate shifter instincts like protection and harmony get lost as you go up the pack food chain. I don't miss it at all.

As the four shifters disappear into the portal, I give Lola an assessing look. "You must really have pissed Nuñez off with that concert trick, huh?"

Her cheeks darken, but she lifts her chin. "Yeah, and the consequences were far worse than I thought they'd be, or I wouldn't have done it. I didn't realize things had changed for Papá. It's never been that big of a deal before."

I soften a little. Big Daddy is silent.

Lola stares into my eyes as if willing me to give her a speech or chide her like Marco probably does. For a long moment, she searches my face. My alpha instincts ping. They've always been good, allowing me to read my packmates and sense their feelings. She's remorseful and worried.

"Let's go," I say gently. "We've got a great little guest house for you to stay in while you're here."

Her lashes flutter against smooth skin.

Holy moons, she's fucking beautiful.

Do you think princess pussy is better than regular pussy? Or about the same?

Goddess, shut the hells up please, I snap at Big Daddy.

After sliding my arm through the handles on three of Lola's bags, I throw them over my shoulder and jerk my head toward the door. Connall grabs the other bags and follows as we cross the cavernous room toward the exit.

CHAPTER FIVE

LOLA

I attempt to steal one of my bags from Richard's Second, Connall, but the redhead shoos me away with a friendly smile. So, instead of carrying my own luggage, I find myself trailing my father's oldest friend out of Ever's portal station holding nothing but my guitar.

I haven't seen Richard since I was a pup. I remember him being larger than life, but I didn't remember him being so...alpha. He stalks across the floor, big strides eating up the distance between the portal and the exit. Thick, muscular legs are clearly outlined in jeans that leave nothing to the imagination. It's not that the cut is meant to be tight; he's just really damn muscular, bigger and broader than most males I know.

A trim waist flares into impossibly broad shoulders, his shoulder blades visible through a thin tee. He's stacked with muscle, tattoos covering both forearms and the back of his neck. Salt-and-pepper hair is slicked back, curling against his nape.

Heat flushes through me. Moons, I'm ogling a man who's basically family and knew me when I was young.

That was a long time ago, though. It's fine as long as I keep my sexy thoughts in my brain and don't say them out loud.

When he grabs the door and swings it open for me with a soft smile, I resist the urge to flirt. *Tamp that down, girl,* I tell myself, slipping through the door with a thankful nod.

Two centaurs stand in front of the station—a dark-coated male and female with black skin. The male, who I think I recognize, wears a shirt that says—oh my gods—it says, "Spread Cheeks. Not Hate." I burst into laughter, covering my mouth with my hand.

He beams and nudges the female. "Told you she'd laugh."

"Thought you'd flipped that inside out," Richard grumbles.

The female gives me a grin as the male steps forward, leaning down to hold a hand out to me. "Princess, I'm Arkan. We've met at Hearth HQ a few times, but I'm now Ever's Keeper. This is my mate, Hana. Let us know if we can do anything to make your stay comfy."

I shake his hand and dip my head politely to them both.

Hana does the same, gesturing to a basket of food in her hands. "This is courtesy of the town of Ever, a gift basket from our wonderful General Store on Main Street, outside of Shifter Hollow. You can follow Sycamore Street all the way there, if you want to explore. There's a grocery here, too, of course, but the General Store has a wide variety from across the haven system."

"Thank you." Goddess, they've done so much for me already, and while I'm primarily appreciative, regret rears her ugly head. I've put people out, all because I tried to do something for myself.

The guilt comes next, because I didn't get a chance to say goodbye to Leo or the Lobos or anyone other than the castle before we left. I can't even comm him from my watch since the only one who can call between havens is my father. Hopefully whatever room they're sticking me in has a comm disk, so I can message Leo and make sure he's alright.

My fingers twitch with the need to do something, anything to get control over my life.

Richard joins us, pausing next to me. He glances between me

and the centaurs. "Let's get Lola to her tree house. She's had a long journey."

Arkan reaches for several of my bags, but Richard shoos him away with a smile.

The alpha places a hand on my shoulder and squeezes, and everything inside me tightens.

That smile.

It transforms him from simply handsome into something powerfully masculine and over-the-top in charge. Dark eyes flash with green and narrow. I can't find a single appropriate word to say when his smile falls, his wolf's emerald shade growing in intensity. For a long moment, he stares. But when goose bumps pepper my skin, he turns toward the street in front of the portal station.

I try not to feel the loss of that focus on me.

Get it together, Lola, you're being weird! I mentally slap myself.

Richard leads the way as Arkan and Hana walk next to me. When shadows swoop overhead, I duck on instinct, but the group laughs together.

I glance up to see two pegasi galloping through the air, their beautiful giant wings beating gracefully. They dive and dance above us before disappearing up into the trees. Goddess, I wonder if they live up there. We don't have any pegasi in Santa Alaya.

Hana chuckles and gestures to the forest around us. "Shifter Hollow comprises nearly a third of Ever's total space within the wards. Unlike many other havens, this one was designed with a forested section specifically for pegasi, centaurs, and shifters. The shifters and centaurs live down here, but the pegasi live up in the treetops." She leans down as if telling me a secret. "There's even a harpy who lives here, so don't be alarmed if you see her. Her name is Celset."

Shock trills through me. A harpy within haven wards is

unusual. The solitary, cannibalistic monsters tend to prefer the untamed wilds of the human world.

Hana's laugh tinkles between us. "Ever is unusual in a lot of ways. It's definitely my favorite haven we've lived in."

Arkan reaches over and places a hand at the base of her spine, stroking her coat with deft, elegant fingers.

I smile up at them as we walk along a broad, flat street through the woods. "You haven't been here long, is that right?"

Hana's smile grows tender. "Our cottage sprang up next to the Community Garden a bit over a week ago. Hearth HQ sent us to help Ever's original Keeper when the warlock Wesley continued to target Ever. The Keeper's mate is a black witch. Wesley attacked her last week, and..." her voice trails off.

Arkan looks around his mate at me. "Morgan killed him. I'm told her power was amazing to see. I wasn't there, but"—he glances at Richard—"Richard could tell you all about it."

Richard looks over the shoulder not weighed down by my bags. "It was terrifying, but she's a hero. Abe retired after Wesley's last attack to spend time with his mate."

"Holy moons," I murmur. "That sounds harrowing."

Arkan looks at me again. "This pack lost a member during the attack, Leighton. If Shifter Hollow feels a little somber while you're here, that's why. Everyone is thrilled you've arrived, but you might sense a tender edge to the Hollow."

My heart drops into my stomach. Jogging forward, I put my hand on Richard's forearm, stopping him. He turns to me with a surprised expression, full lips pursed into a flat, thin line.

"This is a horrible time for me to come here, if you're dealing with loss. Let me call Papá, Richard. There is no need for you to focus on me when you should be focusing on your packmates."

Chocolate eyes soften, and he shakes his head. "You're never a bother, Lola. We're happy to have you here." His thoughtful smile returns. "Sobre todo, familia, remember? That's just as true here as anywhere else, and now that you're here, you're part of my family."

He tries to turn and continue, but I grip his forearm harder. "Did Papá know?" My voice is pure steel when it rumbles from my throat. If Papá sent me here not realizing their pack is in mourning, then I should leave.

Richard glances off into the forest, letting out a soft sigh as if he's weighing telling me the truth or not.

After an interminable silence that's probably only moments, he shakes his head. "Marco didn't know." He gives me a serious look, black brows furrowing in the center. "He didn't ask, and he shouldn't have because your safety is his priority."

Richard's skin is hot through his shirt, nearly burning my palm with his heat. Dark eyes sear mine with intensity as he continues, his wolf's green overtaking his natural shade. "You are not a bother, Lola. Leighton's family is well cared for. There will always be space for you, no matter what else is going on."

At his side, Connall nods. "We're good, Lola. We promise."

I can't ignore the guilt and discomfort that rise in my core, nearly choking me with their strength. All of this because I tried to put the music first instead of my people. How many times has Papá drummed 'pack first' into my brain? We have a responsibility to our people, not our dreams.

I'll never make that mistake again. Shifters as high up in the hierarchy as I am don't get to make those sorts of choices about their lives.

I can see why.

When I say nothing, Richard spins and walks backward, waving his free hand around us. "This is Shifter Hollow's downtown area. The main road, Sycamore, leads to downtown Ever if you go the opposite way. The post office is here, if you need to order or receive a package from another haven. My bar, Bad Axe, will be on your right. I live above it, if you need anything at all."

I look at where he's pointing. The front of the bar is as rustic as it gets, a big neon sign hanging above twin wooden doors with mismatched tree branch handles. Like every other store in the Hollow's downtown, it's built right into the base of gigantic, wide trees so tall, I can't even see the sky.

Above Bad Axe's entrance, a giant rectangular glass box juts out. Another is angled to the side on top of that one. In fact, as I look around, that's true of every second story along the whole street. Angled glass rooms hang out into the street, furniture and art and monsters visible through the clear walls.

I stare in awe at the traditional shifter architecture. I rarely leave Santa Alaya, so I haven't had a chance to see it in person. A potions shop occupies the space next to Bad Axe, and in the glass room above it, a female walks with her hand lifted to her mouth, speaking into her comm watch.

"Little different from Santa Alaya, huh?" Richard winks. "We went old school with the design of Shifter Hollow when Ever was created, but I love it. There's nothing to make you feel connected to your pack like seeing your pack all the time."

"We understand if you want privacy, though," Connall pitches in. "You can blur or solidify the glass with the touch of a button, or the house can do it for you, if you ask. Please don't feel like you have to give us the inside view into your life. We don't expect that."

I'm at a loss for words as the omega a floor above us glances down, notices us, and waves. She seems excited to see our group, speaking rapidly into her comm watch as her hand makes wild motions.

Richard jerks his head to the potions shop. A sign that says "Alkemi" hangs on the glass-front door. Through a giant plate window, rows of potions and crystals are visible. "Alkemi has a potion for anything you need and the owner, Malik, is amazing. And of course, the General Store on Main Street has a limited selection of potions, too."

"It's beautiful," I say, hiking my guitar higher over my back. Is this what it would have been like if I wasn't born the princess? If I was just another shifter omega in a small pack? If the entire haven didn't technically count as my family?

Richard continues his tour as we walk slowly up the street. "We've got the grocery, where you can get supplies." Piles of vegetables are visible through the front window. "There's Pack Gem, your home for all the glittery goodies an omega might want to adorn herself with." He winks a second time.

Shifters' love of beautiful jewelry is well-known—Santa Alaya is full of renowned silversmiths. Wolves come from many other havens to purchase special jewelry in my home haven. I'd have been surprised if there wasn't a jeweler in this one.

Next to Pack Gem, a book-filled window seems mismatched with a sign indicating they sell jewelry.

Arkan looks at me. "The Pack Gem folks moved next door before we came to Ever. My father is currently renting their old space for his books. That location is more of an office right now. Although, you're welcome there at any time. Just know that once you enter"—his tone goes mysterious and dramatic—"you'll be there for at least three hours."

I snort out a laugh.

Richard waves around us, still walking backward. "About a ten-minute walk this way, you'll come to Biergarten, which is a great spot for lunch and brunch. They close down for dinner, though."

My laugh carries on. "So what you're telling me is that at least half of the businesses in Shifter Hollow are related to food? I suppose that tracks."

He beams. "Are we even wolves if food and family aren't every other word out of our mouths?" His expression grows serious.

"I'm sorry to say there are no paleteros in Ever, but there's a kick-ass ice cream shop downtown."

I make a faux grimace. "Paletas will always reign supreme, but I suppose I can deal." I like this playful approach to the town tour. For a minute, I can forget the reason I'm here in the first place.

He jerks his head toward the right. "Like most shifter towns outside of Santa Alaya, our homes spiral out from the main street. The guest houses are interspersed with spoken-for dwellings to help make it easier to assimilate." He levels me with that same smile, but I sense something guarded there, something that brings back the pressure in my chest.

They lost a packmate. Now they have to deal with me. All because I couldn't follow the main fucking motto of all shifters.

I stare around at the stark, forested beauty that's so different from home. Huge dark trees soar above us, so tall they blot out the sky. A sense of claustrophobia hits me at not being able to see across town to the bay. My breath comes faster, tension in my chest tightening until I have to force myself to breathe evenly and not look freaked out.

The last day's worth of emotions are hitting me all at once.

Hana glances down at me, clasping her hands at her waist. "Lola, once you get settled, it would be my honor to give you a tour of the remainder of Ever, if you'd like to see it."

I force my lungs to fill with air, plastering a smile on my face. When I turn to the lovely female, my grin widens. "That would be great. Maybe later this afternoon or tomorrow?"

She lifts her wrist, showing me the blue-banded comm watch that encircles it. "Any time, friend. Simply call me. There is no rush."

We walk quietly along a residential street that arches away from the main thoroughfare. It's quieter here, the sounds muffled by the tree canopy. Just like the main road, giant glass rectangles stick out of the trees in every direction. Through the clear walls, shifters are visible going about their daily lives. It's fascinatingly new, and as I observe everything, homesickness hits.

Connall glances over his shoulder at me. "We hope you enjoy the guest treehouse we picked out for you, Lola. Remember, we have no requirements for you while you're here. Enjoying yourself is enough for us."

Some of the pressure in my chest eases at his words, but, like always, that bone-deep instinct to serve hits me hard. What will I do all day every day if I'm not visiting Lupe and the others and spending time with my pack?

Do they miss me?

I think about the last time I saw her. What if nobody told her I was leaving? What if nobody told anyone at all that I'd be back… eventually?

About halfway up the street, we dip between two enormous tree trunks to walk along a moss-covered stone path. Richard slips an ancient-looking metal key from his pocket as we pause in front of a tall, moss-encrusted door.

He shoves it into the lock and twists. The door opens with a groan and a light turns on inside the entryway.

The treehouse creaks, bringing a smile to my face. Her hello is reassuring, for some reason.

Richard stalks through the door and disappears down a short hall and around a corner. Connall follows, but Hana and Arkan pause next to me.

Arkan grins. "Call us if you need anything at all, even if you just have questions. Welcome home to Shifter Hollow."

CHAPTER SIX
RICHARD

I stride through the dark entry hall, the treehouse turning lights on for me as I go. A wide, circular wooden ramp leads up to the main living level, a cavernous open room with a kitchen on the left-hand side. After crossing the room toward an oversized pit sofa, I drop Lola's bags on it and turn. Connall joins me, the princess right behind him, one hand on her elbow. She rubs the back of her arm as she stares at me.

"This is lovely," she whispers. "Absolutely lovely." But she's barely looking around, even though the treehouse practically quivers with excitement at having a guest.

Instead, a scent cuts through the air—stress.

When I shoot Connall a look, he flares his nostrils and breathes in quietly. Green eyes flash to mine, and, like always, he reads my sentiment. Nodding, he drops Lola's bags next to the ones I carried. Her scent grows stronger as he gives her a friendly smile, and turns to leave.

Her muscles begin shaking as she drops her hands to her waist, clasping them together as she flashes me a big smile.

Fake.

Big dark eyes fill with tears until she spins away from me and looks out of the glass wall opposite the kitchen.

Do. Something. Now! Big Daddy bellows in my mind. His suggestion is pointless—I'm already across the room.

That scent—her scent—calls to the deepest and most instinctual part of my alpha nature. I'm committed—no, it's more than that. I'm *resolute* in my need to support and care for my people.

And that began to include her the moment she stepped into my haven.

I close the space and press my larger frame to hers, wrapping my hands around her upper arms.

She looks up, the first tear trekking down her bronze skin. Her trembling intensifies as I rub her upper arms.

"What's wrong, Lola?" I murmur softly, a purr rolling out of my chest. I don't use it often; it feels rumbly and awkward like an old engine starting up for the first time. But like every time I've purred to comfort, I know it works when her shoulders sag slightly. She presses her body closer to mine, tilting her chin up to stare into my eyes.

"I'm sorry," she whispers. The tears come faster.

"For what?"

"For crying." The tears are full-on rivers now, and despite the fact that she's pressed to me and I'm purring my heart out, the scent of anxiety perfumes the room with a bitter smell that chokes me.

Fixfixfixfixfix.

Big Daddy shoves to the forefront of my consciousness as I dip down and rub my cheek along Lola's. If anything was going to comfort her, it would be that gesture.

But instead, the soft crying morphs into shuddering sobs, her athletic frame shaking as she rubs her cheek along mine. When she abandons the move and buries her face in my chest, I'm at a loss for the first time in a long time.

"Talk to me," I encourage, sliding my hands around her upper body to cocoon her in a tight hug. My shirt is damp from her tears as Big Daddy paces anxiously behind my breastbone. My job is to protect, to soothe, to care for.

Lola pulls out of my arms enough to look up with a deep sigh. "I...messed up, Richard. I did something Papá asked me not to do, and people have suffered the consequences of my actions."

Oh. Ohhhhh. I wondered if it was bothering her more than she let on. I need to hear the full story from Marco, too.

"Do you want to talk about it?"

She gives me a sideways look. "I shouldn't speak badly about my father; it's in poor taste."

Sighing, I put a finger beneath her chin and guide her near-black eyes back up to mine. "You've known me your entire life, Lola. You can tell me anything, and I will keep your confidence."

She pauses for a moment, nipping at black-cherry lips before giving me a quick nod. "I try to play the part of the princess as well as I can, and honestly, I'm really good at it. I put the pack first almost all of the time." Her tone goes bitter, or maybe forlorn?

"I'm sure you can sympathize with this, but the higher up the shifter food chain you go, the more politics come into play, or so Papá tells me. I can't remember a time when we made choices simply because we wanted to."

I've had similar conversations with Marco many times over the years. I chose to move to a small pack in Ever precisely because of what she's talking about. Shifter court, at the highest level where she's from, is all about politics and connections.

"I wanted something for myself, even if it was only a few minutes," she whispers, eyes brimming with fresh tears. "But it turns out I can't have even that. Papá beat my best friend Leo for helping me. And then he demoted Nuñez and sent me here for safekeeping." She jerks her chin out of my hand. "I didn't get to say goodbye to anyone."

Surprised and sensing she needs space, I take a step back and lean against the sofa's low side arm. Marco beat someone for helping her? That's…not right.

Frustration for the situation fills me, most especially for the crying omega in front of me. I keep my tone even and helpful as I try to reassure her. "You can contact anyone you want to from here. I know that won't ease the pain you feel over how things went down, but there's a comm disk in the kitchen that you're welcome to use."

She shoots me an incredulous look. "Papá didn't tell you to hide it or something? He made it seem like he wasn't telling anyone about me coming here."

I shrug. "He won't tell anyone you're in Ever, but if you have a few trusted friends, I don't think it's a big deal for you to call them."

She lifts her chin, leveling me with a serious gaze. "Do you think there's risk in me calling them? I wouldn't want to put Leo or any of my packmates in a bad way due to another poor decision."

I shake my head and reach for one of her elegant, long-fingered hands, bringing it to rest over my heart. I've found over the years that the steady beat tends to calm even the flightiest of wolves. I suppose that's an advantage of being my pack's alpha. The ways I can comfort and soothe are almost too numerous to count.

Lola's near-black eyes drift to my chest and back up as she bites her lower lip.

I clear my throat. "Your father told me about Eliel. I'm aware of that threat. But I can't see a reason that chatting with Leo would be unsafe. There's no way for Eliel to even get to Ever without coming through the portal, and we guard that. You're safe here, Lola."

She grits her jaw, a muscle working overtime as her fingers dig into my shirt. After a long, quiet moment, she continues. "I'd definitely like to check on him since he was hurt because of me."

I cock my head to the side, admiring the innate strength that's so clear in her. Like any good packmate, she worries for others before worrying for herself. She hasn't asked me a single thing about the safety of Ever in comparison to Santa Alaya. About *her* safety.

"There's only one thing I want to be clear while you're here," I say softly, drawing her attention once more.

When she gives me a curious, guarded look, I smile.

"I want you to have fun. I want you to decide how to spend your days and who to spend them with. Do whatever the hells you want, Lola. Okay?"

Her dark lips part into a big smile. "Don't tease me with a good time, Richard. I haven't chosen my schedule since I was a pup!" The smile falls a little, turning into more of a smirk. Her tear tracks are drying, and she doesn't look ready to cry anymore.

"What can I help with while I'm here?" Her question is soft, but there's steel in her tone.

It doesn't surprise me that she'd insist on helping. It's the shifter way. Family first.

I grin. "There's a welcome dinner for you at Bad Axe tonight, if you feel up to it."

"Of course," she says with a playful laugh. "I'm always down for a politics-free party."

My grin grows bigger. "Well...I've got a pack leadership meeting tomorrow afternoon if you miss the politics after a day without it." I slip my hands into my pockets and wink at her. "Technically, you're the highest-ranking wolf here. If you feel like dipping your claws into tiny haven leadership, the door's open."

She cocks her head to the side and purses her lips, seeming to consider it. Finally, she returns my smile. "Yeah. I'd like to know how other havens work. I have so little context outside of Santa Alaya. I don't even remember a time when Papá wasn't the king."

"He won the crown when you were so young," I murmur, remembering his challenge like it was yesterday.

Lola wraps both long arms around her torso. "I remember Mamá being gone and Papá being crowned, but it's all mashed together," she says, turning a soft smile up at me. "I can't remember what she looked like anymore."

Which gives me an idea. I'm pretty sure I have some pictures of Marco, Maria, and me from way back in the day. I make a mental note to find them so I can give them to Lola at some point in the near future. I won't promise her I have them unless I'm sure, though, so instead I push off the sofa and point to the kitchen.

"There's a manila envelope there on the countertop. It's got an Ever comm watch in it as well as our typical new-resident packet. Ever's got a short but rich history."

"Oh, I've heard all about it," Lola says with a ragged laugh. She crooks one brow upward. "Is that whole welcome packet Evenia-approved?"

That pulls the same ragged laugh from my throat, and I shrug noncommittally. "Evenia hasn't personally approved welcome packets in a long time. To be honest, I'm not even certain who's technically responsible for the Ever welcome packet. Just that it seems to magically be updated every time we gain a new resident."

"How curious," Lola deadpans, her grin huge.

I lean in close. "It's Catherine. Catherine does it." Our resident succubus is the only one who could make such a change without getting approval from Hearth HQ, the monster world's ruling body.

Lola leans in conspiratorially. "Obviously. Sometimes I think she does things just to mess with the Hearth."

We share a quick laugh when I nod, and then I jerk my head toward the door. "I'm gonna go make rounds, but get settled and rest. Comm Leo. Do whatever you want."

The smile she turns on me has Big Daddy preening behind my bones.

"Thank you, Richard," she murmurs.

Welcome, Princess, Big Daddy growls in my mind at the same time I voice the sentiment aloud.

~

Big Daddy is mercifully silent for the remainder of the afternoon as I make the usual rounds of Shifter Hollow with Connall by my side. Rounds are a chance for us to be available, to connect, to check in. We do it at least twice daily.

We pass guardian wolves on every other corner, stationed there to keep an eye on the Hollow during Lola's time here. I'm not worried about her safety in Ever, but I want to make sure *she* feels safe, given everything Marco shared.

"She's not what I expected," Connall says quietly as we round a bend in the street, treehouses soaring tall above us. Solidified surfaces are dappled green and brown to match the trees, glass walls interspersed between them lend the architecture a modern feel.

I keep an eye out for anything amiss. "How so?"

Connall shrugs. "Somehow, I was expecting a kid."

I grunt in agreement. I don't know why I had expected time to stop, but the person who stepped off that train earlier was not what I thought she'd be.

Connall's quiet for the next few minutes, until his comm watch pings. He stops in place and nudges me with his elbow. "I've got a session with Leighton's parents in ten minutes, so I'm going to head back. Need anything from me before I go?"

I shake my head, worry for our dead packmate's family filling my chest until it's hard to breathe. I've never lost anyone on my watch. Not the entire time I've been Pack Alpha. Hundreds and hundreds of haven-years.

"How are they?" I manage. "From your perspective, I mean."

Connall sighs. "As your Second, I'm worried they won't stay in Ever, which would be a loss for our pack since they're so beloved. As your pack therapist, I can tell you they're struggling with the shock of losing Leighton so suddenly, and the way he died."

He turns luminescent green eyes on me. "They probably seem like they're doing alright from the outside, but they're in fight-or-flight mode. They're focused on all the things that happen after a death, but as the pack returns to normal, it'll hit them like a ton of bricks, and they'll be faced even more directly with his loss. They'll really need you then."

I shove down intense heartache for my packmates. "What's the best way to help?"

Connall claps me on the shoulder. "Just be there. Keep asking how they're doing. Keep showing up. Sometimes, the worst part about loss is when everybody around you starts to move on, and you're still stuck with the grief. You don't understand how others can behave normally when you're mired in sadness. Keep showing up the way you have been. They might not always accept your help, but the fact that you asked is enough."

I nod. I check on them daily, but I understand what Connall means about those around you moving on. My parents died when I was a pup, and I'll never forget the only person who never stopped checking in with me after his pack took me in and adopted me as one of their own.

Marco.

Connall removes his hand from my shoulder, giving me a gentle, understanding smile. "If you don't need anything else, I'll head out, but I'll see you at the welcome dinner."

Big Daddy remains noticeably silent as I say goodbye to my Second and turn for the forest again.

Hours later, I push a beer across the worn wooden bar toward a chestnut-coated centaur. She smiles shyly at me, grabs the beer and turns into the crowd. Bad Axe is always slammed around dinnertime, but tonight feels especially chaotic, like centaurs and shifters and pegasi are packed in all the way to the rustic plank walls.

We've got a little welcome dinner starting for Lola, but there seem to be a whole lot more monsters in the bar than I actually had Connall notify. I suppose news of the princess's arrival traveled fast.

Big Daddy is quiet in my mind. He has been since Lola arrived. It's odd. I make a mental note to visit Arkan's father, Vikand, to see if he has any insight into my wolf's increasingly erratic behavior.

A hush rolls over the bar, the air electric with anticipation.

She's here.

Time slows as I turn to see Lola at the hostess stand. She's speaking to the hostess, her guitar slung at her back.

Does she take it everywhere? That brings visions of her giving impromptu concerts to my head. I've never seen her play, but I'd like to.

The hostess blushes and dips her head, but Lola's gracious and places her hand on the woman's elbow, saying something that has the other female beaming. They turn toward the room, and Lola's eyes flick up, catching mine across the space.

Her hair's pulled into a thick black bun, but all that hair out of the way only serves to show off the slim, elegant column of her neck. Crimson stud earrings wink from both delicate ears. Random black freckles dot her bronze skin. She's just as casually dressed as earlier—jeans filled out by athletic, long legs; a simple white tee, pert, round breasts visible. It's not an outfit meant to be flashy or sensual. It's comfortable, everyday wear.

She's a godsdamn knockout. There's no way to tamp down the natural beauty that radiates from her.

Flesh. Taste. Herrrrr.

Big Daddy's visceral reaction to the beauty standing at the front of the bar gets me moving. I blink, giving Lola a wave and what I fucking hope is a welcoming smile, and not the smile of a much older alpha whose wolf has turned into a horny teenager with anger issues.

Not anger, he growls into my mind. **Need.**

You can't need her, I snap. *Too young. Too off-limits. Marco would fucking gut us. He sent her here to keep her safe.*

You're wrong, he retorts. But just as I drum up a response about her being hundreds of haven-years younger than us, he disappears from the front of my consciousness, retreating from me but still there, still watching her. He's telling me he doesn't want to talk.

I close my eyes and run my hands through my hair, slicking back the salt-and-pepper strands that refuse to stay put no matter how much gel I throw in them.

Don't stare at Marco's daughter, I remind myself, hoping Big Daddy gets it through his thick skull how very off-limits she is. Being so at odds with him is new and weird, and I hate it. We were always in sync when he was my guiding star and more of a sentiment than anything.

But once he found his voice.

Goddess.

He doesn't deign to respond, so I stalk to the end of the bar and press through the crowd that's quickly gathered around Lola. I expect her to turn to me with a grateful look, but she dazzles them. She speaks to everyone, touching elbows here and there, admiring tattoos, even tickling a fat baby one of the new mothers brought in.

When the mother offers the baby up, and Lola takes the child and sits him on her hip, I go weak at the knees.

"Go, have a drink," Lola encourages the mother, squeezing her forearm. "I've got him for a while if you want."

Perfection, Big Daddy grumbles. **She takes care like she should. Pack is hers right away. This is right. This is good. Sobre todo, familia.**

I can't find it in me to disagree with him on that. The more senior you are in shifter society, the more time you spend caring for a bigger and bigger pack. Lola likely spends a huge majority of her day doing service work with her father—the entire haven of Santa Alaya is technically their family.

The crowd dissipates as she spins toward me with the burbling baby in her arms. She grins, stroking elegant, long fingers down the baby's chubby shoulder. "Richard, isn't he adorable? Look at these darling fat cheeks!"

A hint of accent makes her roll the *R* slightly.

My mouth goes dry.

Yeah, you want her. You're practically panting at how our name sounds coming from her.

Be quiet! I practically scream into my mind.

A darkly satisfied laugh is Big Daddy's only response.

Lola's smile falls, probably because I haven't answered her thoughtful compliment. "Alpha, are you alright?"

Damn. Bet that mouth would feel good on—

"Totally fine," I grit out, forcing a smile. I reach over and tickle the baby under the neck, which gets me a giggle from him and Lola both.

"Goddess, he's cute," she murmurs before looking up and around the bar. "So this is your bar?"

I nod, trying to see it the way she does. Plank wooden walls are covered with ancient artwork of monster lumberjacks. The entire back half is the axe throwing section. Everything in here is dark and moody and smells like beer, so I grin back at her. "No stage, sorry. But if you wanna sing, you're welcome to hop up onto the bar."

She blushes, her color deepening over her cheeks and down her neck.

But when she leans in close conspiratorially, I lean to join her. "I will definitely hop on your bar, Richard."

Big Daddy howls loud as fuck in my mind as all the blood rushes to my head.

And my cock.

Goddess Alaya, help me. This is a problem. This is the biggest of fucking problems.

CHAPTER SEVEN
LOLA

Alaya above, did I just tell Richard I'd hop on his *bar*?! Now that the words are out of my mouth, I feel like an idiot. It sounds like I'm talking about something totally different from the long wooden bar that runs along the left side of Bad Axe.

And we're still standing close, our heads together, breath mingling. His dark eyes are locked firmly on my mouth, his jaw gritted tightly and working overtime. Oh my gods, I'm making this weird. I should step away from him.

Except something locks me in place. My eyes flick to his, his wolf's green flashing from deep within. I'm staring at them both, something that's deeply personal and considered rude to do without invitation. But he's not moving either.

Inside my mind, my wolf stretches lazily and rises, pushing to the forefront of our shared space with wary interest.

I know the moment my eyes start to shine like Richard's, because his blaze with his wolf's otherworldly intensity. A low, rumbly growl leaves his throat—but it's not Richard at all; it's his wolf's voice.

The center of the world spins and moves as I stare into his

wolf's fierce, amazing gaze. The predator inside him eyes me like he's examining every inch of my soul. But then the baby lets out a timely purr and Richard's green focus drops to the infant.

I take a full step away and sway the baby side to side, tickling his fat thigh. A deep sensation of being rocked and shaken swirls through me as Richard clears his throat. He forces a smile and points at my guitar. "Want me to set this behind the bar so you can grab something to eat?"

I nod and shrug the strap off, careful not to jostle the cooing baby on my hip. But at the brush of Richard's fingers along my shoulder, I freeze in place, resisting the urge to step into that touch. His fingers brand my skin as my wolf paces against my chest, focused on him, eager to get another hit of his wolf's attention.

What in the actual hells is going on here? She's never cared about other alphas past a vague interest in my daily life.

Nonono! She cannot care about *this* one. He's off-limits in every possible way. He's Papá's closest friend. I can't!

Richard slings my guitar over his beefy shoulder and waves to the far right-hand side of the bar. "There's a buffet over there. The bar food isn't fancy, but I hope you enjoy it." His grin broadens. "Come find me if you need a drink or you're ready to hop on my bar."

I'd swear there's a teasing lilt to his words, but I can't find it in me to do anything other than give a rushed thanks. As he turns to walk away, my wolf presses to the forefront of my focus, watching intently as the big alpha pushes carefully through the crowd, greeting and chatting with a half dozen shifters and centaurs on his way back to the bar.

Like an idiot, I watch until he disappears behind it. He sets my guitar down in a little nook out of the way. Someone must shout his name, because he turns, face breaking into a huge smile as he chatters back and forth with a patron.

And to firmly cement my idiocy, I stand in place, rubbing the baby's chubby thigh while I stare at Richard and the effortless way he works the room and his pack, checking in, caring for everyone.

A hand on my elbow surprises me, but I turn with a practiced smile. Connall stands there with a big grin on his face. Oh goddess, did he catch me staring at Richard?

"Want me to take the baby, Lola? You can grab some food."

I smile and shake my head. "Nah, I think I'll keep him." I shift the baby up until he nuzzles along my cheek like our people do. "Look how adorable he is."

Connall's incandescent green eyes drift to the baby and back to me. His grin grows broader. "You look like you're having fun, but there's no pressure here to put on a show. If you're tired or wanna get outta here for a minute, find me and I'll help." He shrugs, eyes drifting to Richard. "Or find *him*, of course."

"I'm good," I say with a smile, rubbing my cheek along the baby's as he grabs my chin and lets out a darling little purr.

Connall's gaze goes thoughtful. He reaches out and strokes his long, freckled fingers down the baby's back. The child's purr grows louder, and he buries his face in my neck, snuffling, his breathing going heavy and deep.

"He's falling asleep," I chuckle. "You've got the magic touch, Connall."

His grin goes huge. "Okay, I lied. I came to steal him because I love babies. Can I take him from you?"

When I look up to see if he's serious, he wears such a hopeful expression, I can barely stand it. Goddess, men who love babies are my kryptonite.

I wonder how Richard feels about babies, as a concept. He's never taken a mate, as far as I know.

Mentally, I slap myself and pull the tiny wolf from my arms, sliding him gently against Connall's muscular chest.

The big alpha starts purring immediately when the baby nuzzles into his neck, getting comfortable, his tiny mouth dropped open. Connall looks so peaceful that it surprises me when he stiffens, green eyes flashing as he stares toward the front door. The expression is there and gone in half a second. I'd almost think I imagined it, but then two people join us.

"Yeh look good carryin' a young one, alpha. Yeh on babysitting duty this evening?" A grinning blue sylph joins us with a human-looking woman beside him.

She smiles tentatively at me, both arms wrapped around her torso. I smile back, but her eyes have already moved to Connall. She stares at him with the same guarded look I've seen many times from my packmates. There's caution and reticence there.

I'm missing something. Connall still hasn't answered, and there's obvious tension between the three of them. I can smell it on the air, sour and irritated.

"Princess, good to finally meet yeh," the male says, dark blue lips cracking into a big smile. "I'm Dirk, and this lovely lady is my woman, Louanna."

The "woman" shakes her head with a frustrated-sounding laugh. "Not your woman, Dirk." She glances up at me. "Please call me Lou. Dirk insists on Louanna but he is the. Only. One!"

I chuckle. "I know all about that. I hear my official title a lot, but it is so cumbersome."

Lou beams at me, chocolatey amber eyes flashing with mirth. But it falls as she looks around the bar. Her expression turns worried as she nudges Dirk with her elbow. The blue-skinned sylph turns a thoughtful gaze down on her, blue hands slung through the wide leather belt at his waist.

"I shouldn't be here, Dirk," she says mournfully. "It's not right."

Next to me, Connall visibly stiffens but finally responds, "Of course you're welcome, Lou."

She levels him with an intense look. "Am I, Connall?"

The extreme need to clear the tension hits me the way it always does. As my father's daughter, I'm a peacemaker, arbitrator, friendly shoulder, anything I can do to ease the natural tension that occurs when a pack of predators bands together. Harmony is the job of all omegas. Where alphas are focused on protection, we're focused on keeping a peaceful balance. I desperately want to fix the tension between this trio.

I touch Lou's elbow carefully. "I just got here and haven't eaten. Would you like to come with me?"

She looks tentatively at her companion, who levels her with an affectionate smile.

"Go on, my beauty. Find us a table, and I'll join yeh in a moment. I need a few words with Connall."

The tension behind us amps up as I guide Lou away from the two men, glancing over my shoulder to see them exchanging hissed words. It occurs to me that I should have stolen the baby back to give them space, but it's too late now. I could listen in, but out of respect for Connall, I don't.

We pick our way through tables full of laughing shifters, centaurs, and even a table full of tiny gnome males. The drinks are flowing, and food is stacked high at every place. I get quite a few waves and deferential nods, so I smile back until we get to a long table on the far side of the bar.

When Lou and I stop at one end of the table, the bar shoves a stack of white ceramic plates toward us. Lou takes one and glances up at me, plastering a smile on her face. I recognize that smile though—it's the same one I put on during haven-wide events.

"You okay?" I ask softly, grabbing a plate and gesturing toward the long rows of delicious-looking burgers, tamales, and dips.

Lou seems to consider things for a moment, but then a shroud falls over her face, and she shakes her head. "It'll be alright."

I open my mouth to pry a little further. For some reason, I get the sense she'd let me. Lou gives off a distressed aura. Her expression is neutral, but I read sentiment well after growing up at court.

A rush of wind announces the sylph's arrival. He places a hand on Lou's lower back and dips his head toward her ear. Her scent and posture both calm noticeably. For a woman who says she's not his, that's not the read I get on them. I suppress a grin. Electric blue lightning crackles across his sky-blue skin, which forces my smile bigger. It's something air elementals do to get attention from potential mates.

Lou's eyes flick to the lightning, but she says nothing.

Oh boy.

Purposely, I give them space and grab a plate, piling carne asada and fried corn tortillas on it. I add heaping scoops of crema and chopped onions and let out a squeal when there's even a plate of fried fish. That one is a nod to Santa Alaya. I'm sure of it. The unique preparation I smell is a famous Santa Alaya recipe.

My heart warms a little when Lou reappears by my side with Dirk next to her. She glances at my plate and beams. "You shifters and your insane metabolisms."

I return the smile and add two fish filets to my stack, sucking in a deep breath to ward off a slight sensation of homesickness. I was able to call Leo earlier and Lupe as well. There's nobody else I really need to notify, and the fewer people I keep in contact with, the better.

Leo assured me that he's fine, that he knew my father's reaction was a possibility when we planned the concert. He's already recovered, thanks to shifters' amazing ability to heal. And he suggested I do something I haven't done in a really long time.

"Have fun, cariño," he had murmured into the comm disk. "You deserve it. We'll be fine here."

I can barely spell "fun," much less have it, but as Lou, Dirk, and I work the length of the table, I wonder if I might be able to let my hair down a little, so to speak.

Half an hour later, that mission has been accomplished. Dirk, who's funny as hells, sits next to me, making lewd jokes as half a dozen gnomes climb all over Lou, attempting to teach her how to throw an axe. We're seated in one of the axe throwing lanes, which take up the entire back wall of the bar.

Lou turns to us with a huffy laugh, although it's clear she's not really angry. A miniature gnome male stands on her shoulder, hanging on to her ear with one hand. I have to clap a hand over my mouth not to laugh at her situation—she looks absolutely ridiculous.

Dirk leans forward, resting both forearms on his knees, blue lips turned up in a wicked grin. "Yeh're drowning in males, Louanna. If I were the jealous type, I'd come save yeh, but as it is, I'm gettin' a little hot around the collar."

She snorts, and the gnome on her shoulder rolls his eyes.

The tiny male turns to Lou and pats the side of her head. "Come on, Lou. Based on sheer chance, you'll hit it any try now."

Lou gives him a withering look but turns to the lane with an axe in her hand. Other gnomes clamber all over her arms and legs. One even jumps up to sit on top of her head, shouting directions as she lifts the axe. We all hold our breath as she lets out a battle cry and throws the axe down the lane.

Like the last ten times, it misses the target by a solid two feet.

She lets out a frustrated shout and grabs the gnome on top of her head around his middle, yanking him down to look into his eyes. "Maybe I could do it without a bunch of dudes crawling all over me!" She turns and gives Dirk a meaningful look that has me laughing out loud.

He grins back at her. "If you wanna know what it's like to have a male all over yeh, Louanna, I am up to the task, any day, any time."

I snort and grab my fifth taco, lifting it to my mouth.

Dirk looks over at me. "What'd yeh snort for, Princess? Yeh don't think my chances are good?"

"Not with those corny lines," I tease.

"Thank you!" Lou shouts, setting the gnome male carefully on the ground. The others hop off her and gather together, grumbling about how terrible she is at axe throwing. They disappear into the busy bar as Lou rejoins us, sitting next to me and avoiding Dirk entirely.

Chocolate eyes find mine and wrinkle in the corners. "I heard you're a musician, is that right? My niece, Morgan, said she saw you give an amazing concert in one of the other havens."

My throat constricts at the memory of my last public appearance. I take a bite of the taco to avoid immediately answering.

Lou places a careful hand on my knee. "I'm sorry, Lola. Is music a sensitive topic?"

I shrug as I force the bite down, looking between my new friends. For some reason, I feel like I can talk to them about what happened. I start at the beginning and give them the highlights, and, by the end, Lou sputters indignantly.

"Girl, you better get on that bar and do a repeat. You know you want to!"

Dirk rests both muscular arms on the back of the bench seat he's on, one navy brow curling mischievously upward. "Do it, Princess. Daddy isn't here to see yeh, and I promise we'll give yeh a standing ovation."

My fingers twitch with the need to play. I play every day at home, but I haven't had two seconds to myself until I got to the treehouse. Even then, I was more worried about checking on Leo and letting Lupe know I'm alright. I stand before I can talk myself out of it.

When I glance at the bar, Richard's bright eyes are focused on me. He grins and points at the bar, giving me a questioning look.

When I nod, he beams and turns to grab my guitar.

Here goes nothin'.

CHAPTER EIGHT
RICHARD

Big Daddy has been silent since Lola joined Dirk and Lou for axe throwing. Thankfully, Bad Axe is busy tonight, or else I'd have been checking on her constantly. Something about her draws my attention. I don't mean to be staring at her when her obsidian eyes find mine. She beams when I point to the bar, and when she indicates she's intending to hop on it, joy fills me.

Big Daddy shows up. **Please, for the love of fucking, let her hop on our bar.**

Stop, I command.

Make me. His deep, challenging growl raises the hair on the back of my neck. I don't know how to navigate this, but I resolve to invite Vikand to the leadership meeting tomorrow to see if he's got any ideas. I can't keep going with this constant irritation.

Then fucking listen, he snarls again. **Am I the only one with my head screwed on right?**

I don't answer that, turning to grab Lola's guitar. I set the soft-sided case on a clear section of the bar as she strolls up. She's lit from within with excitement. Her joy is palpable.

"Thanks, Richard," she murmurs, her voice scratchy. She

unzips the case and pulls out a stunning turquoise and pale green long-necked electric guitar.

When I let out an appreciative noise, she sets it on top of the soft case and strokes her fingers along the strings, smiling at the instrument. Her eyes flick to mine. "Papá bought this for me when I came of age. There's a warlock who makes them in the haven connected to ours. He imbues his guitars with magic so you don't need an amp. It's amazing."

I lean over and brush my fingers along the guitar's variegated surface. It's beautiful. A hint of magic zings my fingertips, and I hiss, pulling them back.

The fuck is that? Big Daddy growls into my mind. **Dislike. Not right for pretty omega to shock us.**

She winks at me. "It's magically coded to me though, as I'm sure you just felt."

I ignore Big Daddy and smile at her. "I can't wait to hear it." I'm about to reach across the bar to help her onto it when she scrunches down and leaps, landing gracefully on the surface in a crouched position. Her movement draws attention from the monsters close to us, who give her space as she rises to a stand.

I cross my arms and lean back as she strums the guitar strings softly, listening and adjusting its tuning pegs.

"Any song requests, Richard?"

Gods, the way our name sounds coming from her, Big Daddy whines.

I'm getting pretty good at ignoring him.

"How do you feel about human oldies?" I question, considering a few options.

She beams and slips the strap over her head, settling the guitar against her chest. "I fucking love human oldies."

"Alright. Start with 'Red House' by Jimi Hendrix, then move into AC/DC's 'Thunderstruck.' Or…start with 'Thunderstruck.'" I give her a teasing look. "How hard do you wanna start?"

Harddddd.

Godsdamnit. I keep the smile plastered on my face as Lola grins wickedly at me.

"Let's start hard, shall we?"

I give her a clipped nod, fighting to keep up the easy smile. Big Daddy sits at the forefront of my consciousness, staring at the voluptuous woman on the bar who vibrates with excitement.

She maintains that mischievous smile as she coaxes the first few notes out of the guitar.

"Thunderstruck." Excellent choice.

The guitar's built-in amplifier sends the notes booming into the bar, hitting me in the chest and bouncing off all the glass behind me. The hair on my nape rises as the whole room stops and turns, staring at Lola.

She strums louder, spinning to face the room. Whispers fill the space, then the sounds of chairs screeching as they turn on the plank floor. Lola steps her legs wider and strums harder, but when she starts singing, I lose track of space, of time, of fucking everything. The first notes out of her throat are pure, delicious gravel, like her voice was made for this song.

She gets the entire restaurant clapping and stomping and howling and neighing to the beat until the rustic chandelier in the middle swings with the vibrations. Bad Axe is having fun, the floorboards slapping to the rhythm of Lola's music.

And Big Daddy watches, his focus so intense, my head feels like he's splitting firewood inside it.

When Lola's wolf growls into the final notes of the climax, every one of my hackles rises as Big Daddy shoves as far forward as he'll fit, nearly forcing a shift as I scramble to get control of my body and mind.

And then he whispers one word into our shared consciousness.

Luna.

"You alright, Richard?" Connall's deep voice is full of concern as we make our way through the forest on our rounds the following morning.

I hesitate to tell him about last night, about what Big Daddy said. Connall's my Second; his role is to be my confidant, my guide, my partner in everything. To provide another perspective. But I don't think I can tell him about *this*.

The Luna bond comes from so far back in shifter lore, very little is known about it anymore. It's been over two thousand years since a shifter had that sort of bond. In fact, it's so rare, there's no one alive blessed by it. The only mentions of it are veiled, shadowy texts, most of which sit in Marco's library in Santa Alaya. It doesn't just…happen.

My wolf is wrong.

Not wrong. You'll see.

"Big Daddy's being an asshole, and I'm exhausted by it all." I figure that's as close as I can get to the truth.

But Connall's as intuitive as ever, which is exactly why I picked him to be my Second when my former Second moved. "Mmm. I thought it might be about Lola."

I stop in place and spin to face him, forcing my hands into my pockets. Big Daddy paces behind my chest bone, snarling and being a general dick.

"What makes you say that?" Big Daddy's tone is clear in my voice, but Connall laughs, his smile as knowing as ever.

"You're different since she arrived. On edge, distracted. I'm guessing she's not the person you remember, and maybe that's got you feeling some kind of way?"

Moons. Maybe he's too intuitive for his own good. Is he suggesting I find Lola attractive? Is it that godsdamn obvious?

Luna, Big Daddy snarls again, snapping at me in our shared space.

She's not our Luna, I bark back. *There's no fucking way. There hasn't been a Luna-bonded pair in over two thousand years!*

I sigh. "Big Daddy likes her."

Connall's auburn brows drift upward, a surprised expression replacing the earlier thoughtful one. "And how do *you* feel about that?"

"I wish he'd stop," I admit.

Can't. Won't. Never.

"He likes her a lot," I hedge.

"I see," Connall says softly.

Unfamiliar, anxious butterflies fill my stomach, rocketing around as I stare at my Second, running my fingers through my slicked-back hair. "How do I get him to stop? I can't do this with him… It can't happen."

Connall smiles at me. "Well, I invited Vikand to the leadership meeting like we talked about, so we can discuss Big Daddy's increasing persistence, if you want."

I gulp. "I forgot to tell you that I invited Lola too."

Connall barks out a laugh. "Well, that'll be interesting." He stares into my eyes. "You know, Richard, if Big Daddy feels that way, he's probably onto something."

I know! That's what I want to shout. Every wolf shifter knows our wolves are the most intuitive part of our being. That's why being in lockstep with one's shift is so critically important. And I always have been…

"Did I lose you?" Connall bumps my shoulder with his.

Back off, Second, Big Daddy snaps.

"I'm good," I mutter. "Just need to sort this out."

"Things have a way of working out," he murmurs, green eyes gone soft as he stares into the trees ahead of us.

Suddenly, I wonder if he's not talking about my issue with my wolf so much as his own problems.

I don't get a chance to ask because he jogs off into the trees, continuing our rounds like any other day. Lost in thought, the minutes pass as I follow him. Eventually, he challenges me to a foot race on our way back to Bad Axe. My thoughts are so muddied, I trip and face plant and he kicks my ass, beating me by a solid ten seconds.

Connall opens the door with a smug smile as Big Daddy berates me for not putting him in his place.

"Gettin' slow, old man," he teases when I stalk through the door.

It's on the tip of my tongue to toss him against the wall and bite him, make him cower beneath my alpha nature. It's what most alphas would do. We protect, but we also keep everyone in line. I never really enjoyed that bit of leadership—it's one of the primary reasons I gave up my spot as Marco's Second all those years ago. It's what led me to come to Ever and work with Abemet to start this lovely haven.

I always longed for a more relaxed way of life.

So I push through Big Daddy's insistence and stalk up the dark back hallway past my office and into the bar, where three wolves and a handful of others sit with the princess. Vikand rests his belly on a curved centaur bench, a beer in his hand. Lola stands behind the bar, twirling a glass on the tip of her pointer finger as they roar with laughter and clap.

Perfection, Big Daddy sighs. **Look at that as—**

"Hey everyone," I break in, elbowing Big Daddy through our connection.

Even as my comment causes everyone to turn toward Connall and me, my eyes drop to the aforementioned ass, Big Daddy and I both appreciating how round and firm it looks. High and tight and so damn muscular. The bottom swell curves into fit-looking thighs encased in jeans that leave nothing to my currently wild imagination.

Connall brushes past me, knocking me to one side as he clears his throat. It takes herculean effort for me to snap my focus away from Lola and glance at something else before looking at my leadership crew.

Lola wears a concerned expression, the glass now gripped between her fingers. "Richard, you alright? Is it still okay for me to join your meeting? If not, I'll totally go…" Her words drift off as she jerks a thumb toward the front door.

"Of course not," I say. "You're always welcome."

More than welcome. Come sit on our lap, pretty girl.

I level my crew with a big smile as Connall takes his spot on the far side. Someone else clears their throat as I skirt past Lola behind the bar to grab beer glasses. I fill them as Connall starts the meeting, same as always.

Half an hour later, I'm pouring the second round of drinks, and we've been through the majority of our to-do list. Continuing to support Leighton's family is at the top of it. Connall was stoic during that part of the conversation. Leighton was his friend, and I know he feels the loss even more acutely than I do.

Eventually, we come to a topic that does bring me joy. I grin at my leadership crew. "I'm going to be challenged this week."

A rousing cheer goes up as they all clap. Lola claps too, but there's a tense edge to her forced smile. It doesn't take a genius to assume she's thinking of how Marco's Second is planning to challenge him soon.

I reach across the bar and pat her hand when she puts it down. "It's not a big deal in our pack; it's more practice than anything."

She nods, but her near-black eyes come to mine and flash with worry. "You could still be injured. Fights go sideways all the time."

Let her see our strength, Big Daddy presses.

I lean over the bar as my crew snickers. "You haven't seen me fight, omega. I won't lose. Not today and not any day in the foreseeable future."

One of her dark brows curls upward. "Is that so? Seems a little cocky, Richard."

I shake my head as I slide her whiskey sour across the bar. "No. I'm assured and confident. Those are different things."

Plump lips curl into a smile. "Then I look forward to seeing you fight."

Yessssss, Luna is into us, as she should be. Let's show her our di—

Lola is Marco's daughter—our friend's daughter. She's a fraction of our age. Even if she was our Luna, which she's not, it could never happen. Just stop.

After that, Big Daddy recedes into the farthest edges of my mind, not bothering to respond. But his ire is palpable and painful in our connection. Eventually, Connall does a surreptitious nod toward Vikand, but I find I don't want to discuss my Big Daddy issues in front of everyone right now, so I shake my head. Vikand watches us and seems to read the room, not bringing up how we invited him here but haven't asked him for anything.

I'll take care of this later.

Somehow.

CHAPTER NINE

LOLA

It's fascinating watching a leadership meeting take place within a regular pack. Richard, Connall, and the rest of the small group laugh and drink and carry on, and it's…easy. I can never remember a time it was like this for my father. His leadership meetings are all veiled innuendo and subtle threats. And sadly, no alcohol.

I mull that over as I watch pack members who are obviously close with one another.

Connall slaps the bar with both hands and rises, looking at the group. "I'm gonna head to Leighton's parents' place for a visit."

"I'll be there in the morning with breakfast for them," Richard says, his expression serious.

It's on the tip of my tongue to offer to go with him, but I'm not part of this pack. I'm just…here. And I don't want anyone to feel like they have to take care of me. I shouldn't even be here at all, but for my own stupid mis—

"Lola, would you like to go get some ice cream up on Main Street?" Richard's rumbly voice breaks through my thoughts, pulling a smile to my face.

"You don't have to do that," I say with a laugh, gesturing at his packmates. "I heard your to-do list. It's very long."

He smirks. "It's never *not* long. There's always time for ice cream, I promise." His smirk becomes a full grin, twin fangs peeking out over his plush lips.

Moons, why am I looking at his lips?

Connall shoos the rest of the wolves and Arkan's father toward the door as I nod and rise from the stool, pushing it into place. The front door opens, and they exit Bad Axe. The bar lights twinkle and shine behind Richard, illuminating him as if the bar itself is telling me to stare. That's how I take it, anyhow.

Richard looks up at the ceiling. "Whatcha doin', girl?"

The way he says the word "girl" has me crossing my legs to ease some of the ache there. Slick arousal wets my thighs, my body preparing for an alpha in his absolute prime. My physical reaction is visceral and impossible to control, and I hope to Alaya that Richard pretends not to notice.

My wolf shoves toward the front of my focus, staring at Richard as I shake my head to ease the pressure she generates in my chest. When I rub at it, Richard crosses the space behind the bar and leans over it.

"You okay, Lola?"

Yes.

No.

No.

"Absolutely," I say instead, not looking at him. I don't want my wolf's amber shade to show so obviously through my eyes. Yet, when I turn to look, unable not to, the green of Richard's wolf shows clearly through his dark irises.

"We need ice cream," he says, his voice a throaty, rippy growl. "Right now."

Goose bumps rise to the surface of my skin at the way he and his wolf are staring. I can't even hold my girl back; she's all about this focus and attention from Ever's pack alpha. I try to remind myself who Richard is to me, to my father, but it feels impossible to grasp at those straws when I half-ass try.

"Can't wait," I manage.

For a long moment, the air in the bar fills with heat. Richard is still as a statue, his big chest heaving, and when I look into his eyes, they're fully green. I'm staring at a man who's seconds from a shift, his wolf taking over to do the transition.

Is he…not in control?

Worried for him, I push forward and press my hand to his chest. He's scorching hot, his skin blazing into mine even through the soft fabric of his black tee. His muscles pop and bend, ears elongating to the lengthy, tapered tips of his wolf's. A deep, ragged growl rumbles out of his throat as he grabs my wrist with one hand. His fingers wrap all the way around it, tightening until it pinches.

When I suck in a breath at the sheer dominance he exudes, he gasps and lets go of my wrist, stepping back. He runs both hands through his salt-and-pepper hair, looking deeply into my eyes. His wolf's green is gone.

Come back, I think desperately. *Let me see you.*

"Lola, I'm sorry," he says, his voice filled to the brim with emotion. "That was inappropriate. I—"

A deep-seated need to comfort him and alleviate the situation rises. I'm well acquainted with emotional tension.

"You're in need of ice cream, I can tell," I say with a wink, slipping off the bar. I jerk my head toward the door. "C'mon, Alpha."

He pauses a second, and I worry he'll try to back out on the idea. I'm about to plead my case for why we should still go, but he strides to the end of the bar and rounds it to join me.

"I'm sorry, truly," he murmurs as we head toward the broad, tall front doors.

When he shoves through them and holds the right door open for me, I pause by his side, glancing up into his familiar chocolate eyes. "I'm not sorry, Richard. You have nothing to be sorry for."

He nods, but I sense his unease, so I slip my arm under his and cradle his biceps to my side. "You promised me ice cream, and I feel like you've really talked it up. How fast can we get there?"

He laughs and bends his arm, placing his palm flat on his chest as we head right up the road. "Twenty minutes walking. It's a nice night, too."

I nudge his side with my elbow. "Is it not always a nice night, on account of the controlled weather?"

He chuckles. "Yeah, I guess you're right."

We fall silent as we stride through Shifter Hollow, treehouses and the trees above soaring like silent sentinels around us.

"This place is so cozy," I share, "once I get past the claustrophobia."

Richard laughs. "It's a far cry from your view in Santa Alaya, that's for sure."

I smile up at him. "Do you ever miss it, being Papá's Second?"

Richard shakes his head immediately. "Never. I love Marco like a brother. Moons, he *is* my brother, for all intents and purposes, but, no, I don't miss the political game of being so high up in society."

"I don't get the sense he enjoys it all that much either," I admit, wondering when the last time I saw my father smile was. I can't think of a time, if I'm honest with myself. The shifter court might tout the family-first motto, but it's less accurate at court than anywhere else.

Richard sighs. "Your father was always driven to win. He's the most competitive wolf I know, which is how he's won a few fights he should have lost, by all rights."

I grimace. "See! That's what I mean about how fights can go sideways." I suck at my teeth. "You just never know when some gangly little youngster is gonna pull a tricky move and oust you. It could happen."

Richard barks out a hearty laugh. "Maybe, Princess, but I'm not worried."

We walk in silence for a while after that as I admire the deeply verdant forest on both sides of us. Richard points out a path that leads to a troll bridge where one of the town's leadership monsters lives—Ohken the troll. Newly mated to one of Lou's triplet nieces, apparently. I'm excited to meet them.

We round a corner to see a vintage-looking 24-hour diner on the left, and a two-story building with a line out the door on the right.

Richard points to that one first. "That's Higher Grounds, a coffee shop. It's run by vampire brothers, Pietro and Alessandro. Definitely worth the walk if you're into coffee."

Something pangs in my chest. In Santa Alaya, we grow our own coffee beans. My entire childhood, I played hide and seek on hills lined with coffee trees. Unless they import from our haven, the coffee will be different. And different isn't bad necessarily, but—

"You okay?" Richard murmurs, pulling on the arm still looped through his.

"Thinking about home," I admit, glancing up as we pass between the buildings and take a left on Main Street. But that's when all thoughts of home vanish. Ever's downtown is one long street with shops on both sides. Red-and-white awnings cover each door, and lamp posts with flower baskets throw a burst of color into the picture.

Richard guides me to the left side of the street as I take in how cute it is.

"We're going to Scoops, but next to that is Miriam's Sweets, a candy shop. We've got a movie theater, bowling alley, and at the far end, there's Town Hall and its gazebo, of course. All full-haven meetings happen there."

The scent of ice cream fills the air as we get closer to Scoops' door. Small red picnic tables on the sidewalk are nearly filled with monsters of all species. It's so homey, so different from the paleteros back home who push frozen carts around, dishing out popsicles in every possible flavor.

Five minutes later, we emerge with two scoops—Richard picked chocolate, and I opted for cherry chocolate mint. We find a free table at the very end, next to the sweets shop. I stare at the front entrance as we sit.

Richard laughs. "Wanna go in? It'll remind you so much of the dulcerías back home. There are so many delicious options."

I take a quick lick of my cone. "Yeah, I wanna go in. It looks amazing." My eyes flick to his. "If you have time, I mean."

"I always have time for you," he says softly, his eyes focused. I'd swear the faintest hint of green appears, but it's gone in a flash as he looks around us at the busy street. "This is what I mean about the difference between living in Santa Alaya and a small haven. We've had our drama, for sure, but Ever is so peaceful—usually."

I lick my cone, the flavors bursting across my tongue. As I open my mouth to say something, the door to the sweets shop opens, and Hana exits, holding it for someone else. When a small gargoyle flits out the door to land on her shoulder, I hold back a giggle.

Richard turns to see what I'm looking at, smiling when Hana clops over to our table. I move to stand so she doesn't tower over us, but she smiles and places a hand on my shoulder.

"No need to rise, Lola. Please, enjoy your ice cream." She pats the tiny darling on her shoulder. "This is Ignatius, Iggy for short."

The little gargoyle beams at me as he hops up and down on Hana's shoulder. Blue eyes flash with excitement. I notice he's holding a half-full bag of candy in one hand.

"You're a princess, right? What's it like? Does your dad get to boss people around all day long? Do you have good playgrounds where you're from? Can you jump out of your bedroom and dive right into the ocean?"

Hana glances over at the young one. "That is quite a lot of questions at once, Iggy."

He shrugs, crossing his arms over his tiny chest. "So?"

I pat the table between Richard and me. "Come on down here, and I'll answer them."

Iggy whoops and hops off Hana's shoulder, sliding down her back until he reaches her horse body. Then he slips down her leg like it's a pole, and hops onto the table.

Richard pinches Iggy's fat thigh playfully. "Ig, shall I get you an ice cream while you question Lola?" He winks at me.

"Yeah, go ahead," Iggy says without looking away. When he settles on his haunches, curling his long tail around his feet, I realize he's waiting for a whole story from me.

Laughing, I try to recall his questions in order. "Being a princess is interesting. There are lots of rules."

Iggy's face screws up, his snub nose scrunching in apparent disgust.

"Yeah"—I give him a look—"so many rules. And, yes, my papá does get to tell everyone what to do, but he tries not to be too bossy."

Ha.

"What about the ocean?" Iggy presses.

I take another lick of my cone and smile as I think about home. "I live in the castle, which is high up in the mountains overlooking the town of Santa Alaya and La Bahía de Santa Alaya, which is the ocean," I tack on.

Iggy nods wisely.

"While I can't leap out of my window into the water, it's only a short walk through the town, and I get to visit all of my favorite people along the way."

"Your town is your family, right?" Iggy says, his voice gone soft.

My heart clenches. Richard reappears at the same time, handing Iggy a single scoop of vanilla ice cream covered in sprinkles. The tiny gargoyle takes it but continues staring at me.

"Yeah, the town is my family," I say.

"Do you miss it?" Iggy asks.

Hana clears her throat like she's about to suggest he stop asking me questions about home, but, honestly, I find him incredibly refreshing.

"I miss some things about home," I share. "My best friend Leo, who I play in a band with, for example. I also used to visit the elderly every morning as part of my duties. Except it never felt like a duty to me. I enjoyed it. And I miss seeing those packmates, even though it's only been a short time."

Iggy sighs and digs into his ice cream, munching on the sprinkles. I risk a glance over at Richard, but his expression is thoughtful.

Hana taps Iggy on the shoulder. "Friend, what do you say we deliver the candy?"

Iggy nods and lifts the bag still held in his right hand, showing it to me. "We bought this for Lou to cheer her up. She's been really sad since, well, I'm not sure why, exactly. Dad won't say anything except that it's 'cause of Wesley." He gives me a disgruntled look. "Do you know why that makes her sad? Nobody will tell me."

Richard clears his throat. "She was there when Morgan killed Wesley, Ig. It was probably really scary, and she's dealing with those feelings now."

Iggy snorts. "Yeah, but that was, like, days ago. When Dad tells me to think about my feelings, it takes me like ten seconds."

"You are exceptionally strong," Richard compliments. "No doubt you'll make a wonderful protector one day, like your father and uncle."

Iggy flares his tiny wings wide, his tail lashing from side to side like a cat as he beams at me. "What do you think?"

I boop his nose. "I think you have an ice cream mustache, and it sounds like you owe Lou some candy, so you'd better get that taken care of, sir."

He lets out a hilarious little cackle, as if I just told the funniest joke in the world. "Nice to meet you!" And then he pushes off the table and zips through the air onto Hana's back. He kicks her sides like he's riding a horse. "Giddyup, Hana!"

Hana smiles at us both, waving goodbye as she turns and trots into the street, Iggy bouncing around on her back with his ice cream in one hand and the bag of candy in the other.

"Moons, he's cute," I say, refocusing on Richard.

"You seem to love children," he says.

"Don't all omegas love children?" I retort with a wink. "Pretty sure it's written in our DNA."

His smile becomes a smirk as he licks a path up his ice cream. Heat flares between my thighs. Everything about Richard is alpha in a way I've never experienced with the alphas back home. Maybe because there's never been a strong enough alpha who could challenge Papá. Even Eliel doesn't strike me the way Richard does.

There's innate strength in his body, for sure, but it's the focus in those intelligent, predatory eyes. He misses nothing, which is obvious when he interacts with his people.

"What are you thinking about?" His question takes me off guard as I struggle not to watch him lick the ice cream.

Your tongue.

Your muscles.

Your knot.

Shit, where did that last one come from? I struggle to rein it in as I lick my own cone. It's melting, dripping down over the edges and onto my fingers.

I want you to lick this off me. The request is on the tip of my tongue, my heartbeat racing as I mentally slap myself. I've got to stop making everything Richard does sexual.

"Home," I lie.

He gives me a wicked, knowing look. "Liar."

My heart skips a beat, then picks up, revving like a truck engine as my nostrils flare, soaking in his scent.

"Dime la verdad," he growls. *Tell me the truth.*

Moons, no, I can't. It's far too natural to be playful with him.

I force myself to stop breathing and focus. "I'd like to walk back now." *And get home to my AknottilatorXL because I am heating up too fast.*

Richard's chocolate eyes narrow as he crunches into the cone, biting it in half. He munches on it as, frozen, I stare at him.

After an interminable silence, he nods. "Okay, let's go."

I should be learning and admiring this darling town, maybe figuring out how to help for the duration of my stay, however long that may be. But I can't pull my eyes from him as he pops the rest of his cone into his mouth, reaching for me with his free hand.

I take it, my ice cream melting pitifully, covering my hand with sticky sweetness as we rise from the table. He guides me off the bench and pulls me into the sidewalk, releasing his grip. The loss of his warmth makes my fingers twitch.

Richard slips a palm to the middle of my back, respectfully and horribly far above where I'd rather he put it.

Goddess Alaya, help me, I pray to all wolves' patron saint. Because I am fantasizing about the one wolf I should never, ever pursue. But as quickly as I chide myself, the thought vanishes to the furthest corners of my mind. I smile and walk, trying not to preen at the sensation of Richard's big hand on my body.

We head toward Sycamore in silence, but at the corner, he jerks his head toward the left. "Do you have any interest in seeing the Community Garden? Hana and Arkan live next door. It's beautiful over there."

The heat building between my thighs demands attention, so after a moment to consider it, I shake my head no. I can't walk around a beautiful garden while Richard points out the amazing things about his haven. I'm one sexy comment away from blurting out how attractive I find him.

We turn up Sycamore toward Shifter Hollow, Richard's palm blazing a spot against my back. All of my focus and attention is drawn to the way his fingers curl slightly into my skin, as if he wants to be closer and can't. Or maybe I just hope that's what he's feeling.

I don't realize we've walked in silence almost the entire way back until we pass the lake and he scratches at my tee. When he drops his hand, I hold back a whimper of need.

"You sure you're alright, Lola? You don't strike me as the early-to-bed type, and the sun isn't even down yet."

When I glance up at him, he wears that same smirk that's been getting to me all night. I clear my throat. "So…when will you be challenged, do you know? How does that work in your pack?"

His smirk becomes a full grin, like he's a giddy schoolboy. "Tomorrow, probably sunset. Usually, when I get challenged, they like to make sure it's before the dinner rush."

I snort. "How very thoughtful and convenient."

He shrugs. "It's so different from Santa Alaya. We've talked about that. But you'll see when it happens. There's no one in my pack with political aspirations like your father had. Until I'm very, very old, I won't have any real challengers." He barks out a rough-and-tumble laugh. "Unless I do something really asshole-ish, and then I could be challenged for real. Although, still, there are no alphas here who could beat me."

"Not even Connall?" I joke, elbowing him in the side. Goddess, his side is a rock of muscle.

His smile goes thoughtful. "Most definitely not Connall. Connall will fight tooth and nail for those he loves, but he's not a fighter in general. He's our pack therapist, a role I created when I realized I'm not naturally suited to those conversations. I'm more of a man of action. Connall is an incredible listener, and he gives the best advice of anyone I've ever met."

"You're lucky to have him," I murmur, thinking about Papá and Eliel's tenuous relationship, if it can even be called that.

Richard must read my thoughts. "Eliel was always an asshole," he mutters. "Fantastic at a Second's duties, but your father knew he'd be trouble, so I guess this is that reckoning. I spoke to Marco this morning, by the way. He hasn't been formally challenged yet."

"Yeah." I cross my arms over my chest, irritated at the idea of not being there for Papá when he fights. "I hope he absolutely pulverizes that creep."

Richard bristles. "'Creep' is a very specific term."

I nod. "Eliel follows me around a lot when I'm visiting and doing my duties. He loves to comment on how single I am and how old I'm getting."

A rough growl rips from Richard's throat as he puts his hand on my wrist, stopping us in the street. His dark eyes are earnest as he scans my face. "Does he make you feel unsafe? Marco mentioned he thought Eliel might try to force a bonding if he won."

I shrug. "He's never done anything aside from look at me in a gross way. But Papá is right…Eliel's a threat. He'd take away my choices if he could."

Richard snarls and shakes his head. "You don't have to go back there, Lola. You're more than welcome here. It's a slower pace of life, and we have no beach. But we've got a beautiful lake, if you—"

"Stay here?" The words come out as a whisper, shock registering at Richard's words. "I could stay here?"

A pink blush steals across his bronze cheeks. "Your father would miss you, of course, but if you wanted to make a new, different life here…you could."

Leave Santa Alaya? Somehow I can't imagine Papá allowing that, focused as he is on pack first.

I blink away the shock as my comm watch pings. Looking

down, I nearly choke at seeing Papá's name hovering above the navy-blue band. That's...surprising.

Richard pats my forearm once, drawing my attention. "I'll leave you to your call. Cheer me on tomorrow?"

I nod. "Of course, Alpha."

His blush deepens, and he nods before turning to jog up the street toward Bad Axe. Sighing, I direct the watch to answer my father, but my mind is locked firmly on the idea Richard presented.

CHAPTER TEN
RICHARD

The following afternoon, I'm wiping down the bar and trying not to pay attention to Big Daddy. I haven't seen Lola all day, haven't talked to her since Marco called her last night. Walking away from her rankled. I wanted to stay and hear what he had to say, to make sure she was okay with whatever it was. To clarify that I wasn't asking her to stay for me, but rather hinting that she doesn't have to choose the Santa Alaya life. She could leave it, like I did.

Any guesses on the reason you care, dumbass? Big Daddy's growly bass echoes around my mind, bouncing off it like it's empty except for whatever he thinks.

As I'm thinking about her, Lola enters the bar and crosses the room toward me with both hands slung in her pockets and her guitar over her back. I chuckle when I see it sticking up over her beautiful black hair.

Offer to brush it. Females like their hair touched.

Oh, for Alaya's sake. Seems awfully assumptive to me, but that's how he thinks, in absolutes.

When she stops beside me at the end of the bar, I grin and

thumb the guitar bag. "You planning to play some awesome fight music for me?"

She grins, revealing twin white fangs. "You never know when a little song will ease the tension. Back home, I took my guitar everywhere." Her expression grows morose. "I used to play it for the elderly at the community home. Those were some of my favorite times."

"Honestly, fight music might be exactly what we need," I say on a laugh, hoping to bring her spirits up.

Just then, the front double doors swing wide, revealing the muscular figure of Rowan, one of the younger alphas from my pack. He stands a head shorter than me but he's wider, stockier. His blond hair is slicked straight back, eyes glinting purple with his wolf's aura.

The challenger. Good. Rip him from stem to stern. Protect our Luna.

Not our anything. Focus. This challenge is a lesson for Rowan, nothing more.

Lola sucks in a deep breath that draws my attention. The look on her face is absolute terror, and it rips my soul to pieces to see that.

Fixxxxxxxxx, Big Daddy shouts.

Without thinking, I wrap an arm around her and pull her to my chest, purring quietly. Tipping her chin up to force her to focus on me and not Rowan, I scan her face, drinking in her pitch-black irises and the black freckle on one side of her mouth.

"I'll be fine, omega," I croon. It's a comforting tone, a tone I've used thousands of times with others in my pack.

Not while touching like this, Big Daddy reminds me. **Kiss omega.**

I ignore that, though, listening for her heartbeat to slow. Instead, it ramps up as Rowan's footsteps echo into the bar. The floorboards begin to clatter as Bad Axe welcomes the challenger.

Cheering and shouting follow Rowan as I struggle to pull my attention from Lola.

She places both hands on my chest. "Be careful, please." Her eyes are wide with fear.

I drop her chin and bring my mouth to her ear, the scent of oranges and cream filling my senses. "Say it with me, omega. I'll be fine."

"You'll be fine," she repeats dutifully, her voice never registering above a whisper.

I straighten. "Then it's settled."

She bites her lip and nods, but her scent remains tinged with the bitter sourness of fear.

"It'll even be fun," I say with a growl as I spin to face Rowan. She'll see. This is not like a challenge in Santa Alaya.

The smaller alpha stands in the entryway with the entire pack behind him, as well as a smattering of centaurs and pegasi. Connall stands to Rowan's left, arms crossed and a big grin on his face.

I stand my ground, waiting for Rowan to issue his official challenge. Lola's worried presence is tangible at my side, but I hope once we begin fighting, she'll see that this is a far cry from what Marco will undertake against Eliel.

Rowan presses his palm flat to his chest, giving me an intense, predatory look. When he speaks, his wolf's voice resonates throughout the bar. "Alpha Richard Benton, I formally challenge you for leadership of Pack Ever."

Howls rise in support of him, which is all part of the show. This is a confidence-building exercise at its very core.

I raise my chin, balling my fists as Big Daddy presses to the front of my consciousness, ready to rip through my clothing and attack.

Start in human form, I remind him. *Don't distract me.*

No answer.

I grin wickedly at Rowan. "I accept your challenge, Alpha

Rowan Clayburn of Pack Ever. May Alaya bless you with strength and courage."

His nostrils flare, his challenge clear. "And you, Alpha."

Connall howls into the room, raising the hair on my nape as the rest of the pack joins in. Howls mix with growls and shouts and cheers, a few jeers too. Arkan and Hana and the rest of the centaurs and pegasi stand at the back, stomping in anticipation of the fight. Despite the fact that they aren't technically part of the pack, I've always included their herds in everything as if they were.

"Outside!" I bellow, commanding everyone out of the bar.

Someone swings the doors wide, and the pack and herds flow like a river out into the street, still jeering and shouting. Electric energy fills my consciousness, my senses sharpening and expanding as Big Daddy pushes his abilities into my human form.

"Good luck, Alpha," Lola says, her tone throaty. She slaps me on the stomach as she passes, heading for the exit.

I snarl at the rough touch, every cell of my body primed and ready for violence. Watching her walk away is a special sort of torture because, amped like I am, I'm just as ready to fuck as I am to fight. Pro or con of being a pack alpha, I suppose. We're always the most dominant wolf in the pack. The knot at the base of my cock swells and pulses, eager to be buried deep in her heat.

Dominate Luna after we win, Big Daddy commands, pressing against my bones until my feet move me toward the exit. I'm too focused on the fight to remind him we can't do that with her.

Out in the street, the pack and herds have formed a giant circle. Silver jewelry glints with gems in every shade—cuffs, bars, earrings—the entire pack has on their finery in support of Rowan. Even the centaurs and pegasi have taken on our bejeweled tradition. Arkan and Hana wear matching fetlock cuffs with purple jewels in a ring. They stamp a beat together as Arkan cheers for Rowan.

Rowan stands in the circle's center, raising his arms to urge the cheers higher. Silver studs glint in both his ears, a chunky pendant hanging from his muscular neck. His girlfriend joins him, holding a hand out for his jewelry so he can remove it to shift.

When I enter the ring, I pull my shirt off so it doesn't tear when we let our wolves out.

Luna is looking, Big Daddy growls. **Take off the rest. Let her see you fight with our big di—**

Concentrate, I snap.

Rowan follows my move, tossing his shirt to his girlfriend Bex. She grabs it and retreats to the circle with his parents and siblings.

He springs forward from a complete standstill, but I saw the move coming. I step easily out of the way as he lands gracefully and tumbles, rolling upright. Backing in an arc, I observe. It's laughable how easy it is to track the way he tenses prior to a move.

He lunges again, slicing at my core with his wolf's claws out. Hushed whispers go up in the crowd as I let him get close enough to score four red stripes down my chest and stomach.

End himmmmmm, Big Daddy commands, his claws slipping easily out of my human form's fingers.

"Give me your worst, Alpha," Rowan mouths off, a sneer marring his face.

Before he gets the entire sentence out, I leap forward and bowl him over flat to the ground. Gripping him around the throat and by one arm, I shift and toss him like a Frisbee across the circle. He hits the ground with a thud, the breath leaving his lungs in a deep, painful-sounding whoosh.

A few titters go up from around us.

Every sound, every sensation is brighter, stronger, more with Big Daddy partnering like this. For the first time since he started talking to me, it feels like actual partnership between us. I could almost crow with triumph for how normal that is.

Rowan roars and shifts, ripping his clothes to tatters as his wolf takes over.

I release Big Daddy with a battle cry that shakes the glass-fronted treehouses around us.

And then a scent hits me, filling the air so strong, I drop to all fours and lift my nose to drag in more of that sweet, sweet hit.

Arousal. Need. Surprise.

Her.

Fuck. I groan inwardly as we look around the circle to see Lola standing at one end, her hand wrapped around her throat, eyes wide with her wolf's amber shining through like a gods-damned beacon.

Which is how I don't notice Rowan sprinting across the circle until he barrels into me, sinking his fangs into the side of my neck.

Screaming in pain, I roll, flipping him as I rip my skin out of his teeth. We grapple for control, but I toss him easily off me. I'm on him before he can rise, nipping at his throat to get him moving. I could end this fast, but that's not what it's about. It's practice; it's about control.

Rowan leaps and spins, knocking against me with his shorter but broader frame. But with the angle, it catches me slightly off guard. Good thing I'm always five steps ahead. I snap at his neck, sinking my fangs deep enough into his throat as he whines. I toss him from me, leaping before he even lands. He hits the ground and rolls, and I land in the spot where he just was.

He whips around and snarls, crouching as blood drips into the dirt from the shallow wounds I gave him.

This time, when he surges forward, I'm there and ready, shoving him so hard, he flips onto his back, exposing his belly. Before he can get up, I crush him with my larger body, hovering my teeth above his neck again. He struggles, moving every way he can to dislodge me, but like this it's no match. I'm physically bigger, and I weigh almost twice what he does—the benefit of being much older.

After ten minutes of scrambling and scratching and snapping, Rowan whines and drops his head back to the dirt, fully baring his neck for me. I lie on top of him for an extra minute, a reminder of who runs this pack.

When he remains still and silent under my dominance, I grumble in his ear, telling him we're fine, reminding him that the fight is done, and now we move on. It's an important part of this process, that reconnection at the end of a challenge. The wounds he inflicted on me are his victory, and he will take pride in them, but the ultimate win belongs to me.

He whines at my yips and snaps, staying prone as I rise off him and shift back into my human form. It's a testament to my dominance that I shift while he's still in wolf form—his claws could do incredible damage if he attacked now.

Not that he would.

After another long beat, the silent crowd breaks into heart-pounding cheers and shouts, congratulating him on a good challenge and me on the win. Rowan shifts into human form and grasps my hand when I reach for him. I pull him off the ground, bringing my mouth close to his ear. "Nicely fought, alpha," I murmur. "These damn wounds fucking hurt."

He pulls back and beams, bleeding from a gash over his eye and shallow teeth marks at his throat. "Thank you, Alpha. That was so damn fun!"

"Anytime," I say with a laugh.

"Tattoo!" he shouts, raising his arms. The crowd goes wild, repeating the chant while Rowan and I laugh.

Connall strides into the circle with us, a wooden box under one arm. He pats it and grins at Rowan. "Your turn, alpha. Congrats on a wonderful fight."

Rowan takes the box, then looks at me with a thoughtful

expression. He turns, scanning the audience until his gaze falls on Lola. Then he glances back at me. "I think, technically, the princess is highest ranking here, right? If so, she should tattoo you to record the win."

I shudder as a chill sweeps over my entire body. Technically, Rowan's right. The politically correct thing to do would be to have the highest-ranking wolf tattoo my victory, but the idea of Lola doing it does things to me.

Case in point, my dick begins to harden against my thigh. While I'm naked in front of every fucking resident of Shifter Hollow.

"I'm sure she wouldn't mind if you did it," I offer, praying he'll read between the lines of my tone and tattoo me himself.

Rowan smiles and waves at Lola to come over. I feel her before I even hear her pad softly into the circle with us.

His voice is quiet as he turns to me. "I'd like her to feel welcome. She'd appreciate the gesture, right?"

She joins us then, her dark gaze moving between the three of us, expression full of question. "Everything okay?"

Rowan hands the wooden box to her. "Princess, as our most welcome guest and the highest-ranking wolf in Shifter Hollow, it would be my honor if you would tattoo our Alpha's victory on my behalf."

Lola gasps, throwing a hand over her mouth. She looks between us again, eyes wide and mouth dropped open. When it's clear that Rowan's serious, she eyes the box. "Rowan, there's no need. I know it's a point of pride to do this yourself. Seriously, don't worry about me. I'm only visiting."

No, you're not, Big Daddy rumbles. **We're never letting you leave.**

Rowan shoves the box toward her. "Pretty sure, as a visiting diplomat, you technically can't decline a gift either, right?" He winks at her. "I've got a present for you, Princess."

Oh hells no. Rip his head off. This isn't care. He's flirting.

Cálmate, I command my wolf. Calm yourself.

Lola's eyes glisten as she takes the box from Rowan. "You're correct, Rowan; in which case, I'd be honored to mark Richard up for you."

Oh, fuuuuuck. She didn't mean those words the way I took them, but a sudden vision of her marking every inch of me with her teeth fills my mind as Big Daddy howls with pleasure at the thought.

Connall grabs one of Lola's hands and one of Rowan's and lifts them high, turning them to face the crowd. "Princess Lola is going to tattoo Alpha Richard on behalf of Alpha Clayburn. Let's hear it for a successful challenge!"

All the cheering in the world can't distract me from the only thing Big Daddy can focus on right now.

That scent.

That fucking scent.

Oranges. Clotted cream. She's a godsdamn fever dream spun up into the most sugary, beautiful vision I've ever seen, laughing politely as she cheers with the rest of the pack, pretending not to feel awkward at so much attention on her.

I resist a deep and desperate need to sweep her into my arms and—

Do it already. Big Daddy's tone is bored.

I do my best to disagree with him, but it feels like using a bucket to stay a rising tide. No matter what, you're gonna drown. And that's how I feel watching Lola stand in the middle of my pack with such obvious joy around her.

She belongs here.

No, Big Daddy corrects. **She belongs where we are. Wherever that is. Luna.**

Before I catch my bearings, the crowd floods in, lifting Lola and me up until we're body surfing over their heads toward Bad Axe.

"Someone grab my clothes!" I shout, but it gets lost in the melee. Nobody hears a word until I'm dropped into a seat, naked as the day I was born. They dump Lola more carefully into a seat next to me, and someone shoves her close enough for our thighs to touch. I look over at my best friend's daughter, desperately trying to stop myself from thinking of her the way I am.

Why does it have to feel so natural to stare at her, to flirt, to think of her in a sensual way? Alaya, help me find restraint. Por favor. Please.

I give Lola an apologetic look as the crowd cheers and chants, stomping on the wide plank floor. Lights flicker as Bad Axe cheers along with the pack and both herds.

Lola grins and beams at the pressing crowd. Connall stands just behind her, keeping the group from hovering over her too badly.

She gives me a saucy look. "Put your arm on my leg please, Alpha."

The crowd hoots and shouts. Rowan stands to my right, also still naked. Shifters aren't fussed by nudity. We've all seen each other naked a million times; it's no different than being shifted. But when I lift my arm, placing it across Lola's jean-clad legs, my cock twitches against my thigh. I straighten and shift to the edge of the chair, ostensibly to get more space. But the reality is I need my dick to dangle down and not wave around like a damn homing beacon.

Despite the moving, cheering crowd around us, my eyes drift to Lola. She hands the box to Connall, who opens it so she can retrieve the tattoo gun from inside. It's imbued with magic. Every challenge—its participants and outcome—will be automatically recorded in a book at Hearth HQ the moment Lola tattoos my skin. It's a tradition begun when the haven system was created to ensure that all challenges get recorded and not lost to poor record-keeping. Winning records then get copied into a tome in Marco's office, designed to keep the king apprised of up-and-coming competitors.

Lola clicks the gun on like it's every day she tattoos someone, and turns to me with her painted black lips split into a teasing smile. "You ready, Alpha?"

Big Daddy flashes green through my eyes, and when I speak, his rougher tones echo through. "Mark me up, sweetheart. You promised."

The crowd cheers and stomps and screams, the noise reverberating off the ceiling and echoing back down. But somehow it feels like the only two people in this room are her and me. At my words, Lola's scent flares in intensity. Her eyes flick to mine and hold the stare, her wolf's amber flashing through her black irises.

"There you are," I murmur. I can't even stop myself. "Mark me, Lola," I command again. I'm dancing on the edge of something here, something momentous, something instinctual, something as old as our goddess herself.

Luna, Big Daddy practically moans. **Touch us.**

Lola's beautiful wide eyes drop to my arm. She wraps her left hand around my wrist, and my dick jerks at the possessive touch. A sudden vision of being tied down in my bed while she rides me hits me so hard, I grit my jaw to avoid panting and pulling her into my lap. All wolves are intensely sexual—pack alphas more so. Ironic that I'm not mated, because I should be fucking a pretty mate five times a day to keep my head on straight.

But I never found anyone I cared about enough to bring her into my life like that, much less someone fated to be mine.

You're lookin' at her, Alpha, Big Daddy breaks through my thoughts. **She knows it, you know it, and I know it. All that matters.**

I'm on the verge of denying it when I realize I can't, a wash of heady need flowing over me as she runs her right hand over the tick-mark tattoos covering my entire left forearm.

"So many wins," she murmurs, smiling up at me. "And now you've got one more."

My lips split into a grin as Big Daddy preens behind my bones. Lola finds a set of lines where there are just four, meaning a fifth would split across them and complete the set of five. She leans over my arm and positions the whirring tattoo gun while the crowd goes even wilder.

A glass breaks somewhere, liquid splashing the floor as Bad Axe creaks in reprimand. Someone's behind the bar slinging drinks and doing a bad job. But all of that dissipates at the sight of Lola's head bent low over my arm. She's so close. I want to bury my nose in her hair and scent every inch of her, to toss her against the wall and command her not to move while I touch her skin, learn where every freckle is, taste, lick.

The first pinch of the tattoo gun refocuses me. She presses hard but steady, moving the gun in a clean line. When her fingers tighten around my wrist, her scent blooming, I resist the urge to howl.

This is turning her on. She's dripping pheromones like a leaky faucet and it's all I can do not to drop to my knees and worship her.

Told you, Big Daddy snarks. **Do something about this tension, for the love of our goddess.**

"Good job," I murmur to the stunning woman by my side.

Her scent explodes into my senses, nearly knocking me back in the chair with its strength. My nostrils flare, eyes narrowing as I watch my prey. She cocks her head to the side, concentrating on the tattoo but giving me the perfect view of her neck. There's a spot within reach where I'd sink my fangs so deep, mark her permanently like she's marking me.

She's perfuming for us, Big Daddy howls.

And she is, beautifully. It's her body making its desires clear—

she's attracted to me. There's nothing wrong with that. As nonplussed as shifters are about sex and nudity, pheromones are the same. They can't be controlled, and so they can be ignored when necessary. Scents are the undercurrent of shifter society. We know when to comment on them and when to shut the fuck up.

But to perfume like this, so strong, and for me? It's a target, and I desperately, desperately want to be the arrow in the center of the bullseye.

That's the worst analogy I've ever heard. Admit you wanna sink deep into that sweet princess pussy and filthy lick her from bottom to top.

I shove down the groan that builds in my throat, masking it as a cough as Lola finishes a perfectly straight tick-mark line.

She sits upright with a big, fake smile. She knows she's perfuming, and we're in front of everyone. "Done, Alpha. Congratulations."

"Thank you," I murmur as the crowd goes absolutely wild. Jewelry clangs, hooves stomp, drinks get thrown back. It's a rising cacophony of noises.

Someone starts chanting "pack run" at high volume, and the rest of the residents take up the battle cry. I laugh and look between Lola and Connall. "Pack run? We had planned to do this tomorrow, but moving it up a day works."

"I'm always down," Connall agrees, taking the tattoo gun from Lola when she offers it back to him. He's gracious, ignoring her scent as he tucks the gun back inside its ceremonial carved box. Goddess, he's gonna want to talk about this tomorrow when we do rounds.

Lola looks around at the screaming crowd. "There's no way to say no at this point."

Good, get naked, Big Daddy commands.

Around us, the other wolves have already begun to shed their clothes, shifting and running from the bar out into the street once more. The centaurs and pegasi follow, one nearly knocking the front doors off the hinges as he barrels through them and rockets into the night sky.

This isn't supposed to be sexual, but as Lola pulls her shirt over her head, revealing dark skin encased in beautiful, elegant lace, I let out the groan I'd held.

She looks up at me, releasing the clasp on her bra and tossing it on top of a nearby table. "You alright, Richard?" She reaches for her pants next, pushing the zipper down and stepping gracefully out of the fabric. Matching panties tease me until she slips those down her muscular thighs. She picks the clothing up and drops it into a pile with the bra and shirt while I resist the urge to throw her onto the table and bury my face between her thighs.

My entire body trembles, fingers twitching. I'm certain Big Daddy's light is shining from my eyes. Everyone has left the bar, and she stands gloriously naked in front of me, dark brown nipples pebbling to points under my stare. I drink her in, all the way to a bare, shaved pussy that makes my mouth go dry.

She spins slowly in place, teasing me, showing me the fullness of her beautiful ass, the twin dimples at the base of her spine. Gods. I'm panting, mouth open, nostrils flared as I scent air drenched with pheromones designed to attract me, specifically, because my fucking wolf is right, damn him.

Mine, he agrees.

Rational thought evades me as I step closer to her and press my fingers to her lower back. Flattening my palm, I run it up her spine, goose bumps trailing my touch. When I get to her neck, I tighten my grip around it and spin her to face me.

Wolfy amber eyes flash with need. "Richard," she pants, her chest rising and falling rapidly, her nipples brushing my bare chest.

Her eyes cut left at a sound. Growling, I whip around to see a shadow at the door. Someone's coming. Probably Connall to ask where the fuck we are.

She shifts in a flash. When she's all wolf, I stand in awe of her stunning body. Her fur is the deepest of blacks like her human hair; it even has a soft curl to it. Her coat is shorter than mine, the curly fur flat against her skin. Her eyes are the beautiful whiskey gold of her wolf, the same intelligence shining through.

The door slams open then. Two centaurs and Rowan yell at us to get moving.

I sense them from the corner of my focus, but I can't stop staring at Lola's beautiful wolf.

Big Daddy is anxious to get out and meet her for the first time.

For the love of Alaya, please behave, I caution him.

Pack run isn't for sex, he snaps at me. **I'm not new at this, you know.**

I relax my muscles, allowing my wolf to take over while I pray to Alaya that he doesn't decide to go rogue and mount her right here in the bar.

He barks out a laugh between us as I pray hard and allow him to take over.

My turn.

CHAPTER ELEVEN
LOLA

I've never been so thankful to be shifted. Our human forms are so much more emotional and indecisive and complex. Being my wolf is…peaceful, and moons know, I need that right now.

Because that *touch*.

A shiver racks my frame as Richard shifts in a flash of cracking muscles. His wolf emerges, swiveling his head to look at me. He's far larger than me in wolf form, his fur the same salt-and-pepper as his human form's hair. Those luminescent green eyes are as beautiful and piercing as ever. He stalks forward and rubs his cheek along mine, grumbling softly as he brushes his head and neck along my fur.

I don't think; I simply return the move as if we're the oldest of friends. But as the bar's front doors swing open again, I know we can't hide in here forever. I slap Richard with my tail before trotting toward the door. Rowan and another male stand there in wolf form, holding the door for us.

We jog into the moonlight, and the sight that greets me makes my heart skip with happiness. A huge group of wolves in every color mill around in the street with a few dozen centaurs. A handful of pegasi fly lazy circles above us. I've never been on a run with anyone but wolves. This feels…significant somehow. As if every resident of Shifter Hollow is so much a part of the pack, that even the other monsters run with us.

Richard stops beside me and lets out a howl to indicate the beginning of the run. Because this is such a big group, I wonder how often they do the pack run. We do a parade in Santa Alaya once a year because there are simply too many wolves to do a typical run. It's usually celebratory and done to commune with our goddess, Alaya. But it's also a way for our wolves to connect as a pack, to strengthen bonds with each other and our shifts.

Richard's Second, Connall, leads. He sprints up the street and into the pitch-black night. If this pack works like every other pack outside of Santa Alaya, Richard will be in the back, helping the pups, older wolves and any stragglers. His wolf looks over at me, green eyes luminescent in the night. He steps forward and snuffles my ear, scenting me as my wolf pauses, letting the pack alpha do whatever he wants.

And that's when I know I'll be at the back with him. I'm drawn to be by his side, to be there helping the young and old ones alike. To serve. To bring harmony.

I yip my excitement, and his wolf lets out a happy little chuffed response. We trot up the street after the pack, breaking into a lope as the clouds above us split, the moon's rays shining down in thick beams that spear the forest ahead.

Alaya is blessing us tonight, it seems.

The pack is silent save for the occasional thrilled yip or hoot. We run until we reach the glowing green wards that protect Ever from the outside human world. They form a bubble over the haven, like they do back home, although, I've only seen our wards a few times in my life.

At the ward wall, Connall leads us left, and we run and run and run under the moon. My wolf's bliss is palpable at being with this pack, at the nearly hundred bodies in front of us. The wolves run together, the centaurs galloping on swift hooves through the forest to our left. Hana leads that group, her mate Arkan at the back with another centaur who can only be his father—they look so similar. Above us, the pegasi flit gracefully through the trees, smiles on their faces as their beautiful wings beat the air.

Joy fills me at the connectedness of such a run. And, goddess, do we run. We run for almost an hour before the pups in front of us begin to slow. Richard and I nudge their tails, urging them on. They pick up the pace for a solid twenty minutes before flagging again. The youngest of pups typically remain with their parents, but the young children run at the very back in a group together—a move designed to bond the next generation.

One of the pups stumbles over a tree root and yips, tumbling into a pile as another falls on top of him. The pack continues on but Richard and I stop, sniffing at the pups to determine they're fine, just tired and getting sloppy. The pup who fell whines and flops onto his back, showing Richard his neck and tummy.

Richard's wolf nuzzles the exposed belly before growling at the pup to roll over. When he does, Richard picks him up gently by the scruff and glances at the second one. The pup jogs forward, but he's limping from the fall.

Without thinking, I pick him carefully up in my jaws and take my spot next to Richard. His wolf's green eyes flash at me, and then he's off again, sprinting through beautiful, twisty dark forest. We come to an old vintage-styled gas station with a highway that leads out of the wards. Ah, that must be how newcomers arrive if they don't portal in.

And then it's another solid hour of running, around a motel run by wraiths—the chill from their aura is tangible over my fur as we pass. I shudder as we round the forest outside the property itself. I've stayed at a wraith motel before, and I did not enjoy it. It feels wrong to be surrounded by the spirits of those who are long gone from their mortal flesh.

Eventually we round a beautiful glassy lake, and then it's

another short half hour until the now-familiar sights and scents of Shifter Hollow come into view. The silent pup in my mouth begins to wriggle when we get close. When a big white wolf circles back around and chuffs a thanks at me, I drop the young one. He runs over to her and she picks him up and carries him off into the trees.

Richard's pup begins to wiggle and yowl once we reach Shifter Hollow's main road. Richard sets him gently down, and he runs off into the milling group. Slowly but surely, the crowd dissipates as we watch. The pegasi disappear up into the treetops and the centaurs canter off in a herd.

Connall breaks off from the group and stalks through Bad Axe's front doors when she swings them wide for us.

We follow, reentering the bar and heading for the table where we left our clothes earlier tonight.

Connall shifts first, grabbing his clothing and throwing it over his broad shoulders. "Good run tonight. Thanks for your help, Lola."

I shift back to human form and nod, stretching against the well-used soreness of my muscles. "That was so fun. We don't do traditional pack runs in Santa Alaya, and even when we do, it's mostly through the town at a very slow pace. This was...invigorating."

Connall laughs softly. "We do a lot of things differently, I suspect."

Richard shifts and groans. "Damnit, I have no idea where my clothes ended up."

Connall snorts and gives his alpha a fake salute. "I'll leave you to sort that out. If you don't need anything else, I'm gonna head home."

"All good," Richard says. "I'll be at Leighton's parents' place in the morning with breakfast, if you want to go with me."

Connall nods. "I'll meet you there." Green eyes flash to me and wrinkle in the corners as he smiles. "Night, Lola."

I wave goodbye as he turns to go. When the doors swing shut behind him, I realize that Richard is sitting on the edge of a table, staring at me.

"What are you thinking about?" His deep, rumbly voice breaks through my thoughts.

I turn to face him. "I was thinking that I love how Connall calls me my name, and not my title." I glance around the empty bar. "Nobody here seems to care that I'm the princess, and I find that very refreshing."

Richard shrugs. "We care; we just don't *care* care, if you know what I mean." He jerks his head toward the ceiling. "I never can sleep after a run. Want to come up to my place and have a drink?"

Everything in me tightens at his words. He touched me earlier, and if people hadn't shown up, I don't know where he would have gone next. Is he hoping to do more of that now? I'm not sure, but I *want* to know with a longing so deep and painful, it nearly steals my breath.

Richard leans forward, bringing his mouth to my ear. "I'll take your shocked-looking silence as a yes." He says nothing else, his breath warm on my skin as I resist the urge to cock my head to the side and give him my neck.

My neck.

I've never shown a male my neck before. Goddess, I think Papá would have put a protective collar on me at birth if he could have. He beat the idea into me of protecting my neck from a claiming bite since I was a pup.

And here I am practically offering it to his oldest friend. After Papá sent me here to avoid another alpha forcing the very same thing.

I shrug that thought off like a wet blanket. I don't need that negativity.

Richard turns when I don't answer, stalking gracefully toward the front door as I stare at his powerful back, ass, and legs. Every inch of him is tattooed muscle. Even if I didn't know he was this pack's alpha, I'd know it from the supreme confidence that rolls off him with every step he takes.

At the exit, he pauses, glancing over his shoulder. "Coming, Lola?"

I grab my clothes pile and jog to catch up, sailing through the door when he holds it open for me. I'm well fucking aware that I'm still naked, but so is he. Maybe we'll stay that way, hang out in the buff like it's every day we chill without clothes on.

Richard stalks down the sidewalk toward the left, rounding the building and disappearing into a dark alleyway. I'm right behind him, sticking close. It's not that I'm afraid; it's that I want to be in this man's orbit—to scent him, be near him. Goddess knows I want to do more than that. I should be ashamed, maybe horrified, probably shocked. And I was for about twenty minutes the day I arrived. But I know my wolf, and Richard is the only male she has ever given a shit about. I can't ignore that.

The building bumps out at the back, a singular door visible at the end of the alley. Richard pulls it open and gestures me into a staircase that leads straight up to another door.

I turn in the darkness. "No centaur ramp?"

He thumps my nose. "It's on the other side, smarty pants. Every home in Shifter Hollow has a centaur- and pegasus-accessible entrance. Every bar, every business is built with our taller residents in mind. I insisted on that when we built this haven."

"Santa Alaya has done a lot to make things accessible, but we've always got room to improve," I admit. Our haven was originally designed by wolf shifters for wolf shifters, but one of the things my papá insisted on was upgrading our infrastructure to accommodate other monsters and those with different needs.

"I learned a lot from Marco's programs," Richard says, stepping past me to ascend the stairs. "Everything we designed here is based on what he did back home. Plus, we've got an accessibility council that meets once a year to determine if any improvements need to be made."

"Love that," I say softly. I wink up at him. "As long as you don't fuck with the food or the music or the candy or the coffee or any of the other wonderful things we have back home, you'll hear no argument from me."

Richard opens the single door at the top of the stairs and waves me through. "Never, sweetheart."

I flush with joy at the new moniker. I'll admit to not having a very deep understanding of my preferred kinks—I haven't had much chance to explore them—but pet names and praise appear to be among them, based on the wetness between my thighs.

Blushing, I enter the open space and sigh at how perfect it is. A flat glass wall frames the front of the space where the street is. It's set to transparent, but if it's like most other havens, Richard can set it to translucent or even solid wall depending on his wishes.

Two oversized sheepskin sofas face one another, extra chairs flanking them on either side. A rustic wooden table in the middle holds a decanter of amber liquid and six glasses around it. To my left, a black-and-white kitchen is just as masculine as the rest of the room. A rustic chandelier hangs from the angled ceiling, chunky beams adding to the maleness of Richard's home.

He moves into the kitchen—still naked—and hunts around in the dark cabinets for something. I turn to continue admiring the beautiful surroundings.

"This is exactly what I'd picture a pack alpha's home looking like," I murmur, more to myself than anything, but Richard laughs from across the room.

"The nice thing about being an eternal bachelor is that nobody has opinions on the lack of pillows on my sofa."

When I glance over to see if he's serious, he's grinning at me with a bottle of wine in one hand and two glasses in the other. "How do you feel about merlot?"

I cross the room and slide onto one of the metal and wood barstools. "Merlot is perfect."

Richard sets the glasses down and spreads the fingers of one hand wide. As I watch, long wolf nails slip out of the tips. He grins at me as he digs one into the cork, twisting the bottle with his other hand. All it does is accentuate the stacked, corded muscles of his forearms, biceps, and shoulders.

I watch in utter silence, past the point of caring if I'm staring at him. He invited me here—STILL NAKED—and now we're drinking. When he slides the half-full glass across the table, I take it and swirl it slowly under my nose.

My wolf has been at the forefront of my consciousness since Richard asked us up here. Like every time we're near him, he's her focus. She seems completely unconcerned about Papá and what's going on back home. She hasn't even been pushing me to play my guitar. It's all Richard right now.

Richard and the sweet notes of the merlot he handed me. He leans over the kitchen island countertop and takes a slow sip from his glass. His throat bobs as he swallows, drawing my eye there.

It's on the tip of my tongue to tell him that he's beautiful, that I'm entranced by the energy between us, that I want to know everything about him. Every single thing. I want to hear about every moment of his entire life just so I can be aware of him.

He can probably tell by the scent dripping from me, but if he can, he doesn't point it out. He stands before I can formulate the words, holding his hand out to me. I rise and take it, a lump forming in my throat when he turns and pulls me toward a dark hallway. For half a second, I think we're going to his bedroom, and a shiver runs down my spine. But as soon as we enter the hall, he takes an immediate right and leads me up a skinny set of rough-edge wooden stairs.

Moments later, we emerge on a small rectangular rooftop patio. We're encased in treetops; no other homes or even the street below are visible. Above us, stars wink playfully through the translucent ward.

A giant puffy beanbag sort of chair sits in the middle of the platform. Skinny wooden tables run around it, forming a half-moon shape with the beanbag in the middle. Honestly, it's huge.

Like a nest.

I've only built a few heat nests in my life. My heat isn't predictable or frequent like some omegas. But this oversized, puffy bed-like structure that's big enough for five people? I'd nest the shit outta that thing. I can almost picture it now—mood lighting, candles, plenty of toys…this perfect alpha with his fangs buried in my throat, marking me, claiming me, taking *everything*.

While I'm silently admiring it, Richard sets his wine down and leaps gracefully in, flipping onto his back. He hums happily as his body sinks, supported fully by whatever the nest is made out of. He grins and pats a spot next to him as I struggle not to stare at his dick.

I've caught a few glimpses, but we weren't alone, and I couldn't stare. Even now, should I?

"Come here."

Richard's command hits me with all the power of a pack alpha's directive. It's like he can reach into my body and pull me toward him on an invisible tether. Without conscious thought, I set my wine down and crawl in next to him—not touching, but close enough that his sunshiny scent fills my nostrils.

My eyes drift over his body, the hard planes and lines of him. His chest is covered in tattoos—compasses, north stars, pine trees, wolves. If there's a shifter-themed tattoo, it can be found somewhere on his upper body. But even the dark ink can't hide the dips and valleys of thick, packed-on muscle. His chest is broad, coated with a fine dusting of dark hair. His abs are outlined in detail, a muscular vee leading down his belly like a damn homing beacon.

"You're staring, omega." Richard's wolf is present in his voice, and when I look up, his eyes flash green. "I know you've seen naked alphas before."

A flash of heat runs through me. "Of course." *But they weren't you,* I want to add.

He stretches both arms above his head, tucking his hands behind his neck. "I spoke to your father before the challenge. Nothing new at home."

Papá…riiiiight.

I flop onto my back next to Richard, sighing as I sink into the comfortable surface. "Yeah, I spoke with him earlier today as well. Sounds like I'm here for the foreseeable future, until he feels comfortable bringing me home." Then it's back to my typical grind.

Do I sound bitter?

Richard rolls onto his right side, propping his head up with one hand. "You sound bitter, omega. Talk to me."

I roll to my left, matching his position as I shake my head. "I'm bitter about being a political pawn, about having to think about the repercussions for my father of every step in my life. I *am* bitter, at least a little bit. I don't know what it feels like to be free of the pressures of our court."

Damn, I really laid it all out there.

Richard is quiet for a moment. "When your mother was alive, Marco was different. She was like you—artistic, creative, kind, wise. She never really cared about climbing the political ladder. Marco was always more interested in it. But when they were newly mated, he didn't focus on it so much."

This is news to me. I scratch at the space between us, my fingers needing to do something to dispel a sudden need to know every single thing about my mother that Richard can tell me.

He smiles as if he can read all of that in my expression. "Your mother tempered him. She was the peace to counter his supreme dominance."

I pick at the beanbag's fuzzy surface. "It's hard to imagine that since I don't remember her."

Richard shakes his head. "When Maria died, Marco lost all

appetite for the things she loved. I think it hurt him too much, the memory of her. So he threw himself into politics, rising fast. By the time he became king, I hardly recognized the pup I grew up with." He looks at me with a remorseful expression. "He's a great alpha, but losing your mother broke something in him that he's never taken the time to heal. Which is why he's so cautious with you. And I suspect why he tries to keep you from the music. She loved it like you do."

I grit my jaw at hearing my father described this way. I've gleaned most of this from living with him my entire life. I knew Mamá loved music too. "He doesn't really talk about her," I admit.

Richard reaches out and places his hand over mine, his palm warm and comforting. "What do you want to know, Lola? I knew Maria well, and I'd be honored to talk about her."

Tears fill my eyes. Papá never wants to discuss her for more than a moment. What do I want to know? Suddenly, I can't think of a single thing. My mind's gone blank, too filled with processing emotion to consider what I could learn from Richard about her. Not to mention the weirdness surrounding the fact that the male in front of me, the male I'm lusting after, was friends with my parents before I ever existed.

"Another time," I whisper.

"Alright," he rumbles, the luminescent green from his eyes fading.

Come back, I want to shout. *Let me see you.*

But his wolf has gone, probably leaving because emotional chatter isn't really their thing. Our wolves are pure instinct.

"Your wolf disappeared," I tease. "Guess he's not really into feelings and moms."

Richard groans and removes his hand from mine to rub at his chest. "I've got to go see Arkan's father, Vikand, soon. I've never felt so disconnected from my wolf."

Sorrow fills me for him. I can't imagine that.

"He speaks to me," Richard says softly.

I stare in shock. "Hearing your wolf is supposed to be the highest level of connection shifters can have. I've only ever known a few shifters who could do that."

Richard's eyes shift to the stars as he considers my confusion. After a minute, they drift back to me. "Turns out Big Daddy and I don't agree on much."

It takes a moment for what he said to sink in, and then a hilarious cackle leaves my mouth. It turns into a snort, and then his eyes flash green again as his wolf reappears.

Between giggles, I manage a word or two. "His name…is…Big Daddy?" I roll onto my back to laugh as Richard starts growling, an unhappy noise threaded with his wolf's deep rumble.

"Don't laugh; I'm serious," he whines. "It's a problem!"

That sends me further over the edge until I'm full-on cackling, tears streaming from my eyes. "That is the least serious name I've ever heard!" I snort again, unable to keep it down. "I thought those lucky few who got to talk to their wolves got names like Grey Swiftwind and shit like that."

Richard lets out an otherworldly growl, and that's when everything goes sideways. One moment, he's on his side grousing at my reaction. The next, his enormous body is on top of mine, my wrists in his hands and yanked above my head. His face is inches from me, lips drawn back to reveal twin fangs. He's hot, so incredibly hot, his skin searing mine like a flame. His hips roll, his hard cock resting against my thigh.

Everything in me tightens, pulse racing as I stare up at him. His eyes are full green, glowing as if lit from within. Some deeply innate sense I have tells me I pushed him, but not too far. No. I think he could do with a little more.

"Hey, Big Daddy," I murmur. "Nice to officially meet you. It's kind of a mouthful, though. Is there a shorter version of your name? Maybe…BD or, I dunno, Daddy?"

A ripped snarl raises the hair on the back of my neck, my

breasts rubbing against Richard's perfect, broad chest. His mouth is so close to mine, our breathing rough and heavy, our bodies pressed together.

"Alpha," he commands. "What you call me should only be 'Alpha.' Say it with me, omega."

I force back a smile. "Yes, Alpha Daddy."

He releases one of my wrists and threads his fingers through my hair, yanking my head back so hard, I yip. The move forces me to expose my neck, his breath warm on it. Fluttery tingles radiate out from my core, my body clenching and tightening at his dominance.

The next wolfy growl pebbles my nipples as I hang on the precipice of desperation. I need a touch, any touch—his tongue, his lips, those damn teeth.

I don't get any of that, though.

Instead, something else happens.

My scent. It blooms and soaks the air with pheromones as I perfume for him. I can't control it any more now than I could earlier when he and Rowan fought. It's a natural response, but the moment it happens, he lets out a ragged groan, dipping lower until his mouth brushes my neck.

"That fucking scent," he murmurs, his voice roughshod.

His words drive me to the point of no return, energy building along my skin as I arch into his frame. "Please, Alpha."

Soft lips hint at brushing my neck. "Please what?"

I can't voice what I need. I'm throwing every possible signal at him. Is he going to make me say it?

Richard releases my hair, returning my gaze to his. Big Daddy's green shows through as I reach up and stroke my fingers down the bridge of his nose.

His eyes scan my face. I'm not sure what he's looking for, but I can't take this heat any longer. Propping myself up on my elbows, I lift my chin and brush my lips across his, just a taste, just a tease. Richard hovers frozen above me, eyes flashing wide as I do it again, nipping slowly at his plump lower lip. For a moment, I see him war with unnamed emotion even as Big Daddy's green burns brighter.

His lips open, and I close my eyes to wait for the maelstrom to unleash.

But…it doesn't come.

Richard lifts off me and off the beanbag completely, rising to a stand as he runs his fingers through his hair, staring at me like he doesn't know me.

The shock of what I just did and the sting of his rejection hit me all at once. For a moment, I lie there, chest heaving, staring at him as he stares at me. There's an entire chasm of unspoken things between us, but the only thing I can focus on is the fact that he pulled away.

He pulled *away*.

It's so wrong and horrible, I could cry. So, I do what any sane omega would do when rejected…

I run.

I run down the stairs and across his beautiful home to the exit. And then I shift into my wolf to stop feeling so very much.

CHAPTER TWELVE
RICHARD

Nooooooooo! Big Daddy bellows and rages and bashes against my bones as he tries to follow Lola. But I can't move; I can barely think around a storm of emotion— shock; confusion; deep, instinctive need. I press against the half wall that surrounds my upper porch and lift my head, looking to the moon, praying for her guidance.

Every bit of my alpha nature tells me to follow Lola, because I hurt her. She ran from me, and it's so wrong, I grind my teeth against the sensation of my skin pulling too tight, anxiety building in my chest. I rub at it as logic overwhelms my emotion. Our difference in age isn't a big deal—I'm far, far older than her —but wolves live a very long time.

My king is the problem. If Marco knew she kissed me, he'd rip me in two and toss me into the bay for the crabs.

She said he didn't want her to be forced. And she wants you. Make him understand! Big Daddy's emotions are firmly in the *chase her down now* camp, but I keep my feet planted as I roll through all the possible outcomes of what happened. I'm the pack alpha; I don't always get what I want. Even in an individual haven, as opposed to far up the pecking order where Marco is, I have to be politically smart about the choices I make. I have more freedom than he does, but there are still…considerations.

Luna, Big Daddy whines, morose as he flops down in our shared mental space, dragging his cheek in the dirt. **She was so beautiful, so perfect, so ready. She fucking kissed you, you idiot!**

Luna. I don't know how I'd know if she was my Luna or not. The lore about the Luna bond is sparse, mostly lost to history. But what I do know is that Lola was crafted by the goddess Alaya herself to belong to me, to be mine in every way. It's why we can't stop touching, why I can't seem to keep my head on straight around her. It's why she perfumes so fucking hard for me. She and her wolf are calling for me and mine in every possible way they can. She's my mate. I know that with absolute certainty. I think I knew it before tonight, but when her lips touched mine?

I'm done.

It's fucking cruel, so fucking cruel for Fate to promise me the one woman I shouldn't touch. I've been single a long time—decades. I'd always hoped that if and when my mate, or even just a compatible omega, came to me, it would be uncomplicated for us. Being alpha is complicated enough.

But the godsdamned *princess* of our people?

I growl and shift off the wall, descending the stairs into my main living area. Her anguished scent fills the space as I pause in the hallway, closing my eyes to drink her in. That scent compels me, feet moving without conscious thought. I'm out my door and winding through the streets until I reach her guest house. Her unhappy scent saturates the air, forcing a rumbly whine from my throat.

This is wrong. So wrong.

I'm sorry, I moan to myself. Goddess, what was I thinking?

Thankfully, Big Daddy is quiet in my mind, allowing me to wallow in misery as I stand outside Lola's treehouse, refusing to barge into her space but desperately begging her to come to the door. She doesn't, and when I eventually turn to leave, Big Daddy recedes into the depths of my mind.

∼

Hurting Lola last night opened a wound inside me that's festering, knowing she's feeling pain and it's my fault. Top that shit sundae off with Big Daddy's ire and I didn't get a moons-damned wink.

At 3 a.m. I give up on sleep. Swinging my legs off the bed, I prop my elbows on my knees and run both hands through my hair. The giant circular window in my bedroom is set to transparent, rain pounding the surface. Big Daddy starts immediately in on me.

You rejected our Luna. If I could break out of here and kick your ass, you'd be dead!

I could have bitten her last night, I admit. *I wanted to.*

Good. Bite her. Mark her. Fill her with pups. Goddess, they'd be so beautiful.

Pups.

Heat flashes through me at the idea of Lola swollen with child, of her perfect breasts filled with life-giving milk. I don't think I realized I had a pregnancy kink until this precise moment, but my dick bobs between my thighs, dripping sticky precum to the floor as my knot swells to a painful point.

Needs to get kissed and locked by Lola.

Him giving me that idea does nothing to dissipate the heat. My imagination runs rampant to a vision of her pregnant, on all fours, me pounding into her from behind as her pussy locks tight around my knot, holding us together while I pump her full of me. Of her neck bared for my teeth. Of me cherishing every moment with her.

I fall back onto the bed, my dick a waving flag until it falls hard and hot against my belly. Every instinct tells me to go to her place, but then logic rears its ugly head. It's 3 a.m. She's probably sleeping. It would be a dick move to wake her up for an apology.

Rolling onto my side, I pull open a drawer in my bedside table and retrieve a pocket pussy. The treehouse does me the favor of blurring the window so my neighbors don't have to watch me jack off.

Big Daddy growls as I slip the toy over my cock, grunting at the sensation of all that slick, cold plastic kissing my length.

Go find the real thing, he barks. **Fix this.**

I ignore him as I yank the toy up and down, teasing the edge of my knot. When the toy pops over the swollen ring around the base of my dick with a sloppy slurp, I pant and arch my back. It feels good, too good, and I'm going to come too damn fast. I've gotta take the edge off before I do something rash.

But I keep imagining Lola and all the ways I want to dominate her, ways she'd love because she's built for me. I explode a half dozen pumps later, snapping my teeth as an orgasm ripples through me, hard enough that my eyes roll into my head, lips curling back as my muscles lock with pleasure.

When it fades, I'm coated in a fine sheen of sweat and thoroughly fucking dissatisfied. Tossing the used-up toy on my bed, I stare at the ceiling for a solid three hours, considering all the angles and trying to come up with a solution that feels right. Ultimately I decide that I need more information. It's hard for me to trust Big Daddy's desires given that he seems to leave logic out of them most of the time.

Eventually I stand and head for the shower. If I'm this much of a mess after last night, I can't imagine how my mate feels.

Holy moons. I thought of her that way instinctively. I've got to find her and talk to her. It's not right, the way things happened last night. I know that, I just…the harder I look for my earlier excuses, the more difficult it is to actually find them.

I twist the silver shower knob on, stepping under the cold water to wash away all evidence of what I did.

Big Daddy is silently watchful as I go through the motions of washing up and dressing. He stays silent as I leave my apartment and head up the main drag toward what used to be an empty spot on the street but is now Arkan's father, Vikand's office. It's too early for anyone to be about—probably too early for Lola to be up—but Vikand is here all the time, it seems.

The glass-paned storefront window is full of dusty books stacked in what appears to be complete disarray. Though, having known Vikand for a short time, I suspect he knows where every book is. I grip the branch-shaped handle and open a thick wooden door, a small bell tinkling to announce my arrival.

Inside, the small space is filled floor to ceiling with books on shelves. They overflow the shelves onto the floor in big, misshapen stacks. Ancient-looking papers stick out of about half of them, handwritten notes scribbled right to the very edges.

Muttering reaches me from somewhere in the back. I follow the sound across the small space and around a corner to a standing desk. There used to be a computer on that desk, but now it's just more stacks of books. Vikand stands there, glasses perched on the tip of his nose and a giant open book in one hand as he turns the page with the other.

His black tail swishes slowly behind him, short wavy hair slicked back over his pointed ears. Goddess, he and Arkan look so much alike. Their personalities couldn't be more different though. Our current Keeper is charming and direct with a surprising sense of humor. His father is…none of those things.

When Vikand doesn't seem to notice my presence, I clear my throat and step to the very front of his table.

Black brows scrunch together as he lifts his gaze to mine, jerking back as if startled.

He closes the book and sets it down, lifting his glasses off his nose. He folds them carefully and tucks them in a pocket of his fitted gray vest. "Alpha, what are you doing here?" He looks confused.

I cock my head to the side, examining the peculiar older centaur. "I'm here to discuss my wolf. I thought Connall mentioned it to you when he invited you to our leadership meeting."

Vikand strokes his chin with long black fingers. "Ah, come to think of it, he did. While I was there, I was considering the magic that allowed Morgan Hector to kill Wesley. Gods, it's a deep, ancient magic she called. Do you know—"

"I need to discuss my wolf with you," I interject. "The Wesley issue is done. My wolf is a problem."

Big Daddy grunts deep in my mind, lifting his head to narrow his shining eyes at me.

Vikand crosses his arms, halting the swish of his tail. "Tell me what's happening, and we can go from there."

I sigh. "Right before the Wesley events, my wolf began speaking to me. His voice is clear in my mind, which is usually cause for celebration among our people, as you probably know."

Vikand nods, brows furrowing again as he stares at me intensely.

I continue, "Typically, it's a sign of strength to be able to speak to one's wolf. It's something I always secretly wished for, if I'm honest. But then he began talking, and we are not aligned."

Vikand shifts forward, placing both hands flat on his desk. "Not aligned? In what way?"

A rumbly growl echoes in my throat, Big Daddy making his displeasure at this conversation known. I grunt and shove his ire down. "We don't agree on anything. He fights me. He's dominant and sometimes I feel he lacks the more rational side that allows me to make long-term decisions."

Don't need that. Instinct is best. Like with Lola.

As soon as he's made that statement, he disappears. I sigh and point to my head.

"It's happening right now. He disagrees that he even needs to consider the long term. He says instinct is best." I leave Lola out of it, because thinking about her pain from last night makes me want to flip tables and punch myself.

Vikand nods slowly, glancing off into the book stacks as he seems to mull over my words. He sucks at his teeth and turns back to me. "Have you considered that he's right?"

A satisfied chuff echoes from the depths of my mind.

I grit my teeth. "If I listened to him, I'd be doing things I shouldn't be doing."

"Like what?" Vikand opens his arms wide. "What, precisely, has he suggested you do that would be so bad?"

I debate the merits of sharing all of this with Vikand, so I level him with a serious look. "This stays between us. I haven't even discussed this with Connall. Or Arkan," I tack on.

Vikand nods. "I can keep a secret; although, you may have noticed my boy is incredibly intuitive, despite the charming persona."

"Oh, I know," I mutter. "I just haven't found my footing with him yet. I worked with Abemet for so long, I'm accustomed to his ways."

Vikand smiles. "You and Arkan will find your groove, but that's your path to travel. Tell me what your wolf is asking you to do that's so bad. I won't discuss it with my son."

I sigh. "My wolf is attracted to the princess."

Vikand snorts, stomping one of his dark forelegs. "Princess Lola?"

"Yeah."

He cuts me an assessing look. "How attracted?"

Goddess, this is gonna get awkward. I cross my arms. "The attraction goes both ways. He thinks she's my Luna."

Vikand's mouth drops open. "Do you know how rare that is, Alpha?" He waves the question away before I even get a chance to answer it. "Of course you do—silly question." Wide eyes flash back to me. "Do you disagree with him?"

And there it is, the question at the heart of all my current angst. How can my best friend's daughter be my mate?

"I don't know how I'd know about the Luna part, but she's mine," I whisper. "And her father is my best friend. I was his Second for *centuries*, Vikand. This is impossibly complicated. I hurt her feelings last night, I—" My voice fails as I reminisce on how fucking terrible it felt to hurt her. I was shocked in the moment, terrified of what it meant to open those flood gates.

I don't usually waffle like that.

The centaur male says nothing as he looks to his left at a stack of thick, dusty books. His fingers trail down the pages until he gets to one near the bottom. He grips the spine carefully and pulls the book out, laying it open on the tabletop between us. He pulls his glasses out of his pocket and perches them on the tip of his nose, hovering over the book. Deft fingers find a page and open to it.

He spins the book to face me. The top half of the page is a singular drawing of a shifted wolf, eyes glowing from where he stands in a dense grove of trees. He stands easily a head taller than the few wolves on either side of him. They look like the last line of defense, standing in a row.

Vikand taps below the picture, bringing my attention to rows of unintelligible text beneath the photo. "This book is an account of a pixie living in the wilds in an area with a ruling shifter pack, many, many thousands of years ago. The shifters ruled the forest and kept everyone safe." He glances up. "This was long before the Cerinvalla Act created the haven system, so, of course, monsters were more at risk from dark forces."

He slides his fingers over the words. Most are in a language I can't fathom, much less read—the language of our goddess, Alaya. I've seen the maze-like text in books before. Marco has a whole shelf of them in his office. But I've never known anyone who could read it. No one has. Thankfully, parts of her account seem to have been translated into English.

Vikand continues, "From the sections I *can* read, their pack alpha's wolf began to speak to him, which isn't unheard of, but then they began to fight. He'd have fits where he'd shout at his wolf, bashing his head against rocks and begging for relief."

I gulp. "And what happened?"

Vikand sighs. "He threw himself off a cliff and died."

I snarl. "This is not helpful."

Vikand points to the next page. "Right, but her account continues. After the alpha died, his Second took over, and his wolf began speaking to him. But instead of waiting for it to get to a point where they drove one another crazy, he went searching for answers. Nobody had ever seen an alpha and his wolf disagree. They thought there might be a sickness going through the pack, something to explain the discord. The pixie accompanied him as a scribe, because the new alpha wanted his findings to be passed along to other wolves, if he was able to figure out what happened to his predecessor."

Vikand closes the book and pushes it toward me. "Your answers lie within this book, Richard."

Frustration gets the better of me, a soft growl rumbling from my throat. Big Daddy is quieter than he's ever been.

"I can't read most of this book, Vikand. Can you summarize anything else?"

The centaur smiles, but it's sad, his gaze thoughtful. "I know, but take it anyhow. You might find yourself curious about the details, or perhaps your wolf will have insight. But, yes, this pack ultimately determined one thing." He gives me a wry look. "On their adventures, the alpha found his Luna. And once he cemented their bond, he became bigger, stronger, more powerful. He and his wolf *both* communicated with her, and he never had the issues the first alpha had. Instead, they both came into enormous amounts of power."

All of the air disappears from the room as I grip the edge of the table. *She's* the answer to this discord. Of course she is. I close my eyes and try to feel for her, to call her to me. I need to have this conversation with her directly. If what he's saying is true, then maybe Big Daddy is right. Maybe she and I share this bond, the first pair to share it in thousands of years. I don't know how we'd know other than Big Daddy's insistence.

I just know. Isn't that enough?

I can't find words to answer him. Desperation to speak with Lola rides me until I can barely stand still.

Vikand's voice is low as he continues, "I think you already know what to do, Richard. In a fight for what's right, does your mate come first or your king?"

I thank him and tuck the book under my arm, my mind awash with emotion and focus. I need to talk to Lola.

Now.

CHAPTER THIRTEEN
LOLA

Rejected. I've never been rejected like last night, never even had the chance to because I never gave any males the chance to have me.

But I kissed Richard last night, and he pulled away. He came to the treehouse but I didn't answer; I pretended to be asleep.

I glance to my right where my favorite chocolate chunk ice cream sits in a tub on the bedside table. Oh yeah, I'm gonna finish the tub right now. Leaning over, I grab it, thankful I was a smart girl who didn't even remove the spoon. I dig it deep into the half-melted treat and drop a huge dollop in my mouth.

Chocolate and cherries and a teeny hint of whiskey fill my senses. Inside my mind, my wolf whines for the millionth time. She never liked confrontation, and being at odds with the pack alpha is the worst sort of confrontation for our kind.

Homesickness washes over me so hard and heavy, I nearly choke on the ice cream. Gods, I miss Leo and Lupe and even Santa Alaya, which is hard to imagine since I was always so excited to leave home. I miss the castle and Papá. I miss the sun and the bay and the smell of fried fish down by the waterfront. I miss the band.

I hop out of bed and grab the comm disk off the wall. Jogging back, I tuck myself under the covers again and drop the disk on my lap.

"Call Leo Wild."

Moments later, Leo's handsome face appears. His rakish grin is so familiar, so lovely, that I tear up at the sight of it.

"¿Princesa, qué pasa?" he murmurs. *What's wrong?*

"Miss you," I whisper around the lump in my throat. "Hey," sobs threaten to steal my voice, "can you do me a favor and go down to visit Lupe and the others? I don't know if anybody is doing that in my absence."

Leo's smile falls. "Your papá is doing it, but it seems performative. I'll go in the morning and bring her coffee like we used to as pups."

"Thank you," I breathe. "How's home? I heard Eliel hasn't challenged Papá yet."

Leo shakes his head, sighing as he rubs ring-filled fingers over his face. "No. Any day now, if word on the street is true. To be honest, Lola, I'm glad you're not here. Eliel's been sneaking around, talking shit about Marco. Goddess, I'm glad I'm not the king. Remind me not to ever get into politics."

I snort at that. It's unfathomable. Rolling to my left, I grab my guitar and strum a few notes.

Leo laughs. "You sleeping with that thing?"

I nod and continue playing one of our favorite songs. "Always. Wanna sing with me for a bit?"

Leo nods and disappears out of view. Moments later, he's back with his black electric guitar. It doesn't have the built-in magical amp like mine does, but, damn, it's pretty. Leaning down, he plugs it into his smallest amp so it doesn't sound tinny.

When he plays the first notes, I fall in. We strum and sing for a solid quarter hour before there's a noise somewhere behind him. Leo glances over his shoulder then looks back at me with a sheepish grin.

"We're packing to get outta town for a few weeks. I don't want to be here when shit goes down with Eliel. If he wins…"

My heart clenches in my chest, and I set the guitar down. "You don't think he could actually win, do you?"

Leo hands his guitar to one of the Lobos and shakes his head, slipping his hands under his armpits. "I don't know, Lola. There's talk of Eliel using magic."

I gasp. "Does Papá know?!"

He shakes his head again. "Hard to say, but your father is a political genius, corazón. I can't imagine this would take him by surprise."

I grit my teeth. "I'm calling him as soon as we hang up."

Leo smiles, but he looks sad all the same. "Te ves triste," he says quietly. *You look sad.* "Is Ever not treating you well?"

"I'd be better if you came to visit," I say, feeling guilty. His free time is limited.

He steps closer through the hologram, dark eyes focused on me. "If you need me, I'm there. We've got concerts the next couple of nights, but I can skip those or come in four days. Do you care which?"

I shake my head. "Don't skip. The music would be sad without you. But if you can come in four days, goddess, I'd love that."

"Done," he states, placing his hand flat over his heart. "Te lo prometo." *I promise.*

A weight lifts off my shoulders at the idea of seeing him and showing him around Ever. I think he'd love it here.

We say goodbye, and the moment he disappears from the screen, I dial Papá. Except it's not Papá who answers. It's Nuñez, who tells me in a curt tone that they're already aware of what Eliel's up to. My former bodyguard clicks off before I get a chance to ask exactly what's going on. I stare at the comm disk, experiencing a range of emotions from fury to understanding to worry to resignation. I don't want to be another thing for Papá to worry about, but damn…

In the silence that follows, I stare around at the beautiful guest treehouse I'm currently staying in. Glancing at the ceiling, I let out a wry chuckle. "So, friend, what's a girl to do given the current sad state of my sitch?"

On cue, the giant round window to my right splits in half down the middle and opens like shutters, a breeze blowing into the room and rustling my curls.

I sigh. "Point taken." Rolling out of bed, I dress and put my guitar back in the case. Slinging it over my shoulder, I leave the treehouse and run almost immediately into Hana. Her hand is poised to knock on my door, and she's got a plate of what smells like freshly baked cookies in the other.

"Oh moons," she says with a laugh. "I was about to knock and see if you wanted cookies. I haven't seen you all day."

I beam. "I was just about to make the rounds and see if anyone needs help with anything. Want to come with? We can share the cookies."

Hana smiles, black lips parting to reveal perfectly straight, flat teeth. "I'd love that." Her tail swishes side to side, brushing against her fuzzy dark coat.

I lift the foil covering to see red velvet macadamia nut... brownies? Glancing up, I cock my head to the side. "Are these the fluffiest cookies ever, or did you make cookies into brownies?"

Hana chuckles and glances skyward as if considering her answer. "Umm, technically cookies but you're probably right that they're really brownies? These are Arkan's favorite, so I thought I'd bring them over. He's in meetings in town with haven leadership."

Ah. So Richard isn't around then, unless he skipped.

I take one of the brownies and turn it over, admiring every perfect, moist side. When I take a bite, the familiar sweetness combined with the sugary hit of the white chocolate fills my senses. I moan and shove the whole thing in my mouth, grabbing a second one as Hana smiles.

"I take it they're okay?"

"Two thumbs up," I murmur around a mouthful of brownie.

We head down the mossy flagstone walkway between my treehouse and the next one over, onto the side street. Hooking a left, we walk slowly toward the main drag—in silence, because I can't stop eating the brownies. Shit, I don't stop until there's only one, and I realize Hana hasn't eaten yet.

Grimacing, I lift the foil to show her, but she just laughs.

"Not a problem, friend. I always make two trays—one for Arkan, and one for everybody else."

I grab the last brownie and shove it in my face without further ado. Damn, they're amazing.

"Need that recipe," I manage.

Connall and a shifter I vaguely recognize from the challenge appear around a bend in the road before Hana gets a chance to respond. They wave as they come closer but stop when they reach us.

Connall glances at me. "Lola, Richard was looking for you earlier. I had to remind him that he had a meeting downtown, but he seemed in a rush. Maybe find him later, if you've got a minute?"

My cheeks heat, and I'm thankful for my dark skin tone that covers what I'm sure would be a bright red if I were as pale as he is. "Noted." I gesture to Hana. "We were going to take a walk and see if anyone needs anything."

"Rounds, nice." Connall beams at us. "Don't let us hold you back. There are a group of kids playing Skyball the next street over if you want to go join in. I'm sure they'd appreciate a little grown-up assistance. Plus"—he winks at Hana—"Hana is an all-star."

Hana pretends to brush something off her shoulder and laughs at me. "I used to play on my haven's official Skyball team. I'm pretty good."

My eyes spring wide as I laugh with her. I never followed

Skyball all that closely, but I resolve to look her up if she played for her haven's team.

Connall and the other wolf continue up the street, and Hana and I make our way over to find the kids. It's a mix of shifters, centaurs, and pegasi younglings. For the next two hours, we play, basking in the joy of the children's carefree adoration of sport.

My thoughts take a turn back toward Richard at the end of the second hour. There's a prickle down the back of my neck, like he's somewhere nearby watching. I can't shake the feeling, but every time I turn, there's nothing.

Maybe it's simply instinct, that deep tether that pulls me to him. Just like last night.

I don't know if it's the release of endorphins from playing, but I come to a determination.

I need to talk to him about what happened. He tried, and I was too upset and embarrassed to have the conversation. But I've got a little distance. I don't want it to fester. Harmony is the goal.

Hana trots up to me, the skyball tucked under her toned arm. She smirks at me. "You look very thoughtful all of a sudden, Lola. Why do I get the sense you're about to make some huge move?"

I snort. "Huge move? No. I need to apologize because I already made a move."

Her eyes go wide as her mouth drops open. She zips it partially closed and chuckles. "Well, if you ever want to talk about whatever it was, I'm here."

"Thank you," I say effusively, dipping my head respectfully in the way of her people. "But I need to talk with *him* first."

"Of course," she says. "I'll leave you to it. I'm going to kick some tiny butts a little while longer."

Out of nowhere, a fuzzy pegasus child zooms out of the sky, landing on Hana's humanoid upper half with a battle cry. She pretends to be shocked and staggers to the side as the rest of the younglings attack her, grasping for the skyball.

I'd laugh at their adorable antics, but nerves clang in my

stomach at the idea of seeing Richard. I'm not one to partake in disagreements and drama—I've seen far too much of that living in Santa Alaya. I don't want that for myself, and that's a decision I can actually *make*. While I'm here, at least.

Gritting my teeth, I slip my hands into my back pockets and head toward Richard's place to see if he's there.

Time to face the music.

~

Fifteen minutes later, I worry I'm making a mistake. My hand is lifted to knock at Richard's door. I've been standing here for at least five minutes, heart racing, mouth dry as a desert, staring at the chunky wooden surface. The guitar across my back that I brought for emotional support is making me sweat.

I move my hand and slap my cheek, muttering to myself, "C'mon, Lola. You've got this, girl."

No sooner have I said the words, the door swings open, and Richard appears in the doorway with a smile. He's got a kitchen towel in one hand, but he throws it over his shoulder and leans into the doorframe, one big arm reaching up to grip the top of the frame. He cocks his head to the side and grins at me, fangs peeking out from his beautiful lips.

I kissed those lips. Almost. And they did not kiss me back.

"You gonna keep standing on my stoop talking to yourself? Or would you like to come in?"

Fucking *moons*. Of course if he was home he'd have heard me standing out here. I call on literal decades of princess power to plaster a smile on my face and stride under his arm, into the giant open space.

He's at my back, a quiet, dominant presence as I walk to the kitchen. The countertop is littered with ingredients. He was cooking. Moons, I've interrupted dinner. Maybe he was cooking for someone. Shit, maybe he's got a fucking date. Oh gods. I resist the urge to run. Instead, I sit on one of the industrial metal stools and clear my throat.

He rounds the island and grabs a handful of prepared tamales from the countertop. The familiar scent of corn masa takes me right home to Santa Alaya. I can almost hear music echoing over the bay as I sit on the boardwalk and share a meal with my guards.

Richard glances at me as he stands the tamales upright in a steamer on his stovetop. "I'm cooking pork tamales. I was planning to bring them to you. Lucky that you came to me first."

Oh goddess. How does everything he say manage to sound so sexual?

I clear my throat a second time. "That's thoughtful, thank you. I wanted to apologize for last night and making things awkward. I'm missing home and Papá and Lupe and Leo and…I got carried away." I glance up at him. "I've known you my whole life, and I crossed a line. I'm sorry."

It feels wrong to apologize for something that felt so right in the moment. But it was one-sided, even if I didn't think it was. Maybe the intense pull I've been feeling this entire time is really just admiration for someone I've known forever.

Richard remains quiet until the tamale steamer is full. His dark brows furrow in the middle when he puts the lid on the pot and looks over at me. "You have nothing to apologize for, Lola."

"I do," I press. "You didn't ask for me to—"

"I was on top of you, naked," he reminds me with a lift of one dark brow.

I could scream from the heat that sears through me at that memory. I try desperately to wave it away. "I know, but—"

He turns from the stove, rounds the island, and reaches a hand out for me. "My head and heart have been at war, Lola. I want to talk to you about that, but before we get into a conversation that heavy, let's dance. Then I want to feed you. And then we can have a conversation we desperately need to have."

Oh moons.

"Yes," I practically moan, taking his hand and sliding off the stool.

Richard guides me to the center of the living room and glances up, clearing his throat. On cue, the treehouse moves all the furniture to the far corners of the room, clearing a spot for us. When the music comes on, I could cry at how beautiful it is.

Salsa. Salsa from a band my mother introduced my father to when they were dating. That music style didn't originate in Santa Alaya, but it's beloved at home anyhow. The music is old, but good salsa music will never go out of style. That's a hill I'm willing to die on.

Richard takes my guitar and sets it down. Then he drapes my arm over his shoulder and brings his hand low in the middle of my back. He takes my free hand and places my palm flat over his chest, his nostrils flaring as he pulls our bodies flush.

He dips down, lips hovering above mine. "Lista, Princesa?" *Are you ready, Princess?"*

CHAPTER FOURTEEN
RICHARD

I spent a godsawful three hours today in meetings about haven planning. Arkan has…ideas. Normally, I love that shit. But with the discord between Lola and me, all I wanted was to find her. And after that conversation with Vikand, I feel unmoored by it all. There's so little readable information about a Luna bond. But from the little Vikand was able to share, it's possible…

But here? With her in my arms? Everything is right. Everything feels peaceful. Including Big Daddy, who's lying on his side at the forefront of my mind, staring at her with obvious adoration.

I push forward, moving her body. She follows as if we've danced together for years. We sway and dip around the room, every swing and move of her hips stoking a fire that appeared in me the same day she showed up in Ever.

I slide my hand up between her shoulder blades to the base of her neck, gripping it tight as I press my forehead to hers. Her hand is flat between us, but her fingers curl into the fabric of my shirt. I resist the urge to rip it off and let her dig those fingers into my skin.

The song ends and morphs into the next one. So we keep dancing, spinning around the room, our lips close enough that we share every breath. I lose track of time and everything but the woman wrapped in my arms, her lithe body pressed to mine. I'm half a moment from burying my mouth on hers, conversation be damned. By Alaya's grace, I manage to hold back and enjoy these moments with her.

Still, I can't keep my hands off her, and I drop her free hand so I can wrap my arm around her and hold her tighter. Her fingers come to my waist, digging into the band of my jeans where she holds on.

It's so fucking natural to dance with her. We're in perfect sync. Big Daddy's a silent, contented observer, and that feels good too. This woman has rewired my brain in mere days. Every instinct, every focus is on the way she relaxes into my hold, letting me lead and guide. And the only way I *can* lead is because she allows me to do so. Dancing is such a perfect metaphor for the way alphas and omegas fit together.

Lola closes her eyes and sways with me, her body following mine as I lead us through a dozen more songs, then two dozen, then three. The moon shines brightly through the front glass wall.

But then her stomach rumbles, and Big Daddy's ears prick up.

She needs food, he commands, as if I didn't just hear.

I don't correct him, though. Instead, I dance her back into the kitchen, laughing when I deposit her onto the same stool from before.

"I promised food ages ago," I say with a laugh. "Let me make good on that promise."

She rests her cheek in her palm and stares at me, her expression amused. "Yeah, you did. I ate an entire tray of brownies on the way over here, but I'm starving anyhow."

Take care of her, Big Daddy shouts at me. **Feed her, let her**

bite our fingers. Do all of this in bed, please, for the love of all things wolfy.

This batch of tamales won't be ready for a little while still, but I had prepped a batch for myself before Lola arrived. They sit, now cold, next to where I was making a batch for Leighton's family. Grabbing a frying pan, I wait for it to heat. Lola watches me in silence, but it's peaceful between us.

"What did you do all day?" I question. "I came to your place this morning."

She groans. "I was feeling awkward and not ready to talk to you about my attempt to—well, you know." Her expression is wry, her tone forced.

I toss three bean and cheese tamales in the skillet, loving the familiar pop as they begin to heat. "I shouldn't have let you leave last night." I shift to the right and lean over the counter, grasping her fingers and interlocking them with mine. "I should have kissed you back. Goddess knows I wanted to, Lola. I…" I hang my head. "I thought of the consequences of us pursuing one another."

She looks down at our interlaced hands. "But you feel a pull between us, don't you?"

I nod. "The only pull that matters, sweetheart." When her near-black eyes meet mine again, I bring her hand to my lips and brush my mouth over her knuckles. "It's more than just attraction, Lola."

Her nostrils flare as she stands and lets go of my hand. She rounds the kitchen island and hops gracefully onto it, pulling me between her thighs by the waistband of my jeans. "I want to hear you say exactly what you think it is, Richard." Her request is laced with all the command of a pack omega. Hackles raised, my dominance rises in response to hers.

Reaching up, I grip her throat and run my thumb over her blackberry-colored lips. "Mate," I say on an otherworldly growl. "Mine."

Luna, Big Daddy corrects.

"My wolf thinks you're my Luna," I whisper. "I don't know how I'd even know, but if I know anything at all, it's that, unlikely as it seems, I'm yours." Big Daddy flashes through my eyes. "And I am so desperately sorry I didn't kiss you last night. I'm so sorry you went home hurt, and that I didn't make it better immediately."

Her lips part, the tip of my thumb slipping between them to press at her teeth. Inky eyes flash up to mine. "I feel you in my soul, Richard. Luna or not, whatever that means, I'm here for it."

Our joint admission feels like an oath, a promise, our souls are making as we stand together.

I groan and slide a hand into her hair, gripping her neck. Pulling her head carefully backward, I bury my face in her soft skin and allow myself to drag in a deep, ragged breath of my woman.

My. Woman.

Big Daddy howls with delight deep inside my mind, panting with need.

His desire comes through in my voice as I moan, sucking in desperate, disjointed breaths of her. She's still in my arms, goose bumps covering her silky skin. There's a spot on the side of her neck, right where her shoulder muscles meet it, that I wanna sink my teeth deep into.

As if she read my mind, she cants her head to one side, giving me perfect access.

I can't help myself. And I can't be blamed for what happens after that, because her offering sends me into a frenzy that happens so fast, I can barely comprehend it. Flattening my tongue into the hollow at the base of her throat, I lick a hard path up her throat and to a spot under her ear.

She jolts in my arms, rocking her hips against my waist with a pretty little whine. I open my mouth and strike, sucking at that perfect spot where her neck and shoulder meet. Lola gasps, her breasts smashing against my upper chest as I hover over her, soaking in her taste, her smell.

Alarms blare in the back of my mind. We can't do this simply. There are considerations. But Big Daddy helps me shove all that away to focus on her.

There is only her.

The only thing that matters now that I've found her.

I trail a path of hard bites down to her collarbone, sliding one hand up to move her tee off her shoulder. My teeth trace a path all the way to the edge, leaving hard indents as her chest rises and falls fast.

I sink my fingers into the fabric of her tee, ready to rip it off her when the comm disk on my wall blares loudly. Lola jumps, and I groan.

For a long moment, we stare at each other. Is she feeling the same wonder I am? The same satisfaction? The same worry?

Her glazed eyes flick to the ringing disk on my wall, and her expression morphs to immediate concern. "It's Papá."

I spin to grab the disk, and sure enough, Marco's name flashes over it. Lola hops off the counter and rounds it, reseating herself on her stool as Big Daddy grumbles in my mind.

I drop the comm disk to the ground and direct it to answer. Then I grab my spatula and remove three utterly burned tamales from the frying pan, setting them aside.

Marco's familiar figure hologram rises up from the disk, his eyes flashing when he sees me. He looks to the right to see his daughter, breaking into a smile. "Lola, good, you're here. I was planning to call you next." He looks over at me, glancing at the spatula. "Don't kill my kid with whatever you're cooking."

I snort and slap at his hologram with the utensil. He ducks and laughs, even though it sounds a little forced. He's here with bad news and stalling, for some reason.

I'm not his Second anymore, but I still read him like a book. "What's wrong?"

He nods and straightens, glancing between Lola and me. "Eliel has officially challenged me."

Lola hisses in a breath as I press against the countertop, crossing my arms.

"When?"

"Just under a week." Marco glances at Lola. "Don't worry, mijita, I won't lose."

"I have utter faith in you," she says with a growl. "And I wish you'd allow me to be there to show my support, although I understand your concern."

Marco shakes his head. "Eliel's using magic. We know that much. If he manages to beat me, I'm convinced he'll come for you in Ever. Nuñez agrees."

A snarl rips from me, Big Daddy shoving into my thoughts. At the full green of my eyes, Marco nods sadly.

"I know, old friend. You'll keep her safe, if something happens?"

"Until my last breath." Big Daddy's vehemence is clear in my tone.

Marco takes a breath and looks between us. "When this blows over, I'll come visit for a while. It's been too long since I took Lola on any sort of vacation."

I nod, forcing my hackles not to rise. I'm not ready for a confrontation with him, and he's intuitive enough that he'll take one look at Lola and me and suspect something. We need a plan, fast. "Of course."

He smiles at Lola. "You're glowing, mija. Are you enjoying Ever?"

She returns his loving smile. "Sí, Papá, everyone has been very welcoming, and I feel perfectly safe. Don't worry about me at all."

"Good, good," Marco murmurs. Worried eyes move to me. "I'll need a new Second after the challenge, brother. Come back home. Please, I'll beg if I have to."

Shock steals through me. Leave Ever? Could I do that? And

then I consider the connection between Lola and me, and I suspect Marco's opinion will change the second he finds out.

I shake my head with a laugh. "I don't miss that life, and—"

He cuts me off with a sharp growl. "Consider it, Richard." It's an obvious command, and I bristle against it even as Big Daddy and I both dip our heads respectfully at our king's power.

"I'll talk to you both soon," he says in a softer tone. He clicks off before either of us get a chance to respond.

When I look across the island at Lola, her chest rises and falls with heavy, deep breaths. Her wolf's amber flashes through her irises. They're both worried. I turn the stovetop off and round the island, grabbing her hand. She follows easily as I cross to where the treehouse has moved the furniture back to its original position.

Falling onto my deep sofa, I pull her with me to straddle my lap. I scoot us until I hit the back, then slide my hands up her jean-clad thighs. Dark ringlets fall over her shoulders, dangling down to touch my chest. I grab a handful of stunning curls and lift them to my nose, inhaling deeply. Whatever she washes her hair with smells like the jasmine vines from back home.

Smiling, I tuck the hair over her shoulder and press my nose to the side of her neck. She slides both arms around my neck and starts humming, long fingers carding through my waves. Sharp nails scratch down my scalp, pulling goose bumps onto my skin. Closing my mouth over a spot below her ear, I suck until she yelps and squirms in my lap.

"So," I murmur into her skin, "you know what you are to me, and what I am to you. How do you want to proceed, Lola?"

She slips back, bringing those gorgeous eyes to mine. "You mean because our situation is complicated? Or because Eliel might come for me?"

I nod. "I'd never allow that bastard anywhere near you. I told your father the truth when I said I'd protect you until my last breath. I would have done that despite our connection. I mean about us. You being Marco's daughter presents a challenge. Even then, I'm prepared to face that music. But beyond that, there's a lot for you to think about."

Her eyes narrow, nails clacking against my scalp. "Tell me exactly what you mean, Richard."

Big Daddy shoves forward, about to berate me, I'm sure.

"You heard your father; he wants me to move 'home' to Santa Alaya. But that hasn't been my home in a long time. If we accept our connection, it means being together. You have hopes and dreams, Lola, and those things would be possible if your father won his challenge. Being tied to me might limit you."

She scoffs. "Are you saying you wouldn't come with me if I toured or traveled?"

I sigh. "I can do some of that easily, yeah. But can I travel nine months out of the year and shirk my duties here? Not really." I grip her throat to feel the steady thrum of blood through her veins. "If you wanted me to come with you, I'd figure it out, but these conversations get harder when one person is as settled as I am."

Lola frowns. "I think you underestimate yourself."

"Perhaps," I say softly. "But at the very least, for now, maybe we should take things slowly."

Fuck that, Big Daddy snaps. **You are ruining *everything*!**

Lola grips my chin, forcing me to stare deep into her eyes. "What are you saying in there? I wish I could talk to you."

Bite her and solve that problem. I wanna tell her precisely what we want to do to her, since you seem so fucking disinclined.

"He wants me to bite you," I admit, "so you can hear him."

She gives me a slow, seductive grin that turns my dick into a rock between us. "Tell him I'd love to hear his opinion on this whole 'take it slowly' concept."

I growl, relishing the way it pebbles her nipples when my tone hits her sensitive ears. "Slow isn't his way. To be frank, it would never be mine either if there weren't considerations."

Lola rocks her hips against mine, pulling a whine from my throat. "It makes sense to me to keep this under wraps until things are settled with my father." She leans forward until her lips brush mine. "But after that…" Her words trail off.

Everything in me tightens at her insinuation. I tilt my head up, capturing her lips softly. For a moment, the world stops spinning, every one of my senses rewiring to her and only her.

And then our lips collide with all the force of a storm. I'm more insistent and rougher than I should be, but she gives back just as hard, little growls from deep in her throat sending my lust sky high. Her hips thrust against mine, her heat dragging along my rigid length even though we're fully clothed.

I rub my tongue along hers, both hands roaming over her ass and up her back, into that beautiful hair and back down again. "Can't keep my fucking hands off you," I growl.

She leans down and licks a path up my chin and over my mouth as I groan and part my lips.

"Give me more of that," I command.

Her hand fists my hair and yanks my head backward, her hot tongue tracing a ragged path up the front of my throat. I whine, guiding her to rock against my dick. We're both gonna come like this, fully clothed, dry humping like horny teenagers.

I want it.

I rub her against me harder, faster, as her mouth explores my neck and her breath becomes heavy, needy pants. Slick soaks her jeans and the front of mine, filling the air with her oranges-and-cream scent.

Seed swells my sack and drips from my cock. I'm primed to explode. When I can't take it anymore, and she's gasping with need, I take her mouth again and lick into it, the deepest kiss we've shared. Our bodies jerk together as orgasm hits her first and me right after. Lola returns the kiss, crying into it as pleasure racks her frame.

Release hits me like a damn battering ram, hips thrusting so hard, I nearly buck her off my lap. But I don't let go of that kiss—that kiss is everything. And it's not until some time later I can blink my eyes open at the panting, smiling princess in my arms and know that I will never, ever not be hers.

CHAPTER FIFTEEN
LOLA

I wake in the morning wound tight despite coming a half dozen times with my vibrator. A faint sheen of sweat covers my whole body, my breasts painful and achy. Blinking my eyes open, I note the sun shining through the circular window in my bedroom. It's definitely *not* still early in the morning.

Groaning, I roll over as my comm watch starts ringing. When I lift my wrist, Lou's name flashes over the navy band.

"Answer Lou Hector," I direct it.

Lou's tinny voice rings through the hologram. "Lola? What are you up to?"

I pick at the knot holding my silk headscarf shut. "To be honest, I just woke up," I admit.

Lou laughs. "Late night? I've heard Shifter Hollow has some bangin' parties." Before I get a chance to answer, she barrels on, "Listen, my niece Morgan and I are headed your way today for Morgan to do some work at Biergarten with her black magic. Do you want to come with us?"

"Oh, black magic, sounds cool." I undo my head scarf, my

curls tumbling out of it like a waterfall. "What time are you coming, and where should I meet you?"

Lou's voice goes muffled like she's talking to someone away from the watch. After a moment, she clears her throat. "Half an hour, and meet us there?"

"Done!" I say brightly. "Thanks for the invite, Lou!"

"Absolutely," she says, although I sense something forced in her tone. She's silent for a moment before continuing, "I immediately liked you, and I usually have a good sense about people. But I've been avoiding Shifter Hollow, and I haven't done a good job working on a friendship between us. I'd like to have one, though."

I blink rapidly at her admission. "Same," I murmur without thinking. "I should be better at that; I've been so focused on getting settled here."

"Well, better late than never," she says with a laugh.

Except—late must be her motto. Because forty-five minutes later, I've been sitting at a table by myself at Biergarten, and Lou and Morgan are nowhere to be seen. My guitar is in the seat next to me, and considering I'm the only one sitting outside right now, I think about playing.

I've been mulling last night over and over in my mind—the rightness of Richard, the strength of our connection. Nothing has ever hit me this hard and fast in my life.

And I don't think I could deny him even if I tried.

Unlikely? Yes.

Untimely? Certainly.

Am I gonna say no to him? Absolutely not.

"Lola, hey!" Lou's voice breaks through my train of thought.

When I glance up, she's exiting the main building through the black metal and glass doors out onto the patio. Iggy is perched on her shoulder, one chubby arm wrapped around her head, his purple fingers curled around her ear. A beautiful redheaded woman follows them.

My nostrils flare as I hold back a laugh. "Looks like you brought another friend."

Lou rolls her eyes and opens her mouth, but before she gets a chance to say anything, Iggy hops off her shoulder and onto my table, bringing a box out from under his free arm.

"Hey, Princess Lola! Lou didn't invite me, but I invited myself because Dad says we should always help people who need it. And Lou's sad about things, so I've been making her cookies." He shoots me a proud smile. "I basically adopted her."

Lou snorts and crosses her arms. "Ignatius Zion, I am just fine, although you're a damn good baker."

"Oh," he laughs, "Dad and Miriam do all the cooking." He lifts a tiny white box so I can see. "I do all the packaging though."

Lou flops down in a chair opposite mine and pulls out the one next to her, patting the seat. The gorgeous redhead smiles and sits down gracefully. She's tall and elegant like most shifter women are, but this must be the black witch, Lou's niece.

She leans across the rectangular wooden table and extends a hand to me. "Nice to meet you in person, Lola. Abe and I saw you play recently; I'm honestly fangirling so hard right now."

I take her hand and shake it. Her grip is firm and sure, the handshake of a confident woman. I like her immediately.

Iggy hops across the table, long tail lashing from side to side. He shoves the box toward me and pulls the top open, looking up expectantly. "You want one, Princess Lola?"

I smile and peek inside the box, making a big deal out of examining every available option. Finally, I cock my head sideways and put my face very close to his. "Which one did you work hardest on, Iggy?"

He lowers his voice to a whisper and points to what I think is a chocolate chip cookie, tucked in the back corner.

I grab it and set it on the table in front of me. "Perfect, I'll have this one."

He nods sagely and spins around, hip-hopping back toward

Lou. He puts the box down in front of her. "Eat up, Lou. Cookies are good for you."

She sighs and folds her hands in her lap. "If you say so, kiddo."

A shout echoes from somewhere on the main drag. I twitch an ear to listen, hearing the same kiddos I played Skyball with yesterday. I pat Iggy's chubby haunch. "Hey, there are kids playing in the street if you want to join them. I kicked their butt at Skyball yesterday with Hana."

Iggy's eyes light up, and he lifts off the table, tiny gargoyle wings flapping wildly. He takes off before Lou or Morgan can say a word.

"Thank the Lorrrrd," Lou whines once he's gone. "He's adorable, but he seems to have made me his personal mission to fix."

Morgan leans over and bumps her shoulder against Lou's. "He's intuitive. And gargoyles are protectors; he can't help himself." She grabs the box of cookies and picks one out for herself. "Frankly, I'm thrilled to have all of these gargoyle family members. We'll never run out of food as long as we live."

Lou huffs. "Snack up, shack up, I guess."

It's my turn to snort. "Say what now?"

Morgan laughs, mouth full of cookie. She places her palm over it and chews, rocking side to side as if hurrying herself on. When she's done, she grins at me. "My sister Thea is married to Shepherd, if you've met him. He's on Ever's protector team. Anyhow, when we first came here and he started pursuing her, he told us that was the gargoyle males' motto."

Lou laughs, pink lips splitting into a grin. "I don't believe there's anything official about that motto."

"Absolutely not." Morgan shoves another cookie in her mouth. "He's a comedian," she manages around a mouthful of the sweet.

A pegasus waiter comes up, handsomely dressed in a collared shirt and tightly fitted vest. His long blond hair is tied in a bun on his head in the way most centaurs and pegasi do. I smile up at him and order a mead. Morgan and Lou do the same.

Lou glances at her niece. "Did Ohken make this, ya think?"

Morgan laughs and looks at me. "My brothers-in-law are multitalented. Ohken does, well, shit, he pretty much does everything. But he's a great brewer." She looks back at Lou. "But, no, I don't think he has anything to do with the mead here. I'm not asking a single thing about it, though, because the last time I asked Ohken about a mead I liked, the magical ingredient was earthworms."

We burst into bright, joyous laughter at that.

For two hours, we sit and drink and chat about everything and nothing. Lou and Morgan are both so genuine and kind, I can't bear the thought of our early lunch ending. I don't have many close friends at home in Santa Alaya. It was too hard to maintain those friendships over the years because I could never come and go like others.

It was always Leo for me, and then Leo and the Lovestruck Lobos. Even then, the actual band members seem to change pretty frequently. Leo's been the only constant.

But…it doesn't have to be that way for me. Here in Ever, I think I could make real girlfriends. If I stayed. Santa Alaya will always be home and I love my haven to the ends of the earth and back. But I'm also ready for new adventures. I consider what might happen if I told Papá I simply wasn't coming back.

Morgan clears her throat. "You look lost in thought, Lola. Everything alright?"

I fake a smile. "Yes! I was thinking about how different Ever is from Santa Alaya."

Lou leans across the table and props her chin in her palm. "Do tell."

I look around us to see if there's anyone to notice my admission, but we're alone on the patio. Even Iggy seems to have permanently deserted us.

"I don't love the pace of life of politics, although I love the haven itself." My wolf whines softly in my mind. "Papá has worked hard his entire life to become king, but it's not a path I would choose, if it was up to me. Shifter politics becomes increasingly cutthroat the higher up our ranks you go, and he's at the very top."

Morgan scrunches her delicate, freckled nose. "Eww."

I point at her and laugh. "Precisely. It's just that, when your parents work so hard to build a life for you, it can be incredibly difficult to admit that it isn't the life you want for yourself." Sweat breaks out across my forehead as I pull at the neckline of my tee, my eyes drifting off into the woods beyond the patio.

"Shit, man," Lou murmurs. "You just realized you don't wanna go home, didn't you?"

I grit my jaw and think about what I told the girls. Finally, I turn to them. "I do…eventually. But I'm also having a lot of fun being here."

My thoughts go immediately to Richard and a vision of us living together in Ever. I agree with the need to take things slowly with him, even though that isn't the shifter way. Our situation is complicated, and I can't risk Papá finding out before the challenge.

Morgan laughs and slaps Lou on the leg. "We lost Lola again. Are we terrible conversationalists, or do you think she's not sharing the juicy gossip?"

All the hair on the back of my neck rises as the strangest sensation comes over me. Whipping around in my seat, I stare into the dense forest on the other side of the patio railing. The trees are so close together here that you can barely see between them. Giant clumps of shady ferns are so large, a person could easily stand behind them and not be seen.

My thighs begin to tremble, my heart racing. The sensation of being watched hits me so hard, I rise to a stand, scanning the trees. I resist the urge to leap over the railing and follow my wolf's instincts into the woods.

I stare for a full minute before concluding I can't see anyone.

But I know someone was there.

Watching.

∼

Lou and Morgan had the genius idea to go swimming at the big lake outside Shifter Hollow. We've only been here for a short while, but three mermaids have already shown up to play with us.

"Get nekkid!" Lou shouts, pulling her clothes off and running into the lake.

I laugh and follow suit, a little surprised my new friend isn't fussed by nudity. I've met a handful of humans at court, and they were always dicey about shifters' blasé attitude toward being unclothed.

Morgan chuckles as her aunt dives headlong into the water, swimming out to where the brilliantly colored mermaids splash. "Lou is absolutely wild, sheesh. No fear." She glances at me. "I have questions, like what else lives in this lake? Anything I need to be aware of, like, I don't know, the Loch Ness Monster? But not Lou! No. Lou's just gonna dive right in."

I glance around the lake, looking for anything that would give me pause, but I see nothing. Smiling at Morgan, I point to the edges. "No tail trails in the mud mean there likely aren't water dragons, so you're good there. And aside from them, there wouldn't be another freshwater monster for you to worry about. You're good to go, Morgan."

Her mouth drops open. "I was kinda kidding, but water dragons—that's a thing?"

"Oh yeah," I say with a laugh. "We've got them in Santa Alaya in the bay, but even then, most of them are friendly once you greet them with a gift."

"Ya don't say," she deadpans, staring out over the water to where Lou and the mermaids splash one another.

"No water dragons here," a deep male voice breaks through.

Richard.

My nipples pebble at that incredible baritone, and it's hard not to break into a gigantic smile. I made him come last night. Heat bursts through me, forcing my cheeks to flush.

When I turn, he stalks gracefully out from between two trees, a small box tucked under his arm. He grins at Morgan. "Don't mind me; I came to speak with Lola for a moment."

Morgan smiles at him, then pats me on the arm. "See ya in the water in a few minutes, okay?"

I nod and watch as she walks in, shivering at the water's temperature. When Lou splashes her, she shrieks and dives in.

Richard stops in front of me. "Did you have a good morning?"

"Pretty good," I say with a knowing smile. "Except that I kept getting the sense someone was watching me. You wouldn't know anything about that, would you, Richard?"

He feigns indignation. "Me? Never. A pack alpha would never follow around the beautiful woman who's captivated him just to watch her having fun." He steps closer, bending down to bring his lips to my ear. "I'm quickly developing a soul-deep obsession, Lola."

I resist the urge to put my hands on him, to show him with touch that I feel it too, even though I've been here such a short time. A hot blush steals over me so I focus on the box under his arm. It's a good distraction, and I need that before I tackle Richard onto the rocky beach and have my way with him. I can't... We agreed to take it slowly.

"What's in the box?"

He takes a step back and gestures to the blanket Lou laid out when we first arrived. "Sit, and I'll show you. I didn't want to promise these to you earlier because I wasn't sure I could find them. But I was able to, and I know you'd want to have them."

I drop to the blanket and wait for him to join me. He sinks elegantly to his knees and sets the box in my lap. Big, rough hands come to the carved wooden top and gently remove it, revealing stacks of photographs. The one on top is of him, my Papá and, oh moons, Mamá too. I recognize the hair. And the smile.

My stomach tightens and does somersaults all at the same time.

His fingers move softly over the photograph's surface. "Maria, Marco, and I were friends long before they got together, and just as close once they mated. The photos from this box are from a ton of different times, but flip this one over."

I flip it to reveal manly-looking chicken scratch on the back.

Maria, Marco, and Richard at the spring pack run the year they mated.

"I labeled every one for you this morning," he says softly. "So you'd know what was going on in their lives then."

Emotion crashes over me as tears fill my eyes. Flipping through the photographs, I gasp at how different Papá looks. He's blissfully happy; that much is clear. I wonder if he'd want to see these photos.

"Lola, you okay?"

I glance up to find Lou emerging naked from the water. She joins us and flops down next to me, grabbing a towel and tucking it around her figure.

"Look," I whisper, barely able to find my voice. "Richard found these photos of my parents from before I was born." I give her a sorrowful look. "My mother died when I was young, so I don't remember her well, but now I have all of this to remind me." My eyes drift to Richard's, which are locked firmly on my face. "Thank you for this."

He smiles. "Any time, Lola. There's a sizable stack at the

bottom from when you were a newborn pup. Lots of pics of Maria holding you and Marco carrying you around."

The first tear trails down my cheek then. I can't believe what a treasure it is to have this.

"This is amazing, Lola," Lou murmurs, flipping several of the pictures over. "Good gods, your dad is hot." She waves at her face. Her cheeks are pink.

"Ewww," I grouse, scrunching up my nose, even though I can see what she means. My father is classically handsome and charming. And now single. It doesn't surprise me that she could find him attractive.

Which brings me back to what's going on between Richard and me. This thing we decided not to share with anyone else just yet. I can see it in his eyes, in the way they wrinkle slightly in the corners and Big Daddy's intense green begins to shine through.

No matter what happened in the past, our future involves each other.

If I'm certain of anything at all about my life…it's that.

CHAPTER SIXTEEN
RICHARD

I spent all morning labeling photos for Lola, and then Big Daddy had the genius idea to follow her when we happened to see her walking up Sycamore toward Biergarten.

I resisted for a while—an hour, maybe. And then I gave in, stalking through the woods to the perfect viewing spot beyond the patio.

I'm not even ashamed that I stood there and stared at her for moons know how long. I could watch her all day every day, and it wouldn't be enough. The truth is out between us; the connection is undeniable.

Yet you tried to tell her she might not want to be tied to us. What the fuck is wrong with you?

She's young; she wants to travel and play music throughout the haven system. She wants to escape Marco; she wants something more out of her life.

We'd go with her, obviously.

I can practically feel him rolling his eyes.

It's not that easy, and you know it. Who would be Alpha if we were constantly gone?

I don't know. Figure it out. Make a plan. Bite her as fast as you can so I can talk to her. He pauses for a moment. **Please.**

Navigating this connection between us has been odd, but for the first time, it occurs to me that I have the privilege of making decisions for the both of us. And he hasn't agreed with a lot of mine lately.

He grumbles softly as I focus on the stack of paperwork on top of my desk. I haven't seen Lola since the lake, and it's late now. What did she do with the rest of her day? I left the girls to have fun, although I desperately wanted to stay and play.

Heat rushes through me. I need to see her, to touch her.

I need to dominate her. All wolves get off on power play, pack alphas more than most. Taking things slow couldn't be farther from my desire.

Grabbing a small remote on my desk, I press the topmost button. A familiar buzz starts, the plug in my ass vibrating softly against my prostate. I groan as the vibrations travel through a silicone ring around my balls. Gods, does this feel better than normal, or is it because I'm so ready to fuck my princess, I can barely stand it?

I work my way through the last stack of order forms for the bar, heat building and swirling as my dick goes hard, my body tightening with need. Once I'm done in the office, I'm going to her place. If she's already asleep, I'll slip into bed with her, kiss her awake and then take her…maybe.

My cock drips precum as I grab the remote and press the second button. The head of the toy begins to move in and out, rubbing along my prostate as I hiss and arch backward, gripping the back of my chair as orgasm builds.

I let my mind wander, paperwork be damned. The sensation of being filled brings me to a vision of Lola with a strap-on, fucking me in our bed. Would she be interested in that sort of play? What about tying me up, blindfolded, and doing whatever she wanted? I'm a highly dominant lover, but godsdamn, sometimes I love being fucking taken by an omega.

Never another. Only her.

Yes, I agree with vehemence. *Only ever her.*

Finally, an agreement with him.

The scent of oranges and cream and jasmine fills my office as I smile and roll my hips. Gods, that scent is wired into my brain.

"Hello, Richard." Her throaty voice comes from the doorway as I pop my eyes open.

Godsdamn, look at her.

She stands there in tight-ass jeans and a corset top that pushes her round breasts high. It accentuates the flare of her waist to perfect, athletic hips. Like always, she wears black studded bracelets. They're rocker chic, but I'm getting Domme vibes.

Heat spikes, my ass clenching around the plug.

The soft sound of vibrating is audible in the room. Lola cocks her head to the side and smiles. "Connall told me I could find you here doing"—she winks—"paperwork."

I sit upright, which forces the plug deeper into my ass. Holding back a desperate groan, I gesture to the stack of papers in front of me. "Paperwork's right there, sweetheart."

She stalks gracefully across the room and sits on the edge of my desk, scenting the air. "Doesn't smell like paperwork in here."

My brows lift. I like the direction this is going. "No? Why don't you tell me what it smells like to you, Lola?"

Pitch-black eyes flash to mine as her dark cherry lips part into a seductive, knowing smile. "Arousal, Alpha. The air is soaked with it."

My body clenches tight. "Can I help you with something, Princesa?"

She perfumes as if I commanded it, her pheromones filling the air. The scent wraps around my dick and tugs. There is no headier smell, no deeper instinct than an omega perfuming for her alpha.

Not just any omega. Luna, Big Daddy reminds me.

Our Luna, I whisper back, relieved to be in lockstep with him for once. I don't know how to tell if she's my Luna or not, but if he believes it, I can go along with that. She's mine, and that's all that matters.

She laughs, her throaty chuckle raising all the hair on the back of my neck as my eyes zero in on those gorgeous, plump lips. "Oh, I think maybe there's something I can help *you* with, Richard. What do you think?"

I grab the remote for my toy and slide it across the desk to her. "You're the ranking wolf here. Do what you want to me."

Her wolf's amber flashes through her eyes as she grabs the remote, eyeing the buttons. "What does each one do?"

"That doesn't matter as much as the outcome," I say on a growl. "Start pressing and see what happens."

A soft click sounds as she presses one of the buttons, and the plug starts ramming me with fast, insistent strokes. Gritting my teeth, I fall forward over the desk, digging my claws in as I groan around the swirling, building pleasure.

Lola chuckles again and clicks the setting off. "That's a little much. You'll be coming in half a second, Alpha, and I like this game." Omega command enters her voice with her next statement. It could only ever hit me as hard as it does if she belonged to me—yet another sign that she's fated to be mine.

"Lean back, Richard, and take your pants off."

That command slams into my chest and spreads heat outward from my heart. I could no sooner deny her than stop breathing.

CHAPTER SEVENTEEN
LOLA

I was with Lou and Morgan almost all day. We went downtown and then came back for dinner. It was a blast, but my mind was never far from Richard. Eventually, I ran across Connall and learned Richard does paperwork in his office most nights.

So, here I am.

And, moons, the sight before me is overwhelming. The air is saturated with the combined scents of our arousal. My heart races, fingers twitching on the small remote in my hand.

Richard leans back in his office chair, dark eyes locked onto mine. Big Daddy's green shines through them as he unzips his jeans and slides them down his muscular hips. His cock springs free, bobbing up toward his stomach. It's absolutely covered in precum. My mouth goes dry, the urge to drop to both knees and worship him so strong, I nearly do it.

But this slow game we're playing, this tease, I'm enjoying it far too much.

Richard shifts the pants to his knees and slides them off his legs, kicking them away.

I take a minute to admire the sheer power of his body. Thick, muscular thighs. A perfect, girthy cock with a swollen knot the size of my fist at the base. A thick silicone ring around his sack and knot accentuates the sheer size of it. It's connected to a strip of silicone that disappears between his thighs. Goddess, he's wearing a plug; he must be. That's got to be what's vibrating. And the idea of this alpha edging himself in the office, probably thinking about me, has me ready to leap on top of him.

His shirt is still buttoned, giving me a hint of flexed, taut abs covered in tattoos. Richard's chest heaves softly, and by the time I meet his gaze, slick flows from me like a fountain.

I jerk my head toward his button down. "Take that off." I've never commanded a man like this, but somehow, it comes naturally with him.

His nostrils flare, but he unbuttons the denim shirt and opens it wide, giving me a better view of his naked chest and stomach. "Play with me," he commands on a growl, placing both hands on the arms of his desk chair.

I can't look away from his beautiful body, so I start in the top left corner of the remote, mashing the first button. The humming vibration slows, and he relaxes, a soft smile coming to his face. It goes predatory as he stares at me. "Slow and steady is nice."

But based on the sheer state of him and the steady drip from his cock, I suspect he's been doing this for a while, so I mash button number two. The vibration picks up, and his eyes roll into his head, which falls back against the chair.

Heat flares between my thighs. Goddess, I want that knot. It seems to expand further as his dick bobs and drips a sticky stream of seed onto his abs. His fingers tighten around the chair arms, his wolf's claws slipping out as wood splinters and cracks.

A soft growl rumbles from my throat, my wolf right up front for the show. I can feel her desire as deeply as my own—she wants to see Big Daddy again. And I need more of the scene playing out in front of me.

Richard's abs flex under tattooed, copper skin. Without

looking away, I feel for the third button and press it. He jerks, back arching as his lips curl into a snarl. The chair arms splinter to bits, and he lets go with his right hand, bringing it over his head to hold on to the chair's back. His hips begin to roll softly, his thighs trembling and flexing as his eyes spring open.

I'm so wet and turned on, I debate jumping him and sinking onto that beautiful knot. But I'm on button three of six, and I'm desperate to know what happens with the rest.

"Don't come yet," I command, depressing the fourth button. Pink dusts his angular cheeks as he runs a hand through his salt-and-pepper waves.

Richard snarls and snaps, his hips jerking as precum spurts from him, the flow heavier than before. His eyes still don't leave mine, but his mouth drops open, his panted breaths rapid-fire as he stares at me like he wants to eat me alive.

"What would it be like for you to unleash on me?" I murmur. "Would you be violent, Richard?"

"Fuck yes." He shifts forward and reaches for me. "An alpha's job is to protect everyone, but his omega is another story. She's where he unleashes, sweetheart. She's HIS resting place. His sweetest torment. His hottest fuck. Sweet nothings aren't a pack alpha's style. Dominance, that's what I want."

I stand just out of his reach and kick my flip-flop off, putting my foot in the middle of his chest. Pressing on his chest with my arch, I shove him against the chair and press the fifth button.

He howls and pants, one hand coming to my ankle. His muscular hips buck and rock, his cock bobbing and dripping.

"Tsk tsk, Alpha," I chide on a laugh. "You're making a mess."

A ragged growl rips from his throat, full of Big Daddy's alpha tone. When he speaks, it's a combination of two voices that I hear.

"So clean me the fuck up, omega." His eyes narrow, his grip on my ankle tightening.

I pull out of his grip and lift my chin defiantly. "I'm not done pressing buttons, Richard."

He shifts up out of the chair so fast, I barely track the movement, caging me on the desk between his big arms. His dick presses into my belly, wetting my corset as his mouth hovers above mine. "I'm a hair's breadth from exploding all over you. Take it back to one before I lose my fucking mind."

His demand is laced with a pack alpha's dominance. Obediently, I press the first button. The sound of the plug's vibrations dies down as he grabs the remote from me and tosses it on his desk.

He stands and backs up a step, his dick spearing the air between us. "Take your clothes off."

I push away from the desk edge and pull my shirt over my head. His big hands reach around me, expertly unclasping my bra. He yanks it off and tosses it over his shoulder.

Voices echo from the corridor. I freeze. Goddess, it sounds like a whole group of monsters. Richard grabs me and flips me, placing my hands flat on the desk surface. His hips press against my ass, his breath warm on my ear. "Let's play a little game, naughty girl. I'm going to get you off, Lola, and I don't want you to make a sound."

I whimper, but his hand comes to my mouth and muffles the noise.

"Silence," he hisses into my ear. "Or else you'll be punished."

Oh, fuuuuck. What kind of punishment would he mete out? I want to know—I really, really want to know.

But he's not done commanding me. "Reach down and unzip your pants. Shove them down as far as you can. Be quiet."

The voices come closer, and his damn office door is halfway open. My body is alive with electric energy, fueled by the terror of getting caught. I unzip my pants, and his hands come to mine and help push the jeans down my thighs to my knees.

His big hand slides up between my breasts to grip my throat, his lips still brushing the shell of my ear. "That noise is the gnome cleaning crew. They like to play music and fuck around while they're cleaning. Their hearing is excellent, though."

I bite my lip to hold back a whine as his grip on my throat tightens hard enough that black stars dance across my vision. His breath is warm on my ear, his body all hard planes at my back as he slips his right hand between my thighs. I jerk at the sensation of being touched by him like this for the first time. My mouth falls open when two fingers slip between my legs, curling to stroke my pussy lips with a gentle, practiced touch.

"Fucking soaked," he says on a growl. The following chuckle tightens every inch of my body, pussy clenching on nothing until he slips two fingers inside and strokes.

I gasp and move my hands to grab at his arms, a needy moan leaving my mouth before I remember to quiet the sound.

"Did you hear something?" a tiny voice floats in from the corridor outside.

Tension amps, my heart racing as I consider what would happen if the cleaning crew showed up in the doorway. Would Richard even stop? Or would he just—

"I won't stop now," he croons into my ear like he read my mind. "So unless you want them to see the princess being fucked by her big alpha, be quiet." A throaty laugh rumbles from him, tickling the side of my neck. "Or maybe you like that, hmm? Does it thrill you to think anyone could walk in and see me fucking this sweet pussy with my fingers? Does that turn you on, imagining them bearing witness while you fall apart?"

Slick drips from me like a waterfall as I hold on to his forearm for dear life. His fingers move with steady, deep, slow strokes, hitting my G-spot with every pass as I pant and beg in silence, my mouth open, hard nipples aching and desperate for his touch. His chest is hot against my back, searing my skin like a brand.

When he moves backward, putting space between our upper bodies, I almost cry out from the loss of his warmth. But then he curls over me and licks a flat, hot path up my spine to my neck. He breathes in, scenting me as I perfume like crazy for him. Another rough lick sends flares of heat along my neck and shoulders as I shudder.

Richard's teeth clamp slowly down on a spot where my neck and shoulder meet, his fingers tightening around my throat. His other hand works faster between my thighs, the heel of his palm rubbing my clit with every pass.

He releases the shallow bite. "Come, Lola."

And come, I fucking do. Everything in me builds and swirls until pulsing, throbbing ecstasy radiates from my pussy outward. Richard groans softly as I clench around his fingers, slapping a hand over my mouth to hold the scream that threatens to overcome everything. I curl over the desk, trying to close my thighs against a wash of pleasure so strong, my vision goes black, hearing disappears, and everything turns inward to the bliss.

I don't know how long it goes on for, just that when orgasm finally, *finally* fades, he's still stroking between my thighs.

The faint sound of his plug breaks through my consciousness, giving me an idea. Reaching behind me, I guide his cock between my legs and rock along the length of it, dripping cum and slick all over him.

"Goddess," he groans, thrusting his hips against my ass. "That's it, omega, ride this knot until you come again."

I shift backward as he thrusts, forcing his knot to kiss between my thighs. My pussy lips part around it as it rubs against my clit. Orgasm builds again as I reach for the remote to his plug, mashing the final button.

He grunts and lets out a string of expletives that have me blushing and rocking back faster and faster along his length. Every pass of his cock through my folds drives me higher and higher, our combined breathing heavy and desperate as we rock together.

A choking sound, followed by the jerk of his body, tosses me over the edge. When his cock emerges through my thighs, I wrap my hand around it and milk him, cum spurting all over my fingers as orgasm barrels through me again. Slick splashes from me, coating him and my hands and the floor—and I don't even care.

There's only the fraught silence, the tension of trying to hold back a scream that's on the very edge of my tongue.

Richard's teeth close around my shoulder and bite, a soft, pained grunt whispered against my skin. His chest rises fast against my back, his tongue swirling softly against my skin as the last moments of orgasm force seed onto my eager fingers.

When ecstasy stops, my knees threaten to give out. Footsteps sound outside the door, but I can't be bothered to look. Voices fade as Richard buries his face in my curls and breathes in.

"Luna," he whispers on a soft groan. "My dirty girl, you feel so good on my fingers."

I huff out a quietish laugh and stroke my fingers down his forearm. "Still want me to clean you up, Alpha?"

He groans but releases my throat and pulls his hand carefully from between my legs. Spinning me in place, he dips and grabs me by the backs of my thighs. In one swift move, he tosses me over his shoulder and stalks toward the door.

"Richard," I hiss, even though I can't hold back a laugh. "The cleaning crew is still here!"

"Then be quiet," he commands playfully, smacking my ass. I swear the sound reverberates off the walls so dang loud. But I clap a hand over my mouth as he stalks to the door and opens it quietly.

This should be interesting.

CHAPTER EIGHTEEN
RICHARD

If I ever thought there was a world where I could encourage Lola to look for some life without me, that idea is dead. As I glance out my office door, twitching an ear to listen for the gnomes, it occurs to me that I would follow this woman to the ends of this world and the next if that's what she wanted. I'll go on tour. I'll fight her father. I'll leave it all behind to bask in her presence.

Whatever Lola wants, I'll make sure she gets.

The gnomes are somewhere in the main room of the bar. To the left, Bad Axe opens the back door for us. My mate chuckles under her breath as I stalk down the hall and out the door into the forest behind the bar. Under the dark cover of night, I round the building and dip into my stairwell, ascending the stairs. At the top, the treehouse opens the door for us.

"Put me down, Richard," Lola says, laughing as she pats at my middle back with both hands. "I love getting whisked away, but your shoulder isn't that comfy."

Grinning, I toss her onto my sofa, staring at her tits as she bounces. She grins and lies down, bringing both hands between her thighs as she steps them apart. Long fingers slip through her folds, gathering the moisture there.

"Like what you see?" Her voice is soft, sensual as she rubs a slow circle over her clit.

"Goddess," I pray. "I love what I see, but I'll be right back."

She whines when I turn. Jogging across the room, I hit the bathroom and remove the plug, tossing it in the sink to clean later. As much fun as it would be to play with her and it a while longer, I don't want to lose my focus on her.

When I return to the living room, I cross the open space fast. I drop onto my knees on the edge of the sofa, then lean over her, caging her in with both arms. "Show me more," I demand. Bringing my mouth to the inside of her knee, I suck until she whines. A kiss follows the rough treatment, and I repeat it up the inside of her thigh until she's whining and rolling her body.

"Tell me what you need, omega," I murmur, nuzzling the juncture where her thigh and body meet.

One hand comes to my head, her fingers digging into my hair and tightening. The pain brings Big Daddy rushing to the surface.

Fuck yes, finally, he yowls, panting inside my mind. **Claiming Bite. Do it for the love of Alaya.**

"Mouth," she gasps, curling over to lift her hips closer to my face.

I lean forward, brushing my mouth over her slick mound. She cries out and shudders as Big Daddy loses his mind.

Her scent is stronger here, but I want full immersion, so I drag my nose through her folds, coating myself in glorious, sticky slick designed to help her take my knot. Lola cries out and writhes, her voice ragged and desperate. At the first flat swipe of my tongue over her clit, she unravels, spewing an unintelligible string of words as satisfaction sweeps through me. I reach for her left leg and pull it over my right shoulder, suckling softly at her clit as her scent explodes between us.

Good. Soak the room with it, Big Daddy hollers. **Make this whole place smell like slick.**

Agreed. Help me.

He scrambles forward as I growl into her pussy. Big Daddy's tone deepens the noise, vibrating against her skin. The effect is immediate. Lola wails and curls in half, nearly ripping my hair out by the roots as slick spurts from her to cover my nose and mouth.

Goddess, yessssss. More. Do it again.

Never stopping, I practically moan into our connection as I eat Lola all the way through orgasm. I don't stop until she's trembling and laughing and shoving my head away.

Even then, I flip her over onto all fours and press her into the soft fabric of the sofa, exposing her sweet pussy to me. She's a damn mess, and I've never been more into anything in my entire life. Burying my face between the globes of her ass, I lick and kiss and suck my way from her dripping pussy to the pucker of her ass and back again.

I drag two more orgasms from her before she collapses on the sofa in an exhausted heap. She waves me away when I crawl over top of her to start all over again.

Nudging her thighs apart with my knee, I position myself between them, my cock resting on her taut stomach. "You're a mess, omega," I say with a laugh. Moonlight beams through the big glass wall at the front of my house, shining down on her beautiful, smooth skin. Reaching down, I stroke my fingers down her chest and over, softly pinching her pebbled nipples.

Lola arches her back with a happy-sounding hum, her breast filling my palm.

"Goddess, I'm ready again," I admit, leaning down to pull her nipple between my teeth.

"Fuck!" She wraps the fingers of both hands through my hair and tightens her grip.

My eyes move to her as I mouth her nipple, playing with the hard bud.

"I'm finding it nearly impossible not to ask you to bite me," she admits, "and that is the opposite of taking things slowly."

Big Daddy and I groan as one. Rocking back onto my heels, I admire the beautiful woman splayed on the sofa beneath me. She's perfect—good, kind, wise, so free with her thoughts and emotions.

"There's not supposed to be anything between us," I manage. "This distance is unnatural, but we were right to put anything formal on hold given what's going on with Marco."

She shifts out from underneath me and sits upright, placing both hands flat on my chest. "I agree; I just don't know how long I can keep this up for." One hand comes down and palms my sack, rolling my balls between her fingers. "I want this, Richard," she murmurs. "With a desperation that's got to give sooner than later."

I chuckle, helping her wrap her fingers around my girthy length. "You can have this any time, Luna."

Black eyes move to mine. "You think you'd be able to knot me and not bite me?"

I groan at the very idea of knotting my Luna without that bite sealing us together.

"Maybe," I admit, panting as her hand strokes a hot line down my cock. "I'd...try."

Her throaty laugh rumbles between us. "We don't have to do it right now, but think about it. I need it, Alpha."

Bringing my mouth down, I slant my lips over hers, reveling in the softness of her mouth on mine. Her tongue dips between my lips, tangling with mine as we deepen the kiss.

I break it long enough to say, "Stay here with me tonight. Don't go home."

When her long arms wrap around my neck, her kiss growing frenzied, I take it as a yes.

I wake with the sun like always, shocked to find a lithe, smooth body curled against my front.

Luna. Sleeping.

Last night flashes back to me, how I bathed her and fed her and then tucked her into my bed after we played. Her curls are huge this morning, mussed and tangled. Deep inside me, a sense of unease wars with the absolute rightness of Lola in my bed.

Vikand's words ring in my head—given a choice between your king and your Luna, what would you pick?

Staring at Lola as she shifts and stretches, I know the answer. It's her. It was *always* going to be her. Now I've got to figure out how to convince her father not to murder me until I can explain what Lola and I are to each other. A Luna bond isn't completely unheard of, but it's rare enough that even Marco can't deny that sort of connection. I've read Vikand's book cover to cover—the parts in English—and there's not much he didn't already share.

What's important is what's written in the language of our goddess, and I can't read that.

"I can hear you thinking," Lola says softly, blinking near-black eyes open to smile at me. "Wanna say it aloud so we can tackle it together?"

Perfection, Big Daddy sighs. **She takes care like she should.**

It's something he's said to me before, when Lola first arrived. And he's right. Like any good pack omega, her first priority is harmony. It's how all omegas are wired.

I reach for a stray, tangled curl and pull my fingers through it as she groans and looks at her hair.

"Ugh, I didn't wrap it in my satin hair scarf, and now look at this mess."

I grin as I pull the tangle gently out of her curl and then tuck it in the matted mess of the rest of her poofy hair. "Let me help you fix it."

"You should," she snarks, slapping my chest playfully. "You made this mess."

Heat flares in my sack as I think about how I cleaned her last night. "I'm a huge fan of cleaning up messes." I dip down to press a trail of kisses from her bellybutton upward.

When she moans softly, my body tightens. She's already coated in a thin sheen of sweat, her skin burning against mine.

Too hot, Big Daddy murmurs thoughtfully. **Too hot, too early.**

Too early? What do you mean?

But he recedes into the distance, watching Lola and me through narrowed eyes.

Lola's stomach rumbles, and my need to protect and care for her kicks into overdrive. I roll out of bed and give her a look.

"Let me start breakfast. Come out whenever you're ready, and I'll help you with your hair. I was serious about mess cleanup. I'm nothing if not devoted."

She laughs and sits up, rolling out of bed after me and heading to the bathroom.

Ten minutes later, I'm stacking pork tamales onto a plate when she emerges from my room and seats herself gracefully at the bar. She gives the breakfast a wry look, then laughs up at me.

"Let me guess. Tamales are the one recipe you know?"

I wave my spatula at her. "I don't entertain a lot, and when I do, I do it at the bar. Tamales are my best option."

She grabs a still-steaming tamal off the plate and bites it, eyes rolling back into her head as she chews.

"See." I give her a knowing look. "Tell me that's not damn delicious. I order the pork from Santa Alaya."

She grins and swallows. "I stand corrected, Alpha."

Big Daddy shoves to the front, his green shining through my eyes.

I really want you to bite her, he sighs.

Gotta wait.

No wait. Marco can't deny a claiming bite.

No, no, he can't. But I don't think I'll even get a chance to explain what's going on if we tell him, and I've already claimed Lola.

"I lost you," she murmurs softly. "What's going on?"

I switch thought processes. "I'm going to visit Leighton's parents this morning and take breakfast. Would you like to go with me?"

She smiles, and it's so stunning, I forget to breathe for a moment.

"What?" She cocks her head to the side and her smile softens.

"You're so beautiful, I stopped breathing," I admit.

She beams at the compliment, but what I said is true. I am thoroughly, completely, and utterly besotted. It took all of two days. But all I know is I could never go back to life before Lola.

CHAPTER NINETEEN
LOLA

We eat quickly since Richard wants to take breakfast to Leighton's family soon. I help pack and cover it, and then we grab my clothes and leave. It's hard to resist the urge to glance into the alley between Bad Axe and the next building over to see if anyone notices me slipping out of Richard's place. Not that word of what happens here would necessarily get back to my father, but it's always possible.

Richard strides confidently into the alley, the tray of tamales balanced easily in one palm. When we reach the street and emerge onto the main drag, it's already full of shifters and centaurs going about their daily business. Pegasi fly in smooth lives above the main street. But apprehension fills me. Is it obvious to everyone here that he and I are connected?

His big body moves into my visual space, one finger coming underneath my chin to guide my focus to him. "This whole 'take it slow' thing is for the fucking birds, but I sense your nerves, omega. Remember, I want to be holding your hand and showing you off to every single monster you see. The only reason I'm not doing it is so we can come up with a plan for telling your father about us. But, in the meantime, I will protect our need for secrecy, alright?"

I nod, relief flooding me. He holds my gaze for a moment before moving his finger from beneath my chin. I don't want to hide him either, but it feels wrong showing the pack what's going on without having a conversation with my papá.

Slipping my hands into my back pockets to avoid touching Richard, I follow him across the street and to the left. We pass five or six curved side streets before he hooks a right. Following the street's slow spiral, we walk quietly until we reach a beautiful three-story treehouse halfway down the row.

A giant tree's roots are visible around the first floor, which boasts a door big and wide enough for a pegasus with their wings extended. Richard strides to the door and knocks loudly.

Heat rolls through me, and I wipe at a few beads of sweat as they appear on my brow. Just then, the treehouse doors split and swing inward to allow us entry.

Richard holds one open for me. As I pass him, he leans down and brings his mouth to my ear. "You smell fucking delicious, omega. What are you doing after breakfast?"

What am I doing after this? "Getting into clean clothes," I whisper back, poking his hard stomach playfully. "Because these have been on multiple floors in the last twelve hours, and my hair is still a wreck."

Richard grins wickedly, gesturing for me to continue into the treehouse. Unlike mine, this one has a giant circular ramp leading up to the first and second floors. A huge entryway to the right leads into an open space much like the other treehouses.

An older female wolf comes forward, hands clasped together as she smiles at Richard and me. "Alpha, it's totally unnecessary to keep feeding us."

A male I assume must be Leighton's father joins us from a back room, walking elegantly past a rustic wood bar. He stops by the female and wraps an arm around her waist, squeezing her to his side. Ocean-blue eyes move between us, then he winks at me. "I see Richard's dragging you into the tamales parade?"

I laugh and cover my mouth with one hand, my usual calm failing me. "The tamales parade?" I glance up at Richard. "I knew it. Tamales are the only thing you know how to cook, aren't they?"

We all laugh as Richard shrugs, passing the laden tray to the male.

The female smiles at me, dipping her head respectfully. "Princess, we're goddess-blessed to have you in our home."

"Please"—I take her weathered hand in mine—"it's just Lola."

"Lola," she repeats with a soft smile.

"Maren, how are you today?" Richard's question is met with a thoughtful half smile.

"We're...okay today, Alpha."

When he opens his big arms, she sinks into them and wraps hers around him, closing her eyes and leaning into the hug. His soft purr rumbles in the quiet space of their home as the male rejoins us. He stands next to me as his alpha purrs for his mate, his expression pained.

We're quiet for a minute as Maren wipes a stray tear from her cheek. I'm not unfamiliar with grief. Even at the highest levels in shifter politics, I've seen my papá comfort packmates in this exact same way.

Another few moments pass before Maren pulls out of Richard's embrace. Then her mate is by her side, pulling her back to his front as he rests his chin on top of her head.

Their love is so obvious, so real, it steals my breath. I want that. I *have* that. And I have to hide it.

Maren smiles at me, waving a finger between Richard and me. "You two are cute together. It's lovely to see since Richard has been a bachelor for so damn long."

Richard startles as my eyes spring wide. I'm too shocked at

what she said to summon a response, but when Richard says nothing, I shake my head vehemently.

"Oh, oh, no, we're not... I've known Richard my whole life."

Maren's smile spreads wider. "Dad's-best-friend-to-lovers is a trope in human romance novels for a reason, you know."

I've never read a romance novel. Sounds fun, though.

I can't think of a response, but I pray Richard does. Thankfully, he comes to my rescue.

"Thank you, Maren. We won't keep you, but can I do anything for either of you? Grocery run? Ice cream from Scoops or candy from Miriam's? I'll drive you up to the community garden if you'd like to visit with the pixies."

Maren shakes her head, placing a hand over her mate's. "We're going to stick close to home today, Alpha, but thank you." She smiles at us again. "I can see that, for some reason, you're hiding an obvious connection. But we of all people know how quickly life can be ripped from you." Her expression becomes intense and serious. "Don't let anyone steal a single moment of a single day from you. Take every one for yourself. Live every single one to the very fullest."

Tears fill my eyes as her message sinks in. She's right, of course. Politics and my father be damned. He's going to lose his mind about Richard and me, but should that stop us from pursuing a bond so deep and revered that our people speak about it in hushed, awed tones?

I wipe another bead of sweat from my brow as Richard places a hand on the middle of my back, rubbing a soft circle.

He manages to extricate us from the conversation as I muddle my way through a farewell that probably makes no sense. By the time we get to the street, Richard's hand has slid to the back of my jeans, where he hangs on to one loop.

When Leighton's parents' treehouse closes the door behind us, he presses me to it, his hand sliding around my front and up my shirt to rest flat on my belly.

"They're right, you know," he murmurs.

I glance up and down the street, but it's quiet. There's nobody around. Still, nervous tension has me amped and sweaty, my muscles trembling slightly. I feel…off-kilter. Like things are happening so fast. Finding my mate so early in life should be a joyous event, but we're hiding behind politics, and I hate that. Mostly, I dread letting the cat out of the bag with Papá. It's not going to go well; that's one thing I can count on.

The need to shout to the world about Richard and me is strong and I *can't*.

"Let's get you home," he whispers in my ear. "Just because they can tell doesn't mean everybody can tell."

"That's not it," I whine quietly. "I *want* to tell everyone, and I hate that we can't, even if I think we were right to decide that. I want to be free," I admit. "I want to make choices about my life that don't take shifter politics into account at *all*."

Richard grits his jaw and strokes my curls away from my face. "I will fight every second of every day for you to have that, sweetheart. Every second, do you hear me?"

I press into him, dropping my forehead to his chest where I bury my nose in hard muscle and soft hair. Moons, he smells so intensely delicious. Slick wets my thighs as his scent fills my senses.

"Lola," he huffs.

"I know," I whine.

"C'mon," he says again, pulling away from me.

My wolf lets out a pitiful groan in my mind, which pulls Big Daddy's green to the front of Richard's eyes.

He huffs. "Swear to the goddess, once the three of you can talk together, this is gonna get wild."

I stare deep into that luminescent green, willing Big Daddy to hear me, and since I know he can, I speak to him directly. "I can't *wait* to hear you. I don't think I've ever been so excited for anything in my life. And I don't know what the Luna bond means, precisely, but I'm excited to figure it out together."

Richard lets out a soft growl, stepping closer again. Voices drift toward us from up the street. We move away from one another and head back toward my place. I'm probably making it more obvious that I want to touch him with the way I fold my arms around my body, keeping my hands close to me so I don't reach over.

It was easier in the very beginning when he touched me the same way he touched everyone. But now that touch means something more.

We round the last bend toward the main drag, and Connall's standing there with the elemental sylph, Dirk. Connall's stance is wide, fists balled as he glares at the slightly shorter male.

"What's going on here?" Richard's alpha tone hits Connall and me the exact same way.

Dirk, on the other hand, looks up with a bored expression. "Hello there, yer mightiness. I was jest tellin' Connall he ought to offer his services to Louanna, on account of him being classically trained as a therapist and all." His expression goes tight. "She needs help, Richard. She can't deal with her part in Leighton's death without assistance, and I think Connall's the best one to help her."

My heart clenches thinking about Lou, my new friend. She hasn't talked much about what happened with the warlock Wesley. I only know because of Connall and Richard in the first place.

Connall turns to Richard and crosses his arms. "Please inform Dirk that I'm certified as a counselor for shifters and equinoids, not humans."

"Doesn't matter," Dirk states, matching his stance to Connall's. "It's gotta be yeh."

It's easy to see that Connall doesn't want to do this, for whatever reason. If Lou needs help, and it sounds like she does, her therapist should be someone ready and willing to help her. I give Dirk what I hope is an understanding look. "I can recommend several wonderful counselors at home in Santa Alaya, if you think Lou would be willing to travel. But Connall would know best if he's equipped to help her."

Connall gives Dirk the old "told ya so" look, but Dirk shrugs and addresses Connall directly, "Yeh're gonna help her, whether it's today or tomorrow or the day after that. I promise yeh that, alpha. Because now I've put that thought in yer pretty head, it'll consume yeh. And every time yeh see her, knowing what's going on in her mind, you'll remember that yeh have the power and ability to help her fix this."

For a long, tense moment, the two males stare at each other—Connall fierce and Dirk resolute. I wipe sweat off my brow as I observe their standoff, Richard doing the same thing I am.

Still not touching.

Goddess, it's so wrong.

Moisture breaks out on my upper lip, my muscles trembling. All the stress must finally be getting to me. On top of which, I've had enough tension for the day. I'm desperate for my guitar and some alone time to play.

I glance up at Richard. "I'm gonna head home for a while. Catch you later?"

He gives me a knowing half smile, and there are secrets in that smile. The secret of what we are to each other, of what we've done, of what we will do. Secrets that'll rip things apart and build something new.

"I've got meetings downtown for most of the day, but I'll be back around dinnertime if you want to come to the bar."

"It's a date," I say without thinking.

Connall and Dirk glance over, their standoff seemingly resolved. Or unresolved, but done.

I lift both hands like I've been caught dead to rights. "I mean, not a *date* date. You know what I mean."

Richard snorts. "They know what you mean, Princesa."

Formal title. Phew, good job, Alpha. I make a mock salute with one hand, dipping my head toward the other two. Connall's eyes narrow, but Dirk turns and stares at him again, like he's trying to sort something out.

Zipping my lips, I spin on my heel and head up the main street.

I am in desperate, *desperate* need of a shower.

∼

Hours later, my curls are freshly washed and detangled, and I've got a hellsuva leave-in conditioner in, praying it can repair the damage from a night of zero curl care. Guitar at my back, I leave my treehouse with the box of photos Richard gave me tucked under one arm. Sweat drips in rivulets down my spine despite the lovely temperature.

I don't know if I'm just missing Santa Alaya, or Papá, or Leo, or all of it rolled together. But my mind feels tender and ragged, like I drank one too many tequilas at the bar or completely forgot to sleep.

I took a peek at the Ever Welcome Packet and found a map that indicates where Shifter Hollow's church is. Now, more than ever, I feel the need to seek out my goddess and ask her advice.

After twenty minutes of trekking on a small trail through the forest, I come to a ring of trees soaring tall. They've been trimmed so no branches hang over the circle, giving me a clear view of the sky. Sawed off tree stumps are placed in circular waves around a stone altar in the center. Black smudges cover the top of the stone.

They lost a packmate recently, Leighton, Maren's son. This would be the pyre they would have burned him on, praying for his soul to run with Alaya.

A chill joins the heat skating down my spine as I walk around the church. Many havens have formal church buildings like we do back home. Just as many prefer to commune with Alaya in a more natural setting.

It's quiet here, not even a cricket chirping as I close my eyes and breathe in. Pine. Redwood. Moss. Dirt. The barest hint of a recent rain.

Smiling at the peace those scents bring me, I open my eyes and seat myself on one of the giant stumps. I fold my legs underneath me and take my guitar off, laying it carefully by my side. The box of photographs rests on my thighs. Removing the top, I admire the picture from before, the one of Richard and Mamá and Papá. I'm shocked anew at how carefree and youthful my papá looks.

Setting that photo next to me on the stump, I pick up the next one. A gasp leaves me at seeing my mamá holding me. I'm chubby as hells, all black curls and round cheeks. My arms are so fat, it's hard to imagine my mother ever dressing me in anything but tank tops. But we're both beaming at whoever took the picture.

Tears fill my eyes as I look through the stack. Picture after picture after picture is filled with joy and love and happiness. By the time I'm nearing the bottom of the box, I wonder if Papá realizes that he lost all of this somewhere along the way in his quest to be king. But this? The love in these photographs? It's worth everything and it's just within my reach.

Wind rustles through the trees around me, brushing lightly across my skin as I close my eyes. My goddess is near.

Please, Alaya, I pray, *let this work out.*

I don't usually ask for anything for myself, but to deal with Papá I'll need her by my side.

CHAPTER TWENTY
RICHARD

It was a struggle not to stare at Lola as she left. Her scent is imprinted into my brain, and even after she was gone, it lingered in the air.

Dirk claps me on the shoulder, surprising me. I whip around to see the slightly smaller male grinning at me with his trademark smirk. "Talk to yer Second, Alpha. I need yer help."

That said, he slaps the round disk that connects two leather straps crisscrossing his chest. When he does, his physical body evaporates into thin air. He disappears into the trees on a whoosh of wind.

Connall sighs. "You ready for a day of meetings?"

"Never," I mutter, giving my Second a look. "You ready to talk about why you and Dirk seem to keep disagreeing every time I see you together? Is it just the Lou issue?"

Connall's green eyes flash in seeming irritation. "Leighton was a close friend, as you know. Counseling someone so immediately involved in his death is a conflict of interest."

I jerk my head toward the street, and we begin walking past the shops toward downtown Ever. "She had absolutely no control over killing Leighton, Connall. She's a victim in this."

"I know that"—his voice lowers—"and I can't imagine how she feels. I don't think I'm equipped to help her."

I glance at him as we walk. "Are you willing to even attempt it?"

He grits his jaw, a muscle in the square line working overtime. It's clear he's incredibly set against offering his services to Lou, and I won't force him. That's never been my leadership style unless absolutely necessary.

"I've been so busy with the pack since Leighton's death. Everyone wants to talk about him, to share their grief and their joy, and it's horrible, but it's healing. At the end of the day, I'm emotionally exhausted from it."

"There's got to be more to it than that." I hope my words seem like gentle encouragement. "I've never seen you turn down a client."

"Okay, I'm going to admit something, and I don't want you to laugh."

I clap him on the back. "You know I won't."

He stops in the middle of the street and turns to me with a big sigh. "I'm attracted to her. As in soul-deep, eating-me-alive need. I want her." He says it so simply that I ache to share my own news. For some reason, I don't. Maybe it just feels right to talk to Marco first.

Connall looks up the street and winces. "Not only would that complicate any counseling I could do for her, but she and Dirk are a thing. Or they will be," he grumbles, "as soon as Dirk can convince her." My Second looks up at me with heartache clear in his eyes. "He's been asking me to help her for two weeks. I can't say yes and then act on my feelings. Everything about the situation is wrong."

"You're right that it's complicated, but sometimes the best things are."

At my expression, he sighs and rubs both hands over his face. "Maybe I should—"

A cackling purple figure flies between us, wind rustling my hair as Connall sputters and turns. "Ignatius, you almost hit us," he barks on a warning growl.

Iggy flips in air, a move he's been working to perfect, and zips back toward us, landing on my shoulder. Like every time he picks me for a perch, one hand goes around my head to hang on to my ear. His tail wraps around my neck, the spade-shaped tip slapping flat against my chest. Santa Alaya has very few gargoyles—it's too hot for their liking—and I still feel like I'm getting accustomed to Iggy's open and frequent affection.

"Are you going downtown? I was playing Skyball with some kids, but I've got to go home for lunch. Can you carry me?"

I reach up and tickle his side. "Yes, good job, and yes."

He snickers and pats the top of my head with his free hand. "Okay, let's go because I need to check in with Lou."

Connall freezes, green eyes flicking up to the young gargoyle. "What do you mean, Iggy?"

Iggy lets out a beleaguered sigh. "I adopted her because Dad says we should always help those in need."

My eyes find Connall's. "I promise this is not a plant."

He frowns at me, and Iggy pinches my ear.

"I'm not a plant, silly wolf. I'm a male!"

Connall's cheeks turn pink as he stares up at Iggy. "What do you mean about her needing help?"

"Well," Iggy sighs, "she's living next door at the Annabelle with Catherine since no house has appeared for her. And she cries a lot in her room. I can hear her when I'm outside playing with Kevin. Dad and I make her lots of snacks to cheer her up, and Minnie and I check on her a lot."

I consider Iggy's new pet—Dirk's old hunter hellhound, Minnie—and I'm not sure a flaming dog would really bring anyone comfort, but Iggy means well.

Connall's emotions are easy for me to read as his alpha. Indecision, guilt, worry, regret, resignation. He stares into the distance for a few moments, then back to Iggy and me. "Maybe I should try helping."

"Yeah," Iggy says as if it's obvious. "You'd probably do a way better job than me. She can only eat so many snacks."

"C'mon, gentlemen," I encourage, turning toward downtown again. "Let's go take care of business."

And then I'm rushing home to my woman. I've got ideas for this evening and I can't wait to carry them out.

～

Hours later, I've checked in at Bad Axe, and the bar's raging as usual, but my bar manager has the crowd handled. I'm not technically on the schedule again for a few days, although I end up here every day anyhow.

I comm Lola, but she doesn't answer, so I head to her place to see if she's home. No answer there, either, and when the treehouse lets me in, it's obvious she hasn't been there for hours.

Worry begins to build as I comm her a second time. That call goes unanswered too. I message Connall to check if he's seen her since we got back, and he hasn't either.

On a whim, I head to my place, wondering if she sought refuge there. Maybe I'll find her on the sofa, playing her guitar. Or waiting for me. Gods, what if I open the door and she's naked, or in the bed edging herself until I get there?

My dick leaps in my pants at the thought.

I pick door B, Big Daddy growls. He laughs when his commentary startles me. **Forgot I was here?**

You've been quiet.

Need Luna. Waiting for the moment I can speak to her without praying you'll accurately relay my thoughts.

Your thoughts are all about sex, and sometimes, it's not the right time.

Inaccurate. He laughs. **It's only about sex ninety-eight percent of the time.**

Huffing, I consider that he's correct, for the most part. Aside from random commentary about me needing to manhandle my packmates rather than using words like a grown male, he's mostly focused on Lola.

I mull that over as I ascend my stairs. Her scent is strong here, oranges and cream and jasmine so heady, I pause in the stairwell to suck in great heaving breaths of her.

She's here.

By the time I make it to the top of the stairs, I'm certain she's inside. But I still don't expect the vision when I open the door.

My place is torn apart, all the furniture moved to the sides of the main room. The sofa's been turned away from the glass front wall, and it's piled high with blankets and pillows. The box of photographs I gave her is on the kitchen counter.

Fuck. Yes, Big Daddy moans in my brain. **Bring it on, omega.**

As my brain catches up to what I'm seeing, Lola emerges from my bedroom, rounding the island with an armful of blankets and clothes.

My clothes.

T-shirts and sweaters and collared shirts. All of them, seemingly.

She halts and blanches when she comes flush with the door and sees me. The pile falls out of her arms onto the floor.

"Oh, Richard, gods, I'm so sorry. I just…I needed to see you, but you were busy, of course. And so I came here, and the treehouse let me in, and then I just, I just…" She throws both hands on top of her head as if the words have overwhelmed her.

The treehouse is drenched in Lola's scent, and as I cross to her, it flares wild and bright and strong. She looks up at me with those beautiful, startling dark eyes, her pupils blown wide and lips parted. A thin sheen of sweat coats her neck and chest.

I reach out and stroke the backs of my knuckles along her jawline. "You're nesting, Sweetheart."

"I know," she murmurs. "And I'm so sorry I came here and did it in your—"

Bending down, I silence her protest with my mouth as Big Daddy pants and paces in our shared space. This kiss is tender, adoring, gentle. But not for long.

We part, and I slide a hand up to grip her throat. "My space is your space. Come here any time you want me." Big Daddy's growl enters my tone at the demand.

Her lip quivers. "We said we'd go slowly." She wipes a hand over her brow. "And I know this is fast and messy—*we* are fast and messy—but I want it, Richard. I went to the church and prayed and Alaya sent wind to brush my cheeks and I, anyways, here I am."

I grin and stroke her throat with the tips of my fingers. "Alaya has already blessed us, Lola."

She covers her face with both hands. "But why is it so complicated? Ugh!"

She's right, it is. So I gently pull her hands from her face to ensure she sees how serious I am.

"Do you trust me to help you figure out your dreams later? Because I don't want you to give up a single one, Lola. I want you to tour and play, and I don't know what we'll have to do to make it work, but whatever that is, consider me all in, ten thousand percent."

Her eyes flash, her hands coming to the bottom of my shirt. She slides them up under the fabric, her fingers exploring the dips and valleys of my stomach. "I do, Richard."

Her words make every muscle in my body tense and achy. I've wanted someone for so long. But I was resolved to be single if I didn't find the right woman. And I don't think I realized how much that hurt inside of me until Lola came along.

"Every minute I spend with you is a blessing," I whisper,

pulling her tighter to me. "You're going into heat, Sweetheart, and I can't wait to share it with you, assuming you allow me in there." I jerk my head to where she's turned my sofa into a nest. It's traditional to ask to enter.

She slaps me on the chest playfully. "You better ask nicely, or I'll make you watch me in the nest for a while before you get to come in."

A deep, needy groan rumbles out of my mouth. "Torture me, please, omega. I like the idea of you getting rough with me."

She whines and backs up, pulling me toward the sofa. "Need you now, Alpha."

I halt, pulling carefully out of her grip. "We need supplies, my love. I'm going to run out and grab a few things, and I'll be back shortly, okay?"

She bites her lip, and I expect a protest, but she nods and wraps her arms around her body.

Console her, Big Daddy snaps, but my feet are already moving toward her again.

Wrapping my arms around her, I bury my face in her neck, brushing my mouth along the curve of her delicate ear. "To be clear, this is *not* a rejection of you or your nest. But when I get in there with you, I'm not coming out for days, Lola. I need to be able to be a good partner while you're in heat, and I won't be rational when we're in the middle of it."

She rubs her cheek along mine, whining softly. "Hurry, Alpha. Please?"

It takes every ounce of grit in me to promise I will and pull away from her. Leaving her alone in the treehouse is the hardest thing I've ever done, every step away is wrong. Big Daddy paces anxiously, on edge and snappish as I comm Connall.

The moment he picks up, relief floods me.

"Connall, I need to see you urgently at my office."

"On my way," he agrees. "I'm with Arkan; do you need him too?"

"Bring him," I command, clicking off. Between the two of them, they can manage Shifter Hollow entirely without me for a few days.

But ten minutes later, they're not at my office yet, and my patience is wearing thin. My dick's a baseball bat between my thighs, my body flushed and hot. It's preparing for her heat, to answer the call of her body's intense need. My omega's upstairs, nesting and hot and ready to fuck, and these two are standing in my way.

Just as I ball my fists and head to the door to find them, they sail through. Connall takes one look at me, slipping both hands into his pockets as he flares his nostrils and scents the air. "I'll be damned, Alpha. Is this what I think it is?"

I snarl, "If you think my omega's in heat, and I look like I'm ready to be in bed with her, then yeah."

I've never spoken this rudely to Connall and I regret not telling him everything about her earlier. He's a great listener; he would have understood. Kind person that he is, he gives me a knowing, happy smile instead of berating me for not trusting him with the information.

"I should have told you," I murmur. "I'm sorry, Second."

Arkan snorts. "Gods, it's fun watching wolves lose their minds when a heat comes around." His smirky expression grows bigger. "We'll handle the Hollow while you're indisposed. What do *you* need?"

"I'll send up groceries," Connall says. "Sorry it took us a few minutes to get to you; we were with Leighton's folks."

I wave his concern away. "I was due downtown for a meeting about—"

"I know, Alpha," Connall reprimands gently. "I've got it handled. Where do you want me to say you are, if our packmates ask? You haven't announced taking a mate so I assume this is still a secret? And do you want a heat condom? Have you discussed pups?"

Gods, the politics of this whole thing are a nightmare, and I don't want to fucking hide Lola. But by the time she and I are through her heat, she'll be wholly and irrevocably mine. And knocked up, if I don't do something about that. We haven't had a conversation about starting a family. We were taking it *slow*.

I give Connall a wry look. "You have a heat condom lying around?"

He laughs. "I don't, but I can send one up with the supplies. Consider it done. You'll have it if you want it. Or not."

Lola and I can discuss it, but it'd be better to have it handy.

Just then, Leighton's parents show up at the door with a giant basket overflowing with snacks and electrolyte drinks. Maren beams at me. "Congratulations, Alpha. We couldn't be any happier for you and Lola."

I stare open-mouthed at the gift basket, shocked. "How did you know about the heat?"

Maren grins. "Oh, it was pretty obvious to us this morning when you dropped by to visit. I looked at Petr and said, she'll be in heat within a day or two, so when Connall rushed off, we made a guess."

I take the basket as shock and gratitude flood through me. This is what it's *supposed* to be like when an alpha finds his mate. A shared celebration, adoration, and pack support.

"Thank you," I murmur, "for everything. Lola and I are so grateful."

Goddess, there it is, an admission of what Lola and I are to each other. And, fuck, it feels good to say it.

CHAPTER TWENTY-ONE
LOLA

I whine and pace inside the treehouse. She's done her best to console me by muting the big living room glass and waggling the fridge door to remind me there are snacks. She's even had soft guitar music playing for the last little while. But there's only one thing that can temper the flames burning me up.

And he's not here.

My nest is almost perfect. In an ideal world, I'd have the time and space to put up mood lighting and flameless candles and all sorts of things. I don't know if Richard has any of that at his house, but I'm guessing not, considering he's been alone for so long. That aside, the nest looks amazing.

Sighing, I pause midpace and turn to stare at the sofa. I placed the pillows all around the edge and front to enclose the space. Blankets encircle it to make it smooth and soft, and even though they're mismatched, it feels right to me. I tucked Richard's shirts in each corner between the pillows and the couch, so the whole thing smells like my alpha.

Except his tee from yesterday. I'm holding that one. I bring it to my nose and inhale. In my mind, my wolf groans and rolls onto her side, panting heavily. She's as ready for him as I am.

A chill races down my spine when I think about Richard biting me during my heat. It's inevitable—he will. I know he will, and what's more, I want him to, with a desperation I never thought possible. My soul is calling to his, and they'll never be complete until we permanently meld them together with a claiming bite.

Then I'll hear them both in my mind. I long for the ability to talk to Big Daddy. I always assumed that one day, when the timing was right, I'd mate some nice wolf and settle down and be pretty happy. But I never imagined I'd get to talk to their wolf.

Thank you, goddess Alaya, patron saint of wolves, I pray. *Thank you for this.*

I never could have imagined it would happen when the timing was utterly wrong, or that he'd be my father's best friend. Or that his wolf would be so damn powerful, he could speak to it. Gods, I wonder if Big Daddy speaks Spanish. I mean, I assume so. But I can't wait to hear him for myself.

Just the thought of him commanding me in Spanish has me dripping all over the floor. My clothes are stuck to me, my body coated in sweat as the heat builds and builds. When my knees go weak and buckle, I flop into the nest and roll to the middle, staring at the gorgeous wood beam ceiling.

No sooner do I think about how pretty this treehouse is than the thought dissipates, and all my other rational thoughts go with it. I haven't had a heat in a while, but I don't remember the delirium hitting quite this hard. The tiny logical bit left in my brain, the only small part that's not wrapped up in the heat hormones, prays Richard will return soon.

I don't know how much later it is that the front door swings open. Shooting upright, I surge onto my hands and knees and crawl to the edge of the nest. Richard comes through the door with bags of groceries and a…gift basket?

Flaring my nostrils, I focus on my alpha's scent, growling when he speeds across the room and drops the supplies on the kitchen countertop. I watch as he quickly unpacks them, setting out rows of shit I no longer care about. All I can do is stare at the hard cock outlined in his jeans. Even his knot is swollen and visible.

My mouth waters looking at it.

Richard pauses, glancing over at me. "Sweetheart, I'll be there in two minutes, I promise. Connall rounded up supplies, and I need to put them away." He gives me a wicked look. "Why don't you undress, lie down and show me how wet and ready that sweet pussy is for me?"

Groaning, I fall to my back and rip my clothes off. Spreading my knees wide, I reach a hand down to rub soft circles over my clit. I nearly come, stars dancing behind my eyelids as slick floods from me like a river. Even that feels good.

Responding growls from across the room push my pleasure higher until I do come, choking back a scream as I clench on nothing at all, bliss exploding out from my core. My entire body shakes with the force of the tremors, jerking until the orgasm wrings me out and fades.

I lie there in a state of overwhelm, sound muffled, vision blurred, as Richard comes into view at the foot of the nest. "Omega, sit up and look at me."

His command has me scrambling onto my knees, muscles primed to throw myself at him. Richard stands at the foot of the sofa, unbuttoning his jean shirt one button at a time. His eyes glow with Big Daddy's intense green as he shrugs the shirt off his muscular shoulders, revealing miles of tanned, tattooed skin. He tosses it aside and steps out of his pants and shoes, never moving his intense focus from my face.

Richard's scent swells between us, a mixture of his natural smell and the primal, heady essence of heat. Luminescent green eyes narrow, his nostrils flaring as his muscles tense. "May I come into your nest, Luna?"

My entire core aches at those words, at the enormity of them, at the meaning behind them. They're words I never thought I'd hear. To have that bond…I can't wait to learn precisely what it means to share it.

I put my whole heart into the formal, traditional answer, sitting on my heels with my hands on my quivering thighs. "Enter my nest, Alpha, and service me."

He slides onto the sofa on both knees as I reach for him and drag him closer. Burying my face in his stomach, I drag in greedy breaths. Yesssss.

Him.

Mine.

Need. Knot.

Snarling, I yank at the jeans as Richard lets out a devious, commanding laugh.

"That's not how this works, Luna. My job is to get you off as many times as I can."

He rolls onto his back and grabs me, pulling me to a seated position on his chest. "Shift forward," he growls. "I need to eat, omega." His hands come to my ass and grip hard enough to bruise.

I cry out as I shuffle forward, dropping onto his warm mouth as shock and ecstasy batter my system. Soft lips and a wicked tongue explore my folds with slow, torturous intensity, and it takes me no time at all to flood him with slick and come with his name falling from my lips like a prayer.

But the heat builds, two orgasms just enough to stoke the flames to a wild, raging roar. When I sag over his face, Richard snarls and flips us, crawling up my legs as he grips my left knee and pins it to the sofa, his thighs underneath mine.

He looks down, his free hand gripping his impressive length. He strokes it, squeezing the tip and dripping precum onto my pussy. The satisfied chuckle that leaves his lips as we watch has me curling over to get a better look at all that seed. It drips onto my clit and slides down my pussy lips. That's when I notice the skin-colored ring around the base of his cock. Seeing it results in a frustrating whine with my wolf's tone running through it.

"Con calma, Princesa," Richard murmurs in a soothing tone. "We aren't ready for pups, Lola. If I don't wear this the whole time, you'll be pregnant by the time we're done." He dips down and slaps my pussy with the head of his cock. "Do you agree it's best to wait?"

No.

Yes.

Fuck.

Pleasure shoots through me. Goddess, I hope he's going to manhandle me. I need it. I want it. But still…that ring. I don't like it.

When I whine again, Richard snarls, lips curling back as the intense chocolate of his eyes goes deeper, brighter, an emerald shine that tells me Big Daddy is so close to the surface of their shared consciousness. "You need something else to focus on," he says on a growl.

Heat ravages me from the inside out, demanding something, demanding more than this tease. I'm still not ready when he directs his cock between my pussy lips and thrusts in. My back arches at the sensation of his thickness splitting me so fucking deliciously. He's huge, and my pussy clenches over and over, desperate to adjust, but he gives me no time.

His free hand grabs my right knee and draws it up and out until I'm thoroughly exposed to him. Muscular hips pull back, dragging his length along everything inside of me as I claw at the sheets and pray for the relief only his knot can bring.

The second snap of his hips is so hard, I'm forced back in the nest. I can't tell if I'm screaming or crying or begging when he pulls out and surges back in, huge body covering mine until time blurs. And still he continues the steady, torturous, deep fucking until the swollen edges of his knot kiss my pussy lips.

"Please," I beg. "Goddess, please fucking give it to me."

Richard lets out an otherworldly growl that raises the hair on my nape as his thrusts grow faster and shallower, every movement pushing that enormous knot farther into me. His hips snap, popping the knot into my channel as I come, overwhelmed by the size of him. I don't know how many times I come or for how long, just that Richard's a blazing, searing presence, his heat burning me alive as orgasm batters me against him.

Hours, maybe days later, I blink my eyes open to see my alpha braced above me, watching me with an intense look. His lips split into a satisfied-looking grin.

"You back with me, omega? You passed out after that last orgasm."

I slap his chest. The heat, the pain, the need hasn't abated in the slightest. "Give me another one," I demand, rocking my hips against his. "And another one after that."

He purrs, that deep noise slicking my channel as he wraps an arm around my waist and rolls us so he's seated upright, and I'm straddling his lap. In one swift move, he grabs my ass and pulls me down onto his dick, snarling as he enters me. The sheer dominance of the move forces a gasp from my lips as I fall forward against his burning-hot chest.

"Big Daddy wants you," he snarls into my neck. "I'm gonna filthy fuck you, Lola, and then I'm gonna bite you and give him his time. You ready?"

I can't summon words, so it's a sob that comes out of my mouth in response to his declaration.

Richard snarls and grips my neck. The other stays under my ass. And then he moves.

Big hips snap up, forcing me up and off his cock, but I can't go far with the way he's holding me. He yanks me back down, filling me past the base of his knot as I beg and plead for this soul-rending pleasure to never stop. His pace is blistering, my body tightening and clenching at the sheer force of him.

He brings his mouth to mine and devours me, his lips desperate as our teeth clash together. It's the kiss of a male who wants to imprint his very soul onto mine, and I know it when we part and he tucks my hair over my shoulder, eyeing that spot he's talked about before.

Glowing green eyes come to mine, Big Daddy's deep bass threaded through Richard's baritone when he speaks. "It's time, Lola."

CHAPTER TWENTY-TWO
RICHARD

Lola gives me a sultry, seductive look as her head falls to one side, exposing the spot I've fantasized about since the day we met. It's perfect, that taut bit of skin where her neck and shoulder meet. Her hair is sweaty, stuck to her gorgeous skin as I stare at that spot and the beautiful Luna in my arms.

When I lean forward and lick a flat path up the front of her throat, her pussy clenches like a vise around my dick. Grunting, I nip at her skin. "Easy, omega."

"Need to come," she snaps. "Bite, Richard."

Listen to Luna, Big Daddy growls in my mind.

I move my lips along her skin as she mewls and pants in my arms, milking my cock for all its worth as I try not to fucking come too soon. Focusing hard, I open my mouth and strike, sinking my fangs into the side of Lola's neck.

My mind is thrown into immediate chaos, like being turned every which way by an ocean wave. I can't tell up from down. There is only her and that connection point between us. A shock runs through me before it builds and explodes outward, waves of blissful pleasure screaming through me as I come, hot seed shooting from me to splash her womb. Her pleasure builds and stokes mine until I don't know who's screaming louder, me or her. All I know is that I never, ever want this ecstasy to end.

Threads appear in my mind's eye, snapping tight and breaking and reforming as we bliss out. And then those beautiful golden lines pull taut and form a single shining path between us, a permanent tether that bonds and binds.

She's mine in the most everlasting way our people have.

Pleasure fades eventually, and I release the bite, licking a gentle path over twin puncture marks to seal them with my healing saliva.

Lola groans and falls against my chest, her neck still close to my mouth. *"Goddess, that was fucking incredible."*

I jolt, a smile splitting my face. *"I hear you, sweetheart."*

Lola sits upright, placing both palms on my chest to support herself. She cocks her head to the side as a giant, joyous smile frames her face with happiness. *"Alpha?"*

That's right, baby, Big Daddy growls, moving into the front of my consciousness. **You hear me too, don't you?**

A shiver runs down Lola's spine, forcing her muscles to tremble as her eyes spring wide. *"Moons, I do. I finally do."*

I relax, allowing my wolf this time with our mate. He's been waiting for this for so long. In my mind's eye, I sense him pacing as he decides what to say to her. She stares at me in wonder.

I'm gonna fuck you hard, Luna, and then you're gonna bite me the same way we bit you.

Lola shudders a second time. *"Bite you?"*

Yeah, baby. Bite us, imprint yourself on us, and your wolf will be able to visit me in here. Or I can come there.

Lola's eyes spring wide, her focus on me. "I've never heard of that. Richard?"

I shrug. "Not much is known about a Luna bond, other than the fact that alphas with it grow bigger and might develop other powers." I gesture across the room. "I've got a book about it from

Vikand. We can take a look later, if you want to, but there's not too much new info in there."

Lola closes her eyes. *"Later. I'm gonna bite the shit out of you then, Big Daddy."*

Good, baby. Now get on all fours so I can lick that sweet cream pie.

My omega shudders and crawls off my lap, obeying Big Daddy's order as I grip my dick and stroke. Goddess, I could come just watching her listen. Why is that so unbearably hot?

Because her.

It was a rhetorical thought.

Everything is because of her. For her. About her. In support of her. She is the center of *everything*, he states.

I can't disagree as I crawl up behind her and drag my nose through her swollen, puffy folds. My seed drips from her, coating the backs of her legs and that gorgeous pussy.

You took us so fucking well, Luna, Big Daddy praises. **But we're just getting started, baby. I'm gonna put my tongue inside you and lick every inch until you're coming, and then I'm gonna knot you so hard, you black out again.**

Lola whines and shifts from side to side, her pussy swollen and needy.

I'm drawn by that tether that connects us now, crawling on top of her as I line myself up with her and drive deep.

"Fuck!" she screams into the consciousness we now share.

Yeah, we're gonna. Big Daddy laughs. **Scream for us, Luna. I wanna hear how much you love us while you come.**

I grip her hips and pound into her from behind, her combined thoughts and Big Daddy's salacious commentary stoking the flames of another orgasm from me. She comes when he calls her a good girl, and her pussy flutters and tightens like a clamp around me.

She's gonna fucking lock us, Big Daddy howls victoriously.

And because she can hear our thoughts now, she laughs even

as her body takes over, a ring of muscle inside her channel swelling around the base of my knot to lock us into place. The sensation is like nothing I've ever experienced, like she's swallowing me whole and sucking my soul out through my cock.

Big Daddy fills our shared space with absolute joy as we come, Lola's screams raising the hair along the back of my neck. When orgasm fades, I roll us onto our sides to rest until her lock and my knot deflate enough for us to separate.

She whines, so I stroke her shoulder where I bit her, causing her to shudder and rock against me.

Easy, Luna, Big Daddy admonishes gently. **Don't move your hips, or you could tear, baby. And we don't want that. Because the moment you can separate, I need your teeth.**

Lola whines again, reaching between us to grab my sack and roll my balls between her fingers.

"Sweetheart, if we want things to go down, that ain't the way," I say with a laugh.

"I was thinking about pegging you," she muses, her voice a whisper.

Say what now? Big Daddy's ears prick up with concern.

Rolling Lola over onto her belly, I shift so that she's supported, my hips pressed to hers as I straddle her from the back. Dipping down, I bury my nose in her hair and kiss the back of her neck and shoulders, everything I can reach without moving my lower half. "I want it. If you can think it up, I want to try it. Every toy. Every position. Every fantasy you have, I need to make it happen."

Lola pushes onto her elbows, rubbing her cheek along mine with a happy hum. "Good, because I have a lot of ideas, Richard." Her head dips low as sweat breaks out along the back of her neck. "Goddess, this fucking heat."

Reaching down, I prod at my knot to find it slightly deflated. Her lock pulses and moves around me, forcing a well-pleasured grunt from my lips. But it relaxes enough for me to pull out of her.

Roll over, omega, Big Daddy commands. **Find your spot and bite.**

"You're awfully bossy," she chides him, flipping onto her back and shifting onto her elbows.

All that movement does is highlight her perfect, firm breasts. I can't resist bending down to lick one taut nipple, pulling the tight skin between my lips and teeth as Lola lets out a soft, needy whine.

"Right here," she says, touching a spot just under my chin, right over the most vulnerable part of my throat. "That's where I want to do it."

I shudder and sit upright. I was planning to let her bite me on whatever schedule she wanted, but the idea of her yanking my head back and sinking those fangs into me has me throbbing with need. Blood rushes through me, dick pulsing as I stare in wonder at this woman the goddess crafted for me.

"Where do you want me?" My voice sounds roughshod and well-used.

All that screaming, Big Daddy reminds me with a flick of his tail.

"Hang your head off the edge of the nest," Lola commands, pointing to the very edge. "Go now."

Because she's fated to be mine, her command hits me square in the chest like a punch. Grunting, I roll onto my back and rest my head over the edge. Lola moves to straddle my feet, dragging her nose and mouth up my leg. She pauses at my knee to nip hard, which makes my dick jerk with need. The closer her mouth gets to it, the harder it is not to flip us both over and have my way with her.

I push onto my elbows, desperate to watch the show as her lazy, slow perusal brings her between my thighs. She bends gracefully down and licks a stripe up the underside of my cock as a string of expletives leaves my mouth. Rolling my hips, I try to get the tip between those pretty lips, but she chuckles. Slim fingers come to the base and grip as I resist the need to fist her hair and drag her up and down until I'm coming down that hot, silky throat.

"More," I command. "Harder, Luna."

She moves forward and brings my cock between her lips, sucking hard on the very tip, tongue swirling a circle around the sensitive underside.

Later, Big Daddy whines. **Do this later, for the love of our goddess.**

Lola growls softly and climbs up my body, straddling me as she leans forward, balancing on one arm. "Head back, Alpha," she murmurs, wrapping her hand in my hair.

I obey dutifully, letting my head sink off the edge.

"Do your worst," I whisper, smiling as she drags that sinful tongue up my neck.

Big Daddy paces and whines in my mind, but I don't think either of us was prepared for her strike. Her teeth sink into my throat below my chin, her fingers gripping my hair tight. The vulnerable position, the teeth of a predator right there should put me in fight mode. But it's *her*, so I groan as my hands roam her body—up both her sides, into her hair. I use my leverage to crush her to me.

And that's when everything goes sideways again. The room flips upside down as the sound of doors unlocking and creaking open echoes over and over in my mind. Bliss and pain hit me in equal measure, Lola tensing as the same thing happens to her. Our bond is flooded with confusion and worry and ecstasy and so many fucking voices, all speaking at once. My body is tight enough to split, every inch of muscle locked and loaded.

Lola releases the bite and sits up, panting. I lie there, immobilized, shocked, as all the noise disappears in a flash and my mind is left blank. It reminds me of the utter silence after a midnight snowfall when the earth is completely devoid of all sound.

Lola grins, a surprised-sounding chuckle rumbling from her. "Gods, he's here, Richard. Big Daddy is *here*." She places a hand over her chest.

And when I feel for my wolf, he's…gone.

"Not gone," she whispers, having heard my thoughts, "here with us."

I search our bond, and she's right. Big Daddy's there, he's just distant. He's…playing with her wolf.

"They're so joyous," she murmurs. "Goddess, this is incredible. Let me see if I can—"

There's an odd-feeling jolt, and then Big Daddy is back with me, but there's a new wolf too, Lola's wolf. She steps shyly into my mental space, looking at me with soft, thoughtful eyes. But then Big Daddy nips playfully at her side, and she leaps on him with a lively snarl. They go down in a heap of limbs, twisting and turning and nipping until he rolls over and plays dead, allowing her to bite every inch of him as his tail swishes lazily in the mental dirt.

I glance at my stunning mate where she straddles me, shocked at what's going on in my mind. "I…wasn't expecting this. I've never heard of anything *like* this."

Lola's crimson lips break into a joyous smile. "It feels right though, doesn't it? It's the Luna bond. Big Daddy was right. He must be."

Emotion overwhelms me as the wolves play in my mind. My hands roam every inch of Lola that I can touch.

"Roll over, sweetheart," I urge her. "Let me fucking lavish my love on you with my mouth while they play. I need to taste you again."

One dark brow curls deviously upward, but she obeys beautifully.

I make good on my promise, licking and tasting and cherishing every inch of my woman.

My Luna.

CHAPTER TWENTY-THREE
LOLA

My heat rages for two full days. I lose track of the number of times we make love; I just know I've never been so blissed out and wrung dry by pleasure. Richard's energy never flags, never fails. As many times as I demand he fill my need, he does it. And not just that—he forces us to pause every few hours to drink water and eat fruit. He's a machine, in the best way.

By morning the third day, I'm exhausted all the way to my bones. Every inch of my body aches. He's not much better. Even our wolves are tired, snoozing in a pile in the back of my mind to give Richard a break from their antics.

I can scarcely wrap my brain around this new normal. What I *am* painfully aware of is how filthy I am. Richard kept warm, wet rags handy for cleanup because I couldn't bear to leave him long enough to shower. He even gave me an extraordinarily sexy tongue bath in wolf form, but all that led to was more sex. Goddess, really, really incredible sex.

Even now, I clamp my thighs together remembering how fun it was to play while he was shifted.

"Sweetheart, my dick is gonna fall off if I don't get a day to recover," Richard says with a laugh from somewhere in the kitchen.

"I know," I murmur, reaching up to pull at my curls. They're an absolute disaster, like a bird nested on my head and came back several years in a row to redo that same nest. And the result is the mass of insanity matted to one side of my scalp. When one of the pieces I grab is crunchy, my nose scrunches.

Richard laughs from across the room, piling sandwiches on a tray. He rounds the island, fully nude, and stalks gracefully across the living room.

"There's jizz in my hair," I mutter. "And on pretty much every inch of me."

He sets the sandwiches next to me and hands me a bottle of water. "I'm tapped out, sweetheart, or I'd offer you more."

I snort out a laugh and down the water under his watchful gaze.

His eyes wrinkle in the corners as he eyes the absolute disaster of my curls. "Will you teach me how to do your hair?"

I cock my head to the side. "It's a forty-step process, and it takes ages. I will, if you want to, but it's a marathon, not a sprint."

He stretches one arm over his chest and rubs at a muscle on the back of it; he must be sore. "I'm done sprinting for a day or two. Why don't we shower, and then you can show me what to do with that glorious mop on the side of your head?"

Laughing, I sit up and slap his stomach playfully. He manages to grab one wrist and do some insane maneuver that flips me up onto his shoulder, face close to his bitable ass while he holds on to my thighs and turns for the shower. His fingers stroke lazily over my skin as I prop myself up with both hands on his lower back.

"Honestly, this is just making me want to tackle you, Alpha," I admit into our bond.

"Same," he murmurs aloud. "Fuck taking a break. Let's sort

your hair, and then I wanna wrap it in my hand and use it as leverage to fuck your ass."

"Goddess." I grin as he sets me down in the dark stone shower. This room is so sensual—every surface is dark stone, and moss is growing in nearly all the corners. It's like he brought the outside into the treehouse.

"I did," he whispers into the side of my head. "And I hoped one day I'd share this with someone. That we'd laugh and love and maybe build a family in this home. What do you think, Luna?"

"I think we've got some details to sort out," I admit, "but that sounds perfect."

The wolves roll upright and disappear from my mind. Richard jerks when they appear in his, roughhousing in a tired heap. Their play is half-hearted, and after two tumbles, they flop together and start snoring.

Richard grins at me. "This is so unusual, and I wouldn't trade it for the world. What a blessing, Lola, to have this with you."

I gasp as he stares at me. "Goddess, Richard, your eyes..."

His smile drops. "What's wrong?" He whips around to the mirror, but I join him so we can stare together.

"They used to be green when Big Daddy was focused," I murmur. "Now they're a swirl of our colors. Amber and green together."

He stares hard. "Do you think that's just because they're with me right now?"

"I hadn't noticed," I admit. "But when they come back to me, we can check." Something occurs to me, and I stroke his chest softly. "Do you think we'll ever have our wolves back by themselves, or will they always go together? And if they go together, would you still be able to shift?"

He laughs and reaches around me to turn the water on. "If you had to pick between going with me or going by yourself, which would you choose?"

"Point taken," I say with a chuckle, stepping into the cold

water. "I wish we could read the book Vikand gave you. I'd love to know more about what to expect. I guess we'll figure it out as we go."

Richard gives me a wry look. "According to Big Daddy, we can now. At least, he seems to think we'll be able to. Not sure if that's true, but if it is, we'll document it in case this happens to anyone else."

I pick my jaw up off the ground as Richard eyes the hot water handle.

"Cold shower sort of girl? That surprises me."

I grimace. "Cold water is good for curls."

His expression matches mine, but he steps into the chilly water and grabs the shampoo. "This first, I assume?"

I nod and stand quietly, thinking about what he shared, hands on his chest as he lathers up my hair with shampoo and gently caresses my scalp. His big fingers force a tightening in my body, nipples pebbling against his chest as I close my eyes and let my head fall into his hands.

"Lola," he huffs, "I never would have thought washing hair would be sexy, but if you keep making those noises, I'm not gonna make it past step one."

I open my eyes long enough to see Big Daddy and my wolf's colors shine brightly through his irises. "I'll tone it down, Alpha; it's a promise." My tone is teasing, but Richard places a soapy finger under my chin.

"Never," he growls. "Never tone a single thing down about yourself. Not for me, not for the pack, not for Marco."

My father's name sends a swirl of butterflies through my belly. His challenge is a day away. And my situation with Richard got infinitely more complicated the moment of our claiming bites.

Richard prods me back to the present with a tickly finger to the side. "We'll tackle that later. Let's deal with the hair, more food and water, maybe a nap. And then we can talk through my plan."

I close my eyes as I wave at the conditioner. "That's next. And there's a plan?"

Richard squirts creamy conditioner out of the bottle and brings his hands to my hair, rubbing the conditioner gently in from the tips up close to my scalp. I reach up and run my fingers through the snarls to finger detangle even though they're wet and weighted down.

"I have a plan," Richard says with confidence. "As soon as the challenge has passed, we'll invite him here and talk to him openly. We've done nothing wrong."

I huff out a growl. "You know he won't see it that way."

"He'll have to." Richard's swirling green-and-golden eyes find mine. "There hasn't been a Luna bond in thousands of years, Lola. This is a blessing, a chance to learn directly from the goddess herself. There are words in Vikand's book that I could never translate, but we can both read it now, if Big Daddy is right."

"That's so wild." I grin at him. "I hope it's true."

He nods with a smile, stroking his fingers through my hair. "Big Daddy has been right about everything else. I'm excited to dig in and find out what we can."

I mull that over as we leave the conditioner in while we finish washing our bodies. My hair is still super tangled on one side, but the rest of the steps to fix it start post shower. We manage to make it out with minimal sexual shenanigans. I'm honestly exhausted to a bone-deep level I couldn't have imagined.

We leave the shower, and I snag one of Richard's tees. Moving carefully around my head, I scrunch my curls in the soft shirt.

He grabs a bath towel and hands it to me. "I'm not so much of a bachelor that I don't have towels, Lola."

Huffing out a laugh, I continue scrunching. "Terry cloth is

hard on curls, and they'll get frizzy if I dry too roughly. Remember all those steps I mentioned?"

He cocks his head to the side. "I'm beginning to understand why you sleep with your hair wrapped in silk."

"Bingo." I laugh as he steps forward and takes the tee from me.

Big hands come gently to my hair and scrunch from the bottom up. He's learning fast. He moves all the way around my head, sighing when he gets the matted section on one side. "I don't know what to do about this, though. Honestly, it's a bird's nest, mate."

Mate. That singular word is enough to make everything inside me come alive.

"I'll never get tired of hearing that," I whisper.

"And I'll never stop saying it." He brings his forehead to mine, nuzzling the tip of my nose with his.

We stand for a long moment, basking in the connection as our wolves snore somewhere in Richard's mind. Eventually, he sighs. "Much as I'd like to do this with you forever, we need to take care of this hair."

"And you should check in with Connall," I urge. Being Richard's means this pack is mine in a way that runs deeper than me being a visitor. Leighton's parents drift into my mind. Lou and Iggy follow. I should call her. I bet she's—

"You've gone into pack omega mode," Richard says with a sensual chuckle. "I can hear you."

I blush, running both hands up his stomach to his chest. "It's hard to turn off, ya know?"

His wry smile tells me he knows precisely what I mean. He points to the kitchen. "Go sit. I asked Connall to bring your guitar over plus all the shower stuff from your place. I've got twenty bottles of hair stuff I have no idea what to do with."

Beaming, I cross the room as the tree house pulls a barstool out for me. I pat the counter as I seat myself. Richard reappears from the entryway with a bag full of hair product bottles and my beloved guitar. When he hands it to me, a deeply innate sense of relief hits me. My fingers itch to play, and so I do.

Richard moves behind me and sets the bottles out on the counter, and for the next hour, I guide him through moisturizer and leave-in conditioner and combing and another round of moisturizer.

And I play. And I sing.

And I've never felt so peaceful or hopeful in my entire life as when my mate learns how to wrap a silk scarf around my drying curls.

CHAPTER TWENTY-FOUR
RICHARD

Did I feel happiness before Lola? I mean, I think I was happy. But now, having her here? My heart is so full, I can barely stand it. I feel young and exuberant, like my only priority is to run to my pack and shout about how I found my mate. And not only that, but the Luna bond that'll continue to grow and develop between us, making us stronger, better leaders.

Together.

I feed Lola a hearty lunch of spaghetti and meatballs, then tuck her into my bed. She looks like a goddess-blessed angel curled around my pillow, clutching one of my tees.

For the next hour, the treehouse and I clean up the living room, moving the furniture back where it belongs. With deep regret, I pull the nest apart and put everything away. The blankets and pillows all go in the wash. I open the front window to let in some fresh air, and then I deep clean. Everything gets scrubbed and shined and buffed until the treehouse is back to normal.

It kills me to wash away evidence of Lola's heat. But we've got plenty of heats ahead of us. They'll come more often now that we're mated.

And thank fuck for that. Glory day.

I grin at Big Daddy's reappearance. *You finally back? Her wolf running you ragged, old man?*

A scoffy snort rumbles in our bond. **Not fucking hardly. She's perfect. We're perfect. She needs rest, and I've never been better.**

Does that mean you'll stop fighting me on everything?

He pauses for a moment, his tone unusually serious when he finally responds. **I never wanted to fight you, Richard. I am you. You are me. But you couldn't see what was right in front of you. It's my job to make that happen. And I will never, ever fail in my duty. We are blessed by Alaya herself to have what we have. Don't forget that,** he tacks on.

A knock on my front door rings through the treehouse. Not wanting the noise to wake Lola, I rush for the door and rip it open just as Big Daddy snarls into our bond.

In the doorway stands Marco, his private guard behind him with their traditional silver long swords pointed at me. My king's narrowed eyes move around the room suspiciously before landing on my naked form.

He glances up, his expression full of disappointment as his lips curl back into a sneer. "Where's my fucking daughter?"

CHAPTER TWENTY-FIVE
LOLA

I'm having the most pleasant dream until my wolf wakes me, ripping at our bond until I shoot upright. Shouting rings out from somewhere outside the bedroom. My first thought is Richard. Instinct searches our bond, and he's there, but—

"*Marco's here,*" he warns me.

"Oh fuck," I snap, desperately searching for some clothing before realizing it's a lost cause. I have no idea where my clothes ended up. This'll go better if we face the music right now, even though this isn't how I wanted to tell my father the happy news.

"Lola?!" My papá's voice echoes through the treehouse, footsteps nearing the bedroom as the treehouse stills around us, like she's holding her breath.

I lift my head and emerge from the bedroom, naked as the day I was born.

Papá whips around, eyes narrowed as he scans my figure. When his eyes land on the puncture marks on my shoulder, he balls his fists, chest heaving. "So it's true, what the young gargoyle in town told me when I arrived. You went into heat with Richard? How could you, Lola? This is what I protected you from my entire life! I sent you here for your safety, to keep you protected!"

Papá's voice is thunderous as he spits venom, pointing at Richard, who stands with Papá's guard around him in a half circle.

My mate shakes his head softly. *"I'm not hurt, sweetheart. This isn't ideal, but—"*

Papá rounds on Richard. "How could you take advantage of her like this? You were my Second, my friend. I sent her here to keep her from Eliel doing this exact thing!" His voice rises in intensity as Richard opens his mouth to respond. But Papá whirls back to me. "We're going home, now." He jerks his head toward the guards, who grab Richard around the neck and shoulders and drag him off his feet.

He doesn't struggle, his dark eyes swirling with Big Daddy's green. "Stop, Marco," he commands. His voice is full of Big Daddy's authority. My father and his guard bristle and stare.

"She's my Luna, Marco," Richard says. "It surprised us both, but it was inst—"

"It's true, Papá," I begin, imbuing my wolf's strength in my tone. "I wasn't taken advantage of. Richard is my m—"

"So help me goddess, if you say mate," Papá snaps, shocking me with his anger. "Richard can't be your mate. He's ten times your age. He knew your mother, for Alaya's sake! It's disgusting!" He balls both fists as he continues spewing venom. "I know a place to take you to break that bond. It'll hurt, Lola," he says, his eyes flashing with something else, sorrow, maybe, "but you'll be free. As for you," he barks at Richard, his royal command rolling through the room like a tidal wave, "you'll be staying right the fuck here. Far, far away from my child. And you will never, ever see her again."

At those words, Richard explodes into his wolf, sending my father's guard flying. Males hit the walls and shift as the treehouse flaps all the windows and doors in anguish.

"Stop, everyone!" I shout. "Hang on for a second!"

I knew my papá would be angry, but I hoped he'd be able to see reason.

"Cease, Richard," he commands. Every wolf in the room halts and slides to a stop, whimpering. Except for Big Daddy, who stands huge in the center of the room, green eyes narrowed as his long tail lashes from side to side.

"I'm going nowhere without my mate," I say calmly, focused on defusing a situation that's getting worse by the second.

"He can't be your mate," Papá snaps. "He's been my best friend for hundreds of years! He carried you around when you were a pup! Don't you see how wrong this is, Lola? I don't know why he bit you, but we will undo that. He took advantage, why can't you see it?"

"Why would he?" I shout, crossing the room to stand beside my Alpha. "Why the hells would he even do that? Our bond surprised us as much as it's surprising you now, but we have the *Luna* bond, Papá." I point to Richard's enormous wolf. "His wolf can come into my mind, and mine can go into his."

"Silencio," Papá thunders. "You don't know what you're talking about." When he jerks his head toward Nuñez, I move to shift. But then one of the guards tosses something at Richard, a powder of some sort. It explodes when it hits Big Daddy's face, and my mate goes down in a heap.

I round on my father. "How dare you deny this, unlikely as you think it to be."

"Cállate!" Papá shouts. His command, the command of my king, hits me square in the chest like a punch. He's never told me to be quiet like that. Not a single time.

"No!" I scream, fury barreling through me. "I've been dutiful my whole life, served when and where you needed me to. I've played the part of the perfect princess ninety-nine percent of the time but I am done! He's mine, Papá. You don't have to like it, but you do have to accept it!"

My wolf slinks back into my mind, whining as we stare at Big Daddy's prone figure in the middle of the floor.

Papá's face turns red with rage. "We're going home, now," he says with a warning growl. He waves a dismissive hand at Big Daddy. "Don't even think about refusing to come, mija. I'll run a sword through him and leave him here to die for what he did. He has you fooled, Lola. This male isn't yours."

"You wouldn't do that," I snap, balling my fists as I call my wolf for a fight. Fuck this. "If you touch a hair on his head, I'll—"

"I will use my alpha command on you if I have to," he says quietly, malice flashing in his eyes.

Shock hits me. Even as a child, he never used it on me, and he's already done it once tonight. I glance around the room at familiar faces, but I don't see friends here. No. I see wolves under the king's command, and I can't fight them all. My best bet is to go with Papá and come up with a plan B. But for now, I can't risk anything happening to my Alpha.

"Don't hurt him," I say softly. "I'll go with you. But this conversation isn't done."

The need for harmony slaps me. Everything about this situation is wrong. I want to fight, I long for it, to rip into my papá for denying Richard and me. But I can't win that fight against guards who've trained since before I was born. So I'll be smart and bide my time.

And even though it kills me, and my wolf howls mournfully the entire time, I follow the king, surrounded by guards, back to the portal and through it.

CHAPTER TWENTY-SIX
RICHARD

"He's coming around."

"'Ey, Alpha, rouse yerself. We've got shit tae do."

Groaning, I flop onto my back. Dirk's navy smirk is the first thing I see, followed by Connall appearing out of the corner of my eye with a glass of water.

Memories flood back, and I shoot upright, lurching forward. But my feet don't work, and I immediately crash into Dirk, knocking us both onto the sofa in a heap.

"Godsdamn," he grunts, shoving at my back. "Is it jest me, or do yeh weigh a fooking ton?"

"Let's get him uprightish," Connall commands.

My brain is moving so slowly, it might as well be tar. I'm struggling to put anything together as the two males pull me off the sofa and manhandle me into a nearby chair. I flop into it, attempting to keep my head up.

Big Daddy's not much better, whining and crawling on his belly.

Luna. Took Luna.

"Marco took Lola," I snap.

"We know," Connall says grimly. "I tried to stop him, but he used his pack alpha command, and I literally couldn't." He looks away. "I let you down, I'm sorry."

I shake my head, trying to reach up and run both hands through my hair. "You can't deny the king's command, Connall. It's not your fault."

"We need a plan to get 'er back, obviously," Dirk states, crossing his muscular arms. "Yeh got anything in mind, Alpha?"

I glance up. "I need to get to Santa Alaya and talk to the king. How the fuck did he know what was going on anyhow?"

Dirk sighs. "Unfortunate series of events. Yeh were here doing yer wolfy thing, and Lou and Ignatius were hanging with me at Bad Axe. Apparently, the king decided to show up and surprise yeh, wanted to see his daughter once before his challenge. Little gargoyle man let it slip that you 'n' Lola were indisposed for a few days. He put it together right quick and took off for yer place while I called in backup." He gestures at Connall.

A door to my left opens up, and Arkan clip-clops into the room with a determined expression, black brows furrowed. "We couldn't prevent Marco from leaving for a wide variety of political reasons I'm sure you're aware of. I shudder to think of what Hearth HQ would do to this haven if they felt we were undermining the system in that way. However"—his eyes flash to Dirk—"we're not without options."

"I need time to talk to Marco," I growl, "to make him understand. Nobody can deny a Luna bond, not even the king."

Arkan nods. "I thought you might say that. Dirk and I were speaking about this earlier, and we think we've got a plan."

I snarl. "Just how long have I been out for?"

"A solid three hours," Connall says gently. "We weren't sure what they did to you. Vikand's been all over the book about Luna bonds, but of course he can't—"

"Big Daddy thinks I can read it," I bark. "Grab it for me, would you?"

Dirk clears his throat as Connall leaves to find the book. "I've got security clearance to all havens on account of my hunter duties. I can bring yeh through the portals to Santa Alaya, but we'll have tae move quickly. HQ can shut my portal clearance down with the flip of a switch."

I cock my head to the side, feeling like I'm seeing the happy-go-lucky, charming sylph in a new light. "All portal travel is tracked through HQ. You'll probably lose your job over this, Dirk. Are you prepared for that?"

He shrugs, his smile growing softer, more thoughtful. "As it turns out, Alpha, I'm an absolute sucker for love, so yeah, I'm ready."

Connall shows back up with Vikand's book and hands it to me, along with a stack of fresh clothes. He and Dirk pull me to my feet and hold me steady as I dress. Connall's already got a bag tucked over his shoulder, and he claps me on the back gently when I look around at the three males.

Arkan smiles, pointing at his shirt. Today, it reads "All You Need Is Love."

"Ready to go get yer woman?" Dirk questions.

"Fuck yes," Big Daddy and I growl.

Even though I can't hear Lola from this far away, I send love into our bond anyhow, hoping she can feel it even over the distance.

I'm coming, sweetheart, hold tight.

CHAPTER TWENTY-SEVEN
LOLA

Teeth tightly grit together, I run my fingers down the spines of the books in my father's library. When I was a pup, there was a whole section about Luna bonds in a language I couldn't understand. He couldn't either; he just told me it was the language of our goddess, and it was his job as king to protect that until the day came when someone could read it.

Well, today is that fucking day. I've been alone in his office for easily two hours, stewing in fury, and in that time, I've looked through every single one of these ancient texts. The chunky letters almost look like tiny maze icons, they're so intricate. But I can read them now. Big Daddy was right about that.

And I've learned a lot through these old books. A plan is slowly coming together. When a sudden pang of pain zips down my spine like a blade, I clench my teeth tighter and fall into the nearest chair. Thanks to the books, I understand my Luna bond with Richard is deepening, and because I don't hear my wolf's voice the way he hears Big Daddy's, I'll develop other powers.

Scary powers, maybe. The ability to shift into multiple animals. Who knows. Every Luna has been different. Once upon a time, one of my powerful ancestors developed the ability to control the ocean.

Grimacing through the pain, I settle into it, wrapping my mind around it as my body twitches and jerks. I grip the edges of the chair, grunting and murmuring Alaya's name over and over to center myself.

This would be terrifying if I didn't know what was happening. I wish Richard was here with a desire so deep I could choke on it.

I search for him in the bond as my back arches, pain slicing through me as my muscles twist and rip and *grow*.

Around me, Papá's office flaps every window and the rug beneath his desk. She's calling for help, desperate to fix whatever's happening. It hurts too much for me to find words to calm her, so I place a hand on the table next to my chair and will her to understand that I'll be okay.

I lose track of time through the pain, but when it dissipates, the room is clearer to me, sharper and full of edges I couldn't see before. The sound of water washing up on the shore is audible, even up here in the rocky hills. Flaring my nostrils, I scent the fish stands down by the boardwalk. I can hear the mercado in full swing, vendors hawking their wares.

Smiling, I raise my hands to look at my fingers. They're longer, the nails black and sharp. I stand on shaky, trembling legs to cross the room and look in a singular, ornate mirror. My face looks the same, but on the side where Richard bit me, I've got black markings all the way down my neck.

No, not just markings. Jaguar spots.

I read about this in one of Papá's books. There was a Luna-bound omega once who received her bond and could shift into anything she wanted. I focus inward on my wolf, but she's in as much shock as I am, trying to navigate how she feels. When I think about shifting into something else, though, I find we're both too tired from the transition to attempt it.

The door slams open, Papa's footsteps ringing up the short

hallway. He enters the room with all the aggressive energy of a pissed-off king. I'm having none of it. Clasping my hands together, I turn to face him, keeping my expression as neutral as possible.

"Sit, Lola," he commands, striding around his desk and flopping into his well-worn chair.

When I don't, he glares at me.

But before he can open his mouth to repeat the directive, I lift my chin. "No thank you. And don't even think about using your alpha bark on me again. That was low. Just one of the shitty things you've done to me today."

He blanches, regret flashing through his eyes before he steeples his fingers and stares hard. "I had to get you away from him, to get you home so we could talk."

"We could have talked like adults in Ever," I remind him. "You could have trusted me to know my mind, because I can assure you that I do."

His eyes—eyes the same color as mine—narrow. "I mean just you and me, not that fucking asshole I thought was my friend."

I examine my brand-new, longer nails. "You took me from my mate. It doesn't seem like talking is really what you have in mind."

He shakes his head and rises, banging a fist on the desk. "The challenge has been moved up to tonight, Lola. I came because I wanted to see you one more time, to remind myself what I fight for. And imagine my shock to find you shacked up with a man old enough to be your father."

I sigh and glance out the window, over sun-drenched Santa Alaya to the sparkling blue bay. "Richard is mine. You'll see soon enough, because he's coming for me." I say it with all the surety I feel in my heart. My alpha won't let a little thing like haven security stand between us.

"The portal's locked down," Papá growls.

I smile, because to me, he's missing the entire point. When I bring my eyes back to him, I let the smile fall. "What happened in Ever was entirely unexpected by both of us. Believe me, we struggled to wrap our minds around the impossibility of it. But we share a Luna bond, Papá, the first Luna bond in over two thousand years. Even you can't deny that."

He pales and slumps against the back of his chair. "You don't know anything about the Luna bond, Lola. I don't know what Richard said to you, what he did to make you believe this is true, but it's all lies. It has to be."

"Why?" I question. "Because you can't bear to believe that your daughter and your best friend are destined by the goddess to be together? Is it really so awful for you that you'd take away my choice? Because what you've drilled into me my whole life was how my choices matter. Except now you're saying they don't because they don't align with your plan for me." My voice rises as the fury rears up and overtakes me. It's a struggle not to yell and scream, except that'll get me nowhere.

Before Papá can answer, I barrel on. "You've kept me caged in this haven for my entire life under the guise of protecting me from others making choices on my behalf. But you're the worst one because, when I finally do choose, it's not good enough for you to accept. But you know what's Parenting Fucking 101? Supporting your children when they take a different path in life than the one you thought they would!"

His mouth drops open, eyes wide as the door opens again and Nuñez appears. If he heard any part of our conversation, he gives no indication. "I'm sorry to interrupt, mi rey, but the challenge begins at sunset, so you've got less than an hour to get ready. We need to take you both to the formal dressing room." He glances over at me, then back to my father.

Papá sighs as he stands, rolling his long shirt sleeves up his muscular forearms. Has he even noticed that I'm taller? That there's a giant tattoo down the side of my neck and shoulder?

No. He's so wrapped up in anger, he isn't noticing anything at all.

"Buena suerte, Papá," I whisper. "Que luches bien." Good luck. *Fight well.*

His gaze softens as he rounds his desk and stares into my eyes. He blanches, finally noticing we're the same height. "We'll talk more afterward, mija." Chocolate eyes fall to the tattoo on my neck, a muscle working overtime in his jaw.

Still, he says nothing.

As I watch him leave the office with Nuñez, it occurs to me that a male who isn't noticing basic things, who's so wrapped up in anger that he can't see reason, is not in a good position to fight off a well-armed alpha. A male this distracted could easily lose against a well-armed opponent.

Alaya, please, I pray to the shifter goddess, *let my plan work.*

CHAPTER TWENTY-EIGHT
RICHARD

Dirk swipes a hand over the portal's glossy green surface, the magic of his security clearance seeping into the shimmer. We step back as the portal explodes into the room and then dissipates, opening for us.

"Last portal, Alpha," Dirk murmurs. "Are yeh ready for this?"

I grit my jaw. "As ready as I can be to challenge my oldest friend."

"Eh, don't think of 'im that way," the sylph cautions. "He's keeping yeh from yer woman. He is the enemy."

Despite what happened in Ever, I still hold out hope that, with the initial shock past, Marco can be made to see reason. But if he can't, I'll challenge him to become king, and as his Second for a longer duration than Eliel, I'll be allowed to fight first.

Focus, Alpha, Big Daddy growls into our bond. **Get our girls back. We've got a day to prep. The challenge is tomorrow.**

That's right. We'll find a place to hide; I still have friends in Santa Alaya. We step out of the portal, and shock ripples through me at being in my adoptive haven for the first time in decades.

I expected guards to be stationed here, but there aren't any.

Marco must be so confident in his ability to keep Lola from me that he doesn't even need to guard Santa Alaya's only entrance.

Dirk looks around. "Beautiful Santa Alaya. I've long been of the opinion that she's the most stunning haven, don't yeh think?"

I stare at the pristine blue waters of the bay and the multicolored city rising up through the hills to a pink-and-white fairytale castle. All I see is a barrier between me and my Luna.

"Hello, Alpha," a throaty voice whispers in my mind.

Relief floods me at hearing her. I hoped we'd be able to connect once I was inside the wards.

"Lola, where are you?" My question carries all the urgency I feel. Now that I'm here, I want to run to her.

"Castle. Come to the ballroom. They've moved the challenge up—it's happening in fifteen minutes."

Urgency fills me as I turn to Dirk. "Lola says the challenge is in fifteen minutes in the ballroom. We've gotta go."

"I'm coming, sweetheart," I purr into the bond. Relief and satisfaction fill our shared mental space.

"Hurry."

Dirk grins like a feral cat. "That means I've gotta carry yeh, Alpha. "Yeh're not my mate, so this is gonna hurt a little bit." He opens his arms like he's expecting a hug.

I stare at the round blue disk connecting two leather straps that crisscross over his chest. Sighing, I step into his arms.

"Godsdamn, yeh're big," he grunts, reaching between us to depress the disk.

Wind whooshes, and then everything disappears.

Screaming wind stings my skin, peppering me with a hail-like sensation that causes Big Daddy to snarl and pace in my mind. My hair whips around my head as I keep my eyes tightly closed. I don't want to see us flying over Santa Alaya with Dirk in elemental form.

When the howling wind stops, I blink my eyes open. He's dropped us into the corner of the ballroom terrace, which is full of wolves in their finest dress and swankiest silver jewels. A few turn when we appear out of thin air, but mostly they're engrossed in conversation—gossip, if I had to guess—and they pay us no mind.

"Let's go," I growl to Dirk, pushing my way through the crowd to the giant terrace doors. Inside the ballroom, hundreds of wolves mill around in small groups. The center of the room is left clear for the challenge itself, with Marco's silver-etched throne at the head of the room. A wall of doors at the back lead to the rest of the castle and his office.

Goddess, I do not miss this place. How did I serve as his Second for so long? Speaking of which, when I take a quick peek around, I don't see Marco's current asshole of a Second, Eliel.

Dirk taps my arm. "Yeh want me to zip around and find 'er? Or are yeh taking care of that with the old mind-meld action?"

Before I can answer, drums begin to beat from deep within the castle. The castle herself swings a set of coral-pink doors open wide, announcing the king's arrival.

"I'm in the ballroom, sweetheart. As soon as you come through, Dirk and I will—"

Her sweet voice is honey to my soul when she responds, *"I've got a plan, Alpha. Follow my lead."*

Anxiety rockets through me. A plan? Instinct and Big Daddy tell me to rip her away from Marco and get the hells out of here. But I trust her with my life, and if she has a plan, then *we* have a plan.

A tall figure stalks gracefully through the open doors. Marco wears only low-slung black dress pants. He's barefoot and bare-chested, hair slicked casually back. He looks every bit the king who's unconcerned about the upcoming challenge. He doesn't bother to address the crowd. Instead, he crosses the crushed-shell floor and seats himself on his throne, throwing one leg over the silver arm.

It's a power play, something I would have told him to do

before facing Eliel, especially if the rumors are true that Eliel's employing magic. It's not technically disallowed; it's just considered uncouth. One should win based on their own abilities, not because they needed magical intervention.

It means that if Marco wins, the victory will be that much sweeter.

Not that we give a shit about his victory right now, Big Daddy reminds us. **Where's my fucking Luna?**

Our fucking Luna follows, sailing through the doors in a traditional gown that takes my breath away. It's the palest cream see-through gauze that wraps around her shoulders and connects around her waist, revealing her stomach and entire back. Dark nipples are visible through the fabric. It's thicker around her hips, trailing long behind her.

"I picked this one out for you," she purrs into our bond. "When this is all over, I need you to rip this off me."

"Lola, what's the plan? I need to know."

"Patience, mi amor," she murmurs. "Just be here."

My anxiety ramps sky-high as the wolves who'd been standing around form a tight circle around the room's center. A figure appears on the far side—Eliel—surrounded by his closest packmates. He wears the traditional fitted dress pants for a challenge. Silver cuffs gleam around both of his wrists, a matching collar slung low around his muscular neck.

I bristle, knowing it's this asshole who made Lola uncomfortable in the past. The tangy, metallic fragrance of magic rolls off him in waves.

Lola ignores everyone and strides elegantly to the center of the circle, turning to face her father. She'll announce him in the traditional way, and then she'll announce Eliel and the challenge will begin.

Challenge them both, Big Daddy snarls. **We can take the king like this. The Luna bond is stronger than him, I'm sure of it.**

"Don't," Lola cautions. Her focus moves to Big Daddy. *"Trust me, please."*

Always, Luna, he growls, whining and dropping to his belly as we watch her. Dirk is a silent presence by my side, waiting to take his cue.

Lola beams around at the crowd. "Welcome, Santa Alaya, to our challenge!"

The crowd erupts into a cacophony of cheers as I tense. When she spins back around in my direction, I gasp at the dark, circular spots running down her neck and shoulder into the dress strap.

"Told you I had this covered," she teases into our bond.

Something happened to her, she's different.

"Lola," I murmur, overcome with the possessive need to stalk through the crowd and pull her into my arms. As it is, I remain surrounded by Pack Santa Alaya, waiting on my princess.

"We have a lot to catch up on," she admits. *"Later, though."*

She walks a slow circle with her hands clasped at her lower back, eyeing the crowd as tension amps up in the room. Every wolf is silent, staring at their princess as she makes aggressive, predatory eye contact.

Finally, she grins and points at Marco. "You came to see a challenge tonight, isn't that right? To see my father crush his Second, Eliel?"

The crowd screams and stomps, howls cutting through the air as goosebumps prickle to the surface of my skin at her taunt.

"What the fook is yer woman doin'?" Dirk mutters, leaning into me.

Lola throws her head back and laughs, turning to her father with a deadly glint in her eye. "Instead, I challenge you, Marco Garcia Rosas, Rey de Pack Santa Alaya, for the throne."

∽

You could hear a pin drop in the room as a hush falls over the crowd. Marco rises from his throne, fists balled as he glares at Lola. "What are you doing?" he growls under his breath, stalking down the dais toward her.

An angry howl cuts through the air as he reaches her. On the far end of the cavernous ballroom, Eliel yanks his shirt over his head and shifts, sprinting into the circle.

I move without thought, urged on by Big Daddy's overwhelming desire to protect our woman. But to my intense shock, Lola winks out of sight, and where she stood, there's nothing but an empty gauzy dress on the floor.

Wait—not nothing. I still sense her, even as Eliel skids to a halt and Marco roars for the King's Guard.

As Eliel reaches us, Lola pops back into view. Except, this time, she's not a wolf. She's a gorgeous black jaguar with slightly darker black spots. Eliel pauses, and in that moment, she slides beneath him, sinking her teeth into his throat.

He spins and dives to the ground with Lola hanging on by the teeth. Marco moves to shift, but I slap a hand over his chest.

"Don't." Our eyes meet. "This is important to her; I can feel it."

He snarls and rips my hand away, then swivels to stare at his daughter.

Just as Eliel manages to pry her off him, she disappears again, and he's left standing there, looking around. When she reappears in the form of a giant anaconda, he whimpers and backs up. She strikes as he backs away, sinking curved fangs into the flesh of his neck as she coils her body around him. He struggles, but his wolf is no match for the enormous snake.

The entire room is quiet as a grave as Lola squeezes Eliel until his head goes limp. She unwinds from him and tosses him aside, his chest still rising and falling slowly. He's not dead, simply beaten by her in mere moments.

Murmurs begin to echo through the crowd, whispers of

power, of the Luna bond, something so rare, it's never been seen by anyone living.

My mate shifts into human form and stalks naked toward us, head lifted high. She stops ten feet away, hands on her hips, bright joy filling our bond. "Well, Papá, are you ready to fight?"

Marco sputters, raising both palms. "This is madness, Lola. I won't fight you. What are—"

"Then concede," she demands, her voice carrying her words as they echo off the ceiling. "You don't have to fight me. But if you don't fight, then you'll yield the throne to me now."

When Marco sputters, she lifts both hands, imploring him in a hushed tone. "Richard and I share a Luna bond, Father, as you can see. I can shift into anything I want. I read the old texts in your office. A Luna-bonded omega can challenge the king, and he must respond. What's your answer?"

The crowd is frozen, murmured words echoing off the high, glossy ceiling.

Luna. Luna. Luna.

CHAPTER TWENTY-NINE

LOLA

I stare at Papá, willing him to make this easier on all of us.

He looks around the room at our whispering, shocked pack, at the hundreds of gathered wolves he's ruled over for centuries.

When he looks back at me, I know his decision.

"I concede," he roars, loud enough for the room to hear. Dark eyes flash to mine and narrow. "You know what comes next, daughter."

He spits the last word, as if he can't bear to be connected to me. I know he's hurt right now, but I hope with time, we'll be able to fix this. I banked on him being unwilling to fight, but there will be consequences for forcing him into this decision.

Glancing at Richard, I implore him, "Come with me, mate?"

Papá lets out a warning growl that Richard ignores. My love reaches for me with one hand, and when I take it, he guides me across the room to Papá's throne—no, my throne—and steadies me as I sit.

Richard's voice booms into the shocked, silent room. "Allow me to present your new queen, Lola García Marquez, First Queen of Pack Santa Alaya. Long may she reign!"

I don't have my princess crown with me, but no matter.

The ballroom is awkwardly silent as Papá approaches the throne, looking at me like he has no idea who I am. Maybe he doesn't recognize this woman who never wanted anything to do with politics but now sits on his throne.

I don't recognize her either. But when I returned home, I read the ancient texts and knew what I had to do. Being Luna-blessed by the goddess comes with great power. It's my responsibility to use that power for my people, and I want to. Santa Alaya deserves the best, and I'll do right by my home. But I'll do it in my own way, on my own terms. I don't want to rule the way my papá did. I can't live like that.

Papá drops gracefully to one knee and bows his dark head, swearing his fealty to his new queen as a rush of sorrow and victory trill through me.

At his move, the room explodes into victorious hoots and howls. The King's Guard shows up and drags Eliel's prone figure away. Moons, I'll deal with that later. Waiters twirl into the room with food piled high on ornate platters. But all I can think about is my mate and my papá, and how things are far from settled.

To my surprise, Dirk the sylph shows up, stroking long blue fingers down the carved wolves on the back of my throne. "Well, girl, yeh've shocked the shit outta me. Princess to queen in the span of a moment. And yeh turned into that gods-awful giant snake. I hate snakes myself." He leans down and winks. "What else yeh got in there, Princesa?"

I slap his chest playfully. "Anything I want, Dirk. Would you rather see a spider? A monkey? A shark? We could go swimming?"

He beams, showing both rows of sharp, conical teeth.

The room is a whirl of activity around us. I'm sure I'm in for a long night of greeting people as their new queen. But I need time with my family first.

I jerk my head toward my papá's office hallway, looking at him and Richard. "Let's chat, shall we?"

Papá stalks off without a word. Richard pulls me up out of the throne, his warm lips coming to my ear.

"Want me to retrieve your dress? Or would you like to have this talk naked? I'll warn you, if you choose naked, I may end up fucking you on Marco's desk, whether he's there or not." An accompanying growl lifts all the hair on my nape. I can't wait to get my alpha alone.

"Let's not flaunt our bond quite that boldly," I say with a chuckle. "I don't know if he'll ever get used to this. His problem, though, not ours."

Richard beams at me and stalks into the center of the circle to grab my dress. When he returns, I slip it on, and we head for Papá's office. As we leave, the party starts in earnest, sound exploding as people gossip and howl and celebrate.

We move through the castle and enter to find Papá standing at the wall of windows at the back of the room, staring out over Santa Alaya to the bay. He lifts a shot glass of tequila to his lips, not turning when we enter. I consider sitting at his desk and asking him to sit across from me, but the last thing I want to do is lord my new role over him.

"Papá," I murmur softly, "we need to talk."

He turns with a sneer. "How long have you been planning this for?"

I run my fingers down the ancient tomes on his library shelf. "Oh, about an hour. I read these, you see, and I knew what I had to do."

He scoffs. "Because of the Luna bond."

I nod. "That's right. It carries the weight of heavy responsibility. Reading these old words opened my mind to possibilities I never considered before tonight."

His dark eyes flash between Richard and me. "I don't know what you did to her while she was under your care, but—"

"Enough," I snap. "He protected me, he cooked for me, he made sure I felt welcome, he introduced me to friends, and he loved me. I've never been so happy in my entire life."

Papá blanches like I hit him, then sets the glass down hard on the window ledge. "Why take on the throne, Lola, if it's so damn bad being here?"

"*Here* is not the problem," I manage. I continue in a softer tone. "Unity is important to me. Harmony and happiness are important. Santa Alaya and our people are the most important. You're my father, and Richard is my mate, blessed by the goddess herself. I want to spend the rest of my days with both of you in my life. Challenging you was the best solution I could see. Not to mention that the Luna bond gives us the power to rule in a way no one else can."

"I don't know if I'll *ever* be alright with this," he states, waving a hand between us.

"You don't have to accept it," Richard warns, "but if you try to take us from one another again, I'll kill for her."

Marco sneers and returns his eyes to mine. "Where do you want me to go, Lola? As the new queen, you get to dictate that." His tone is frustrated, bitter. I didn't expect to have a deep conversation about the Luna bond right now; I knew he wouldn't be ready to hear it. But I hope one day soon, he will.

Here's the last bit of my plan that I hope and pray works out.

"I want you to be my Second," I say softly. "I'm a young ruler, and I could use your guidance. Plus, I'd like you to act in my stead when I'm not here. Santa Alaya will always be home, but my mate's responsibilities lie in Ever. We'll need to work out the logistics of that."

Papá's eyes spring wide. "¿Qué? You want to rule, but you don't plan to move back?"

"Both havens deserve a present, focused leader." I clasp both hands at my waist. "I could no sooner leave our pack behind than Richard could leave his. We'll discuss the logistics of how to ensure that's done well. For your part, I'll give you the night to think about it. I have one more person to visit before I can return to the party, but please, go enjoy yourself if you like."

Papá picks his tequila back up. "I'm going to stay here, if you don't mind. I've got a lot to think about." He dips his head, his expression softening a little. "I'll consider your request."

I cross the room and slip into Papá's arms, pressing my cheek to his warm chest. "Te amo, Papá," I whisper. "Please help me do this. I need you."

His free arm wraps around my waist as he rests his chin on top of my wild hair. "Yo también te amo, mija." *I love you too, daughter.*

I sink all my love into the hug, willing him to see that, while I'm not the same woman who left Santa Alaya a short time ago, I'm still Lola in meaningful ways. When we part, I smile up at him and pat his chest lovingly.

I turn to find Richard waiting for me, hand outstretched. We leave a sullen Papá behind in his office, meeting Dirk outside the door.

"Yeh need accompaniment, wolves? Or can I go party? I imagine it won't be long before the ole boss calls to ask what the fook I was doin' using my clearance to break through a king's portal lock."

I lay a hand on Dirk's muscular forearm, admiring the lightning streaks of pale blue that move across his skin. "I'll call Evenia myself, if it helps. I can never thank you enough for bringing Richard to me."

"Oh, it wasn't entirely altruistic," he says in his thick accent. "I told Richard that I'm a sucker for love, but I'm hoping a certain someone will notice how far I'm willing to go for it."

I snort. "When we get back home, I'll make sure to tell Lou all about your heroics here tonight."

"Excellent," he says with a feral smile. "Make sure to tell her all about how bravely I fought, and how I was nearly killed, but I managed to—"

"We get it, Dirk," Richard says with a laugh, pushing the big sylph up the hall. "Go enjoy yourself."

Dirk winks at us and slaps the disk on his chest, disappearing into a gust of wind as he travels toward the party.

Richard presses me to the wall, reminding me how we fit in every way.

"I need alone time with you," he murmurs into my ear. "As soon as possible."

Sliding my hands around his neck, I rub my cheek against his. "I want to introduce you to someone first, and then I have to allow the pack to officially greet me. But I promise we can leave as soon as that's done."

Good, Big Daddy snarls into our bond. **You made promises about ripping that dress, and I need to do it.**

Shivering, I unlace my arms from around Richard's neck. After threading my fingers through his hands, I pull him toward the back hallways that lead to the courtyard and the rest of Santa Alaya.

∼

Half an hour later, Richard and I walk quietly through empty, familiar streets, past La Iglesia Santa Alaya, and hook a left along the oceanfront boardwalk. When I move through the coffee shop and up a set of stairs, he follows, a quiet, steady presence at my back. I open the door to the elderly wolves' home to find that even the front desk wolf has abandoned her post.

When I stalk the halls to the common room, Lupe is exactly where I thought she'd be. She's half asleep in her chair, staring out at the bay with a coffee cup perched precariously in her lap. I cross the room and take it, setting it on the open windowsill like always.

She blinks her eyes fully open, looking from me to Richard as she sputters and pulls me close for a hug. "Lola, my darling. You disappeared, and then Leo came to tell me you'd been taken to Ever. What is going on?"

I squeeze her tightly, then encourage her back into her chair. "Everything is fine now, Lupe. But I want you to meet someone." I reach for Richard, who joins us and sinks into the chair across from her, pulling me onto his lap.

Giggling, I wrap my arms around his neck. "Lupe, this is my mate, Richard. Richard, Lupe is one of my dearest friends in the entire world, and I have missed her greatly."

"It's wonderful to meet you, Lupe," Richard says in that deep baritone I adore.

Lupe's eyes go wide, and she leans close to me. "Older male and a pack alpha to boot? Bien hecho, corazón!" *Well done, my heart.*

"Oh, there are more surprises to share," I say with a laugh. For the next half hour, we tell Lupe about how we fell in love, how Papá stole me away, and how I'm now the queen.

She listens in utter silence, and then she tells us what she's been doing in my absence. Drinking coffee. Listening to music. Staring at the blue waters of La Bahía de Santa Alaya.

We sit with her for a long time, staring at my beautiful home haven. I could no sooner leave Santa Alaya than I could my mate. No matter what comes next, I'm resolved to be a good ruler. Perhaps a different sort of ruler than my father, but hopefully the queen my people need.

CHAPTER THIRTY
RICHARD

Santa Alaya hasn't changed a bit. But seeing it with my mate, my queen, by my side makes everything seem a little different. Big Daddy fled my mind the moment he could, sprinting into Lola's consciousness. He's fascinated by her wolf's ability to turn into anything. Even now as we head back toward the castle, he's poking her wolf to turn into something else in our shared consciousness.

I can't keep my hands off Lola, though, and every step we get closer to the castle reminds me of how we have hours of people greeting ahead of us before we can sink into bed and fuck. I need to worship her before we go back there.

And I'm in total awe of what she did tonight.

"Lola, stop," I murmur, pulling her to face me.

When she obeys, I drop to both knees in the middle of the street and bury my nose between her thighs. Her hands come to my head, a happy sigh ringing off the colorful buildings around us. The cobblestones beneath my knees aren't comfortable, but I can't find it in me to care too much as I pull the sheer fabric of her dress aside.

Her pussy lips glisten with slick.

"Just being around you has me in a damn constant state of need," she says playfully.

Big Daddy and Lola's wolf slink off into the darkness together, receding from the forefront of our thoughts.

I can't find words as I slip my tongue between her thighs and lick a soft, flat path over her clit.

Her answering jolt stokes my lust sky-high as I grip her ass cheeks and hold her to me. When I growl, she steps her legs out wide enough to give me better access. Snarling, I go wild, sucking and licking and biting as her cries ring louder and louder, surrounding us until it sounds like the whole of Santa Alaya will hear her pleasure.

When she comes with a choked scream, curling over my head and ripping my hair out by the roots, I groan and spurt into my pants. Goddess, I need to knot her before I die of lust.

Sensing my thoughts, she laughs. "I suspect this is the first of many times duty is going to get in the way of us making love. I'm sorry about that, but I promise we'll figure it out."

I rise from my spot at her feet and cover her mouth with mine, silencing her train of thought. Of course we'll figure it out. Together. Her people need her, and I'm determined to ensure that she gets what she wants out of life too. However I need to make that happen, I'll do it for her.

Our tongues tangle as she opens for me, hopping into my arms. We kiss under the fading evening light. We kiss for a long time before I'm willing to let her return to her duties. It feels like *hours* that we kiss under Santa Alaya's beautiful moon. But eventually, it's time to return to the castle.

∼

Hours later, I've had my fill of politics. I don't know what our future state looks like—a lot has changed tonight, and she and I didn't get a chance to discuss any of it before it happened. That can't be helped, but I swear to the goddess, if one more wolf comes up to—

"Mi reina, congratulations on your ascension! My name is—"

Fuck. Yet another wolf now stands in front of Lola. This one is older, and he must see the look on my face because he stops mid sentence. "Ah. You know what? I'll come back another time. It's been a long night."

Lola shifts forward off the throne and lays a hand on the elderly male's forearm. "I would love that. Please do come back. It's been quite the evening, but that doesn't make our meeting any less important."

He smiles thoughtfully and nods, disappearing into the crowd. But even the crowd is beginning to dissipate now. Couples and throuples leave in droves, emptying the once full ballroom.

Dirk is nowhere to be seen. Marco hasn't emerged from his office.

Lola grabs my hand. "Come, mate."

I let her lead me through familiar halls to her room, but by the time she enters the door, I'm hard and aching. Our wolves are with her; my mind is quiet save for a seething, dark need to take my queen.

When we enter her room, I don't expect the blast of pink and turquoise coloring every inch of the place. But I laugh—she must have done this after I left Santa Alaya. As a pup her room was a neutral palette.

Lola slaps me playfully on the stomach. "I can hear you, you know. Don't laugh. It's still beautiful." She strokes the door frame as she smiles at the ceiling. "My perfect room, right?"

The pink-washed ceiling beams creak, the chandelier in the middle of the room swaying softly.

I take a moment to walk around the space and get insight into the woman who captured me so completely in such a short time. The corner boasts a mini concert stage with photos from what appear to be a dozen or more different concerts over the years. Lola's only in one or two of them.

I point to the collection of photos on the wall. "Are these all concerts you missed?"

She nods softly, sorrow filling our bond.

Gripping her throat, I press her to the wall against the pictures, hovering my mouth above hers. "No matter what happens, I will never let you give up this dream, do you understand?"

Lola laughs, the throaty sound seeming to echo in the high-ceilinged room. One beautifully dark brow slants upward. "Is that a command?"

I brush my lips over hers. "Command. Demand. Request. Plea. Promise. It's all of that, Luna. We will find a way to manage this, alright? Somehow, we'll take care of Santa Alaya and Ever and your dreams."

Her smile grows softer, but she nods. "I used to be scared of ruling like Papá does, scared of the wrong turn or the wrong connection or the wrong alliance. But I suspect you and I will do things a little differently. And we'll still have his guidance, of course."

I growl at that. I'd like to say we don't need it, but the reality is that I plan to push a shitload of responsibility onto Marco's shoulders so Lola gets the chance to travel. He was always a genius regarding alliances and contracts and the more technical things related to ruling Santa Alaya. He always liked that part of it best, I think.

Lola is going to be a queen of the people; I can feel it. She's not going to spend all of her time in boardrooms discussing trade. She's going to be down among her packmates helping, visiting, supporting. I know it.

"There's one thing I want to do before we leave," I murmur, sliding my hand down her exposed chest to the gauzy belt that holds her dress together.

"Rip this off me, I hope." She brings both arms around my neck.

"And deal with Eliel," I remind her. "Not only was he going to force you, but he attacked you."

"During a challenge," she reminds me. "It was fair game then."

It's my turn to raise a brow. "I hope you don't expect me to let him off the hook?" My fingers return to her throat and squeeze. "I don't think I can do that, mate."

"Well, I think I'm gonna let him stew for a little while, and then I'm going to have a little heart-to-heart with him."

I open my mouth to protest, to tell her that having a heart-to-heart won't change who Eliel is. The only thing we can do is banish him to somewhere he can't hurt others or brand him officially as a criminal. That brand will make him unwelcome in any pack in any haven.

Lola growls, pulling my attention back to her. "I believe you made me a promise about this dress, Alpha. It's time to make good on that promise."

My eyes drop to the see-through fabric. Dark nipples peak the front, and my mouth waters at my Luna's obvious need. Big Daddy stalks along the bond from her mind to mine, muscles tight as he focuses on—

Hot damn, Luna. Lookin' good.

"Thank you, Big Daddy," she croons into our bond. *"You're not lookin' bad yourself, sir."*

He puffs his chest out as I roll my eyes and lean down to bury my nose just below her ear. I breathe in deeply, pulling her scent all the way into my lungs as I try to infuse her inside me. "Need you rough, Luna," I growl into her ear, dragging my lips and fangs down to her shoulder. When I lick over the now-healed marks from my bite, she jerks in my arms, head falling back against the wall.

Big Daddy urges me on as I bite a hard path down the front of her throat and along her collarbone. By the time I get to her shoulder, ragged snarls rip from my throat, Big Daddy's claws tipping my fingers. Continuing a trail with my teeth, I bring both hands to the gauze belt holding her dress together. Curling my fingers into the translucent fabric, I pull with both hands. The fabric rips and tears, Lola's body jerking with the force as I yank again, and again, and again, tearing the front of the dress in half. I shove the straps down her shoulders and slant my mouth over hers.

Hauling her hands over her head, I press both wrists to the wall. With the other, I reach through layers of torn fabric and slide two fingers between Lola's thighs. When they come away wet, I laugh and lift them to my mouth, sucking the taste of her off them.

Lola's dark eyes flash with her wolf's amber, her mouth dropped open, breathing fast. Her heartbeat is a rapid staccato against her chest as I suck and lick my fingers clean.

"You're wet," I growl, Big Daddy's deepest tones threaded through mine.

"Do something about it," she challenges, lifting her chin as she struggles to release herself from my grip.

Goddess, yes, Big Daddy groans. **She wants to fight us. Absofuckinglutely, omega.** Into our bond, he focuses on her and her wolf. **Run, girls.**

I drop her wrists long enough for her to slip out of my embrace, then I spin in a circle and hunch down to watch my prey. Her bedroom is big, but not that big. Lola darts with a shriek across the room, pausing on the other side of the bed with eyes wide and a big smile on her face.

"We need a bigger space for a chase." I slide both hands through my hair as I anticipate tackling her on the bed.

Her devious thoughts filter down our bond as I tsk, shaking my head at her. "No shifting into something tiny, Luna. Stay in this form."

She pouts, but I'm halfway across the room already, leaping across the space and landing with a crash in the middle of her bed. The frame creaks and cracks as Lola spins to run. Surging forward, I knock her to the carpet on her hands and knees, trapping one of her legs with mine so she can't escape.

When she snarls over her shoulder at me, I reach down with both hands and unzip my dress pants. Pulling my thick cock out, I slap her ass crack with it.

"Fight, woman," I command. "I love it when you get wild with me."

In a move I somehow didn't anticipate, she yanks her leg out of my hold and flips onto her back, kicking me square in the chest with both feet. The move shoots her backward, and she executes some kind of amazing ninja flip, landing upright like a godsdamned dancer.

Laughing, I rise and kick my pants off. When I rip my shirt over my head, she makes a move. I tense for an attack, but the sound of footsteps on stone echoes back.

She ran out of the damn room!

Snarling, I toss the shirt aside and glance to the patio that runs the length of her room. Her shadow flashes past a window.

I follow, pumping my arms as I slide onto the patio and scramble to catch her. She's nearly to the end, and if she gets there, I have no doubt she'll jump off it and do some crazy maneuver to get down into the street. And if she does that, she'll have the whole of Santa Alaya to hide in and tease me from.

My strides eat up the distance between us, and, just as she leaps for the railing, I grab her by the waist. I haul her back against me so hard, it knocks the breath from us both as I use my hips to shove her against the elegant stone railing outside of her bedroom.

My dick slips between her thighs, seeking her heat as she throws her head against my chest and looks up at me.

"Goddess, that was fun. Let's fight all the time."

"Only as a prelude to fucking," I promise, reaching down to guide my cock between her sweet pussy lips.

She gasps when I enter with a quick punch of my hips. Wrapping my arm around her waist so she doesn't get hurt on the balcony, I fuck hard and deep and slow, curling the fingers of my left hand into her hair to give myself leverage. The rough treatment does nothing but amp her lust higher, orange and cream and jasmine exploding across my senses as her lust saturates the air around us.

I drag her head to the side so I can bury my mouth against the skin of her neck. "Mine. I godsdamn love you, Lola."

Her wet, hot heat clenches around me, milking me for all I'm worth as her lock begins to swell.

"Don't lock me yet, sweetheart," I grunt, pulling out and stepping back. I can't rip my eyes from the panting omega with both hands on the railing who spins in place and glares at me.

"You fucking stopped? Oh no. Oh, moons no. No, you did not."

I turn casually and head for the double doors back into her room. "I'm not done, sweetheart. But I want you to come and take it from me."

My woman lets out a battle cry and shifts into a giant eagle. I'm so shocked at seeing her in any other form that I don't react quickly enough, and she snatches me up in her talons, sailing through the large doors. She drops me onto the mattress and shifts back to human form, sinking down to straddle my chest, her pussy dangerously close to my face.

Her eyes flash with her wolf's intense amber, and that challenge calls mine to rise, my dominance and hers warring together in the most perfect of ways.

"And for that insolence, my king, you'll feast before you get to come."

"Get up here," I command, pointing to my face.

As she settles over my mouth, soaking me with need, I grin up at her. "Before we leave, I need to fuck you on the throne with just your crown on. Make it happen, my queen."

"If you're a good boy," she says with deviant, triumphant joy. "Now put that mouth to good use, Richard."

EPILOGUE - LOLA

It took longer than I wanted to get things settled in Santa Alaya. But Papá did agree to become my Second, although he still won't look at Richard. I hope it'll just take time for him to realize that our love—unlikely as it might be—is worth everything. We're back in Ever for a few days to update the Ever pack and talk through plans for co-ruling both locations. Hearth HQ is reformatting some of the portals between Ever and Santa Alaya so I can return home more quickly.

"Girl gimme a beer, stat." Lou's throaty voice pulls me from my thoughts, and I look across the bar at Bad Axe. She slides onto one of the bar stools with a big grin. "Pretty glad to see you back in one piece, sister."

I shake my head with a thankful smile. "It's not, like, perfectly sorted, but my friend Leo should be arriving today, which means I'll get to play guitar with him, and honestly, that's about all I need. That and for Papá and Richard to not be at each other's throats."

Lou laughs. "Well, I got to hear Dirk's firsthand impression of the whole thing. You can turn into a snake?"

My laugh matches hers. Of course Dirk would focus on the snake. "Yeah, or anything else. Any animal."

"Damn," Lou mutters. "That's cool as hells, Lola. I'm so happy for you and Richard."

I pour her a beer and slide it across the bar. "What about you, Lou? Sounds like Dirk found you pretty quickly once we came home?"

She rolls her eyes. "If by find me you mean stalk me like a creeper then, yes, he sure did."

I rest my elbows on the table, putting my chin in my hand as I wink at her. "You don't really seem to mind all that much, if we're being honest."

Pink dusts her freckled cheeks. "I mean…attention is nice, sure. But he's like…always there."

It's my turn to pry. "Have you kissed him?"

"What?" Lou sputters. She brings the beer to her lips and takes three huge gulps. "Why would you ask that?"

"No reason," I say. "It's just that he was super heroic in Santa Alaya, and I thought you might be interested in knowing how he—"

"Lola, First Queen of Packs Santa Alaya and Ever, your presence is requested in, well, the middle of the street." The request rings through the bar, but when I turn toward the front, the doors are swinging shut behind whoever spoke.

Lou takes another gulp of her drink. "Hoboy, I'm gonna head outside."

I stand and cross my arms. "Louanna Hector, do you know something about this?"

"Okay, byeeeee," she draws out the final sound as she grabs the beer and heads for the door.

"Lou, get back here!" I shout, laughing as I jog toward the end of the bar and catch up with her. When I get there, I sling an arm around her neck. She's so much shorter than me now. I'm probably close to six feet tall at this point with the Luna transition.

Bad Axe swings the doors wide for us, and just outside them, the entire pack, as well as the centaurs and pegasi, all stand in the street, chanting my name. In the very middle, Richard stands with one hand on the back of an empty chair.

My mouth falls open as Lou disappears into the crowd. Everyone is here. All the wolves. All the centaurs. All the pegasi. Literally everyone.

Richard pats the back of the chair, his other hand slung casually through his belt loop. "C'mere, sweetheart."

A rousing cheer starts on one side of the circle and echoes across to the other. Catcalls and jeers ring out as I push through the crowd and join my mate.

"What are you up to?" I eye my deviously smiling Alpha and the empty chair by his side.

Richard laughs, and it's Big Daddy's voice that comes through as my wolf sits with him in Richard's mind. **Sit here, baby. We're gonna put on a show for you.**

Heat flushes through me as the crowd screams.

And then I hear it.

Music.

Not just music.

Leo. I'd know the way he plays anywhere.

The crowd parts, and my best friend appears in the space, plucking at his black electric guitar. It's an old song, a song we played as pups, a song we've been playing together for decades. His dark eyes flick to Richard, and he beams. Lupe stands by his side, a weathered hand holding onto his forearm.

I turn to my mate with an incredulous expression. "You got Lupe to come? How?"

"Tell you later," he murmurs. "Take a seat, mi reina." *My queen.*

Dutifully, I sit in the seat as the crowd goes wild. Leo walks slowly around the inside of the circle, strumming and singing just loud enough to be heard over the crowd as Richard unbuttons his shirt.

Heat swirls in my belly as he unveils all those miles of tattooed skin. He stares at me lovingly as he speaks, voice carrying across our packs and the rest of Shifter Hollow.

"Welcome, Pack Ever, to the formal presentation of jewelry from myself to my Luna."

At the word "Luna," everyone goes wild, but in our bond, Richard's voice is resonant and clear.

To new beginnings, Lola. To beautiful partnerships. Long may you reign, my love.

THE END

++++++++++++++++++++++++++++++++++++++

Lou, Connall and Dirk are the next HEA in Ever. Preorder Slaying With Sylphs now!

Wanna know what happens after Richard's public dance? Spoiler alert — it involves a collar and leash, some skyscraper heels and a strap on. Need to know more? Sign up for my newsletter to access the spicy bonus epilogue where all that (and more) transpires.

BOOKS BY ANNA FURY (MY OTHER PEN NAME)

DARK FANTASY SHIFTER OMEGAVERSE

Temple Maze Series

NOIRE | JET | TENEBRIS

DYSTOPIAN OMEGAVERSE

Alpha Compound Series

THE ALPHA AWAKENS | WAKE UP, ALPHA | WIDE AWAKE | SLEEPWALK | AWAKE AT LAST

Northern Rejects Series

ROCK HARD REJECT | HEARTLESS HEATHEN | PRETTY LITTLE SINNER

Scan the QR code to access all my books, socials, current deals and more!

@annafuryauthor
liinks.co/annafuryauthor

ABOUT THE AUTHOR

Hazel Mack is the sweet alter-ego of Anna Fury, a North Carolina native fluent in snark and sarcasm, tiki decor, and an aficionado of phallic plants. Visit her on Instagram for a glimpse of the sexiest wiener wallpaper you've ever seen. #ifyouknowyouknow

She writes any time she has a free minute—walking the dogs, in the shower, ON THE TOILET. The voices in her head wait for no one. When she's not furiously hen-pecking at her computer, she loves to hike and bike and get out in nature.

She currently lives in Raleigh, North Carolina, with her Mr. Right, a tiny tornado, and two sassy dogs. Hazel LOVES to connect with readers, so visit her on social or email her at author@annafury.com.

Printed in Great Britain
by Amazon